SLAUGHTERED

BY

K.A. Lugo

Tirgearr Publishing

Published by Tirgearr Publishing
Ireland
www.tirgearrpublishing.com

ISBN 978-1-910234-34-1

A CIP catalogue record for this book is
available from the British Library.

10 9 8 7 6 5 4 3 2 1

DEDICATION

Always for Peter

ACKNOWLEDGEMENTS

There are so many people who helped make this book possible.

First, I want to thank all of my family and friends who supported me through this project. Going from romance to murder is a big step, and I appreciate the handholding along the way! Especially my husband, who's been my rock through this project. He was subjected to my rants and raves from the moment I typed Chapter One and right to The End, and still let me lean on him.

I want to thank three special ladies: my editor, Sharon Pickrel, who was patient with me every step of the way; my proofreader, Lucy Felthouse, whose fine-toothed comb teased out the final tangles; and to Cora Graphics for creating the perfect cover for this book and set the theme for the series. Thank you, ladies!

I also want to thank my wonderful team of beta readers, each who gave me unique and helpful advice on how to improve my work—Charlotte Howard, Dellani Oakes, Kat Simons, and Carol Warham—all amazing writers in their own right.

A special thanks goes out to Detective Adam Richardson at Writer's Detective: www.writersdetective.com. I can't say enough about this wonderful experience. His professional advice and inspirational words have meant so much. Anyone turning to crime writing should tune into his amazing podcasts. And join his group on Facebook: www.facebook.com/groups/writersdetective.

A big shout out to the wonderful folks on my Facebook author page. I put out a call for help naming some characters in this book, and so many wonderful people chimed in with their suggestions. Unfortunately, I couldn't use them all, but these ladies gave me two of the names I did go with (Violet and Jasmine): Laurie Atchison, Kimme Browne, Kandis Caringer, Sharon Caringer, Candy Hake, A.D. Keller, Brandy Messenger, Evin Bail O'Keeffe, Teresa Eland Reitnauer, Linda Rowswell, and Patricia E. Sharp. Thanks so much, ladies! I know I can always count on my readers.

Finally, to my readers: To my new readers, thank you for giving my books a chance. And to those following me over to thrillers . . . welcome to the dark side!

SLAUGHTERED
BY
K.A. Lugo

CHAPTER ONE

San Francisco, California

Wednesday

"Is it her? Is it Leah?"

Jack Slaughter's heart hammered a hole in his chest as he watched the rail-thin form of the newly-made detective, Paul Travers, stride toward him. If he could read the man's expression and body language, Travers seemed more amused by Jack's presence than annoyed.

When Jack started lifting the crime scene tape to duck under it, Travers pushed him back with a firm hand on his shoulder.

"You gotta stop turning up like this, Jackie." Travers' flippant voice grated on Jack, almost as much as the man's ruddy complexion and brassy hair. His voice edged on being just a bit too high and too nasal to want to listen to for long. Jack didn't know how his best friend and former partner, Ray Navarro, could stand it.

With a hand still on his shoulder, Travers nudged Jack back. He made a shooing motion with his other hand. "Why don't you just go on home and let the professionals do their jobs?"

Travers' condescending tone made Jack want to punch him in the throat.

"Where's Ray?" He followed Travers' gaze over the man's shoulder and saw Ray standing over the victim's body several yards away. It appeared to have been deliberately positioned at the foot of a tall pine at the dead-end of the road. "I want to talk to him."

Travers caught his gaze and looked back. "Go home, Jackie.

1

You don't belong here." He emphasized the word *you*. They both knew why Jack was no longer Ray's partner, nor on the force.

Ignoring the little pissant, Jack shouted over the man's shoulder. "Ray!" His friend looked up and gave a quick wave to acknowledge he'd seen Jack. He finished up with a CSI, then made his way over.

"What are you doing here, Jack?" When Ray reached up to shake hands, Jack palmed his cell phone into Ray's.

"I told him to go home . . . *partner*."

In Jack's opinion, Travers seemed to take every opportunity to rub it in that he now occupied Jack's former position. It didn't escape his notice that Ray also cringed at the word *partner*. Jack knew his leaving the force had been a blow to his friend too.

He gazed directly into Ray's eyes, struggling to keep the anxiety he felt from his voice. "I got another one."

"Jack—" Ray sighed, gazing down at the phone's screen to the open text—*Spreckels Lake*.

Since the very first text he'd received—*You'll find your wife in the Panhandle*—there had never been anything more than the next location. The texts came every three months, as if on schedule. Every one of them led Jack to a body, but none of them were Leah. If the texter was intent on driving him crazy, it was working. But he couldn't risk the guy was crying wolf. Even after three years, Jack still showed up . . . just in case.

Ray handed back the phone then threw his hands onto his hips. Jack could almost hear the gears working in his friend's head as he gazed around Spreckels Lake with obvious concentration.

This was a beautiful location. Jack remembered bringing his family here but pushed the memory from his mind. He gazed away from the water, forcing himself to breathe. He knew the answer, but he had to ask it anyway. "Is it her?" Even *he* heard the waver in his voice.

"You gotta let me do my job, man. You gotta trust me. If this was Leah, you know I'd tell you."

"I know, but—"

"No buts, Jackie," Travers cut in, edging up closer to him as if posturing. "You're not a cop anymore. You don't belong here. Go *home*."

2

Jack stared at Travers with a look he hoped said, *go ahead and touch me again, pissant, I dare you.* He must have got his point across because Travers hesitated before stepping away, his back noticeably erect.

"I'm sorry. Paul's right. You don't need to be here. It's not her." Ray's voice remained calm. Jack knew the tone, as he often used it to try defusing situations with suspects and distraught families.

"You're just a distraction, Jackie."

"Paul!" Ray's warning tone made Travers jump, as it did those around them.

In his heart, Jack knew when a victim's family turned up on a crime scene, or tried insinuating themselves into an investigation, it only disrupted the process. More times than he could count, the time he'd spent dealing with the family would have been better served on the investigation.

Jack shrank away from the crime scene tape, his energy evaporating. "You're right, Ray. I'm sorry. I just can't risk that the one time I don't respond to the text, it really will be Leah."

"I know, Jack. I know." Ray put his hand on Jack's shoulder this time. "But this isn't her. Go ho—" Ray stopped short. They both knew Jack hadn't been *home* since that night three years ago. "Go back to your place. I'll stop by after my shift. We'll talk then, okay?"

Jack looked past Ray's shoulder to the lifeless body. He watched as technicians carefully placed a protective tarp over the victim, telling him the CSIs had retrieved all the scene evidence they needed and now waited for the coroner's removal.

Dumping the body at the lake had been a bold move. Even at this dead-end in the road, Golden Gate Park attracted a huge number of people, visitors and homeless alike. Someone had to have seen something.

"Can you use an extra hand?"

"Sorry, Jack. You know I can't. I gotta get back. I'll see you later, at your place."

"Don't bother." Jack didn't have to look back to know Ray watched to make sure he was leaving.

From behind him, he heard Travers ask, "What's with that guy?"

"Lay off, Paul," Ray said. "You'd react the same way if your daughter had been murdered and your wife was still missing."

CHAPTER TWO

"Bless me, Father, for I have sinned. I can't remember the last time I've been to confession."

Jack knelt with his hands clenched before him, his head lowered in submission, though it felt more like defeat. Had his eyes been open and his gaze lifted, he would have only seen the shadowy figure of Father Nicholas on the other side of the lattice screen partitioning them.

"I remember, Jack." The old priest's deep, graveled voice softened here in the confessional, but the normal timbre came from a more streetwise, albeit aged, man. Jack knew the man had come to the priesthood in his later years, but didn't know much of his younger life, nor what had brought him to the church so late in his life. If forced to guess, the priest had to be in his eighties. "It was the night you lost your family, and you came to me, asking for forgiveness for an act you *intended* to commit."

Jack recalled everything from that night. He and Leah had been frequent parishioners of Saint Gabriel's Church, just a few blocks from their house in the Sunset District, so it had been natural to seek out Father Nicholas in his greatest time of need. While he no longer attended mass—how could God have allowed this to happen to his family? —Jack returned to the church for the priest's counsel each time he received a text.

In recent months, Father Nicholas moved from Saint Gabriel's to the Shrine of Saint Francis of Assisi in the city's Little Italy district. From where he now lived above Tommy Wong's Chinese Restaurant, the twin spires of the church stretched above the district, as if beckoning parishioners into the Church's welcoming

5

arms. He preferred steering clear of the Sunset District and his former home, so the priest's move to a closer church wasn't a boon Jack was about to question.

"You received another text." It wasn't a question. They both knew what these regular visits were about. For a moment, the priest let the silence linger between them. Jack hoped the quiet would calm his racing thoughts and lift the constant weight he felt pressing down on him. "Jack," the priest finally said, "would you rather we just talk, or do you now require that absolution and penance?"

"I haven't found him yet, Father. I just don't know where else to go."

He couldn't go *home*, and he couldn't immediately go back to Wong's. Every time he stepped into his apartment-cum-office was like a slap in the face at how horrible his life had become. Even though he no longer attended mass, the church offered the quiet solitude his mind needed after being turned away time and again from crime scenes the texter had sent him to.

"Come on."

Jack gazed up and watched the priest's arthritic hand slide the shutter closed over the partition, cutting off the conversation. He heard the door creak open and the man step out.

Jack stood and parted the curtain over his side of the confessional and met the elderly priest beside the pews. His already small frame seemed more hunched since Jack had last seen him, but the man was still spry for his age and moved without the use of a cane or walker.

Silently, the priest led him through the church to a door opposite the altar. Jack knew where they were going. He followed the old man through the door, down a short hallway, and into the priest's office. Jack entered and threw himself into one of the two stuffed leather chairs in front of the desk.

"I assume you walked up." The priest closed the door before going to a small cabinet at the edge of the room. He withdrew a bottle and two glasses.

"I did, Father," Jack said, acknowledging their ritual.

"You know it's Nick when you're in my office."

Nick poured them each a short measure of whiskey, handing one to Jack with arthritic fingers.

After three years of similar meetings, he and Nick had developed a relationship that went beyond that of priest and parishioner. Sure, Ray was his best friend, but Jack always felt he had to hold back part of himself. It was the nature of being a cop—an absolute dedication that didn't allow for weakness, on or off the job, which invariably spilled into any relationship that evolved between partners. But they still had their secrets. Until that night, Leah had been his only confessor. Now Nick filled that role.

Ray had also been there for Jack when he needed him. Ray and his wife, Maria, had taken him in until he could get his shit together and decide what to do with the rest of his life. Jack's family and upbringing had pretty much dictated his future, until the unthinkable happened. Not in a million years would he have ever anticipated his life taking this kind of twisted turn.

Ray had been, and still was, a steadfast friend. But Jack needed more from a confidant. Nick offered that kind of friendship. Jack knew without hesitation that whatever was said between himself and Nick, even here in his office, the priest would take to his grave.

Jack took the offered glass and watched Nick slowly lower himself into the opposite chair.

"So . . . do you want to tell me what's going on?" Nick asked.

"Same shit. The bastard sent me to Spreckels Lake this time."

"And it wasn't her."

Jack shook his head, focusing on the amber liquid warming in his hands. The scent of it slowly filled his nostrils. He could almost smell the history rising off the Jameson 12 Year Old whiskey. He knew he'd only get the one, so he waited until the time was right before emptying the glass.

"It never is, but I keep going. Just in case," he said, quickly glancing up at Nick. "You know?"

"What—" Nick hesitated. "What would happen if you didn't go?"

Jack chuffed sarcastically. "With my luck, that would be the time it *was* her and I wasn't there."

"But if it was her, at least you could put all this behind you. Why drive yourself crazy like this?"

Nick was right. Over the last three years, Jack had beat himself up many times over the same conundrum. His brows pressed together and turned his gaze back to the glass in his hands.

"I don't want her to be dead."

"Of course, you don't."

"What I mean is that I already know the bodies I'm being sent to aren't Leah's. I go with that knowledge. But until she's found, in my mind . . . in my heart . . . she's still alive."

"And by going to all those locations, you're just confirming your belief, is that it?"

Jack nodded. "I suppose."

"You know, Jack, for a while now, I've wanted to ask you something."

"What?" He met Nick's gaze and held it.

"Have you ever thought that Leah might have had something to do with what happened that night?"

"No!" Jack glared at the priest. Anger instantly burned his skin. That question had gone through his own mind. Once. He knew in his heart Leah would never harm their daughter. Or their dog, Trax, who'd also lost his life that night. What happened in his house had been beyond anything any sane person could have done. And most certainly not Leah.

"Think about it from a practical standpoint. There hasn't been a ransom note. There aren't any clues in the house. It's been three years, and you're no closer to finding her, or finding Zoë's killer, than you were from day one."

Emotion crossed over Nick's face—worry tinged with reality, but mostly honest concern.

"Don't you think I haven't already thought the same thing?" His vision blurred, and he blinked repeatedly until his sight cleared. "Leah had the gentlest soul I've ever known. For fuck's sake, she couldn't even kill mice that came in off the beach. She set live traps and walked them across the road to the beach to set them free. Kill Zoë, and Trax? No way."

"I had to ask. I'm sorry I've upset you."

"It's okay. I just—"

Just what? His body shook with helplessness and a sense of things spinning out of control.

"You're still struggling with your guilt, Jack. You *know* there was nothing you could have done to prevent what happened."

"I should have been there, Nick. I could have been home earlier." Jack's voice hitched.

From the corner of his eye, he saw Nick calmly gazing at him. Were priests trained to remain composed around people who were on the verge of insanity? He was on that knife blade. Every goddamn day.

"Were you ever home earlier?" For a moment, silence floated between them. "And how much earlier? Five minutes or an hour? Who's to say this wouldn't have happened on another night?"

Jack scrubbed a shaking fist across his forehead, trying to stop the building pressure there. "How many times do you think I've beat myself up over that?" He shot his gaze back at the priest, unintentional anger rose in his voice as he spoke. "Had he already tried on other nights? If I had been home earlier *that* night, would he have tried again on another night? Was he going to keep trying until he could finally get in when I wasn't there? Or was he really after *me*, but instead took his anger out on my family?" He stopped short; he was now practically yelling at the priest.

His heart pounded hard in his chest, nearly robbing him of breath. The frustration of being so out of control was almost too much to bear.

He gazed intently into the glass in his hands, as if somehow the whiskey's amber depths foretold his future. How much more could he take before it became too much?

Not for the first time, he swallowed hard at the thought of eating his gun. He couldn't—not before he found Leah and administered his own justice on his daughter's killer.

"Jack." Nick's too-calm voice seemed to echo in the quiet room. "Don't let this pull you into the darkness."

Had the priest read his mind? Jack downed the whiskey in one go. "Too late."

9

CHAPTER THREE

Thursday

A sharp sound beat inside his head, jarring him from a fitful slumber. Jack lay on the tattered, old sofa set along one wall in the front room of the untidy apartment that doubled as his office.

He hadn't planned on living in the office space he'd rented above Tommy Wong's Chinese Restaurant, but he couldn't go home. Or rather, back to the house where he'd lost his family.

In an odd turn of events, he *was* home. He'd grown up in San Francisco's Little Italy district. Wong's was located on the corner of Columbus and Broadway at the end of a row of Italian restaurants, where Little Italy bordered with Chinatown.

Tommy was a longtime local boy too; they'd gone to school and played together as kids. When he found out Jack was in need, he offered the apartment for a song. Living upstairs from the restaurant had its perks for them both—all-you-can-eat free food, and no one messed with Tommy when there was a former cop on the property. While he was paid in as much food as he wanted, lately Tommy was getting the better end of the deal.

The city center location was ideal for attracting clients. And he couldn't beat the view. Had the worn, thin curtains been open, he would see the Bay Bridge directly ahead.

Known locally as the Trans-Am Building, the Transamerica Pyramid was to the right, and across the street was the famous Condor Club.

To the left through an angled corner window, the twin spires of Father Nick's church jutted up behind a triangular shaped building that occupied its own block.

And just outside his windows was the *Language of the Birds* sculpture by Goggin and Keehn, a collection of twenty-three suspended books that looked like birds taking flight. At night, small lights automatically switched on so passersby could read the text on the pages. The display was just one thing drawing tourists to this part of the city. Another was the bold jazz mural dominating the entire front of the building above Wong's.

Jack had wanted to find a place somewhere in the city where he and Leah didn't have history but found it nearly impossible. The familiarity of Little Italy had seemed a safe bolt hole, at the time, but he hadn't considered the number of tourists just outside his door. The city had changed since his childhood.

In reality, he probably should have just left the city, perhaps for the more tranquil Monterey two hours south along the coastal route. But he couldn't leave. Not until his family's case was solved.

Right now though, he didn't care where he was. He just wanted to lie in the relatively quiet darkness and forget. But even on the top floor, light and noise from the busy city streets filtered into the room through the thin curtains; the heat of the day was trapped behind closed windows, making the scent of garlic and stale Asian spices cloy at his sinuses.

As it often happened when he was turned away from crime scenes the texter had lured him to, memories of that night slammed into him like a wrecking ball. And as usual, he tried pushing them away with liquor. Not the good stuff offered by John Jameson, but the cheapest stuff he could find with the highest alcoholic content.

His head pounded. Ignoring it, he let the whiskey fuzz envelop him again, and fell back into the darkness . . . into his dark dreams.

Until that night, Jack had been a creature of habit. Every night after work, he'd called Leah, letting her know he was on his way home. On arrival, he'd park his Harley in the small garage and make his way into the house through the internal kitchen door where he'd greet his family. Their dog, Trax, rushed to greet him as Jack made his way across the kitchen to kiss Leah. He missed being away from her while he was at work and made sure his kiss told her how happy he was to be home. Having outgrown her highchair, Zoë would be in her booster seat at the head of the table in the small dining area where she could watch Leah prepare dinner. Zoë giggled with delight at the sight of her daddy coming through the door and kissing Mommy and then collapsed into new fits of giggles when he lifted her from her chair to spin her around and kiss her cheeks and blow bubbles on her neck.

Even after the seemingly endless trail of horrible cases crossing his desk on a daily basis, seeing his family at the end of a long day always made the work he did worthwhile. Despite what he saw on the job, he loved the work. He would do everything in his power to protect Leah and Zoë, and to do that, he had to be the best damn cop he could be. His many citations were testaments to that goal.

They'd had the perfect life.

He was happy.

They say you never remember trauma in great detail, but Jack remembered everything about that night. Every last second. If it wasn't bad enough the memories were etched into his soul, Jack was forced to relive it every time that damn texter sent him on a wild goose chase.

On that night traffic had been light, so he'd arrived home within half an hour to their small Victorian in the Oceanside area of the Sunset District. The night played out in Jack's drowsy, whiskey-fogged memory.

Leah's 1965 pale yellow Mustang had been pulled over in their driveway so he could get his black Harley Fatboy into the narrow single-car garage located under the living room. He'd smelled Leah's homemade marinara as he climbed the stairs leading up to the kitchen door, but he couldn't get through. He'd had to push against the weight pressing from the other side of the kitchen door. He looked down and saw Trax's shaggy, dark tail. He would have chuckled at the retired service dog, knowing he often found places to sleep that may have been comfortable for him though not so convenient for those around him, but his tail lay unmoving in a dark puddle on the floor.

Jack pushed into the kitchen, smearing blood across the floor. A distinct metallic scent tinged the air, mingling with the contents of burnt marinara still simmering on the stove.

His cop instincts collided with instant panic as he surveyed the scene, scanning from the lifeless dog across the bloodied floor and into the dining area where Zoë sat slumped in her highchair.

At that moment, everything seemed to move in slow motion.

His heart had squeezed into his throat when he raced across the short space to his daughter and lifted her face in his palms. Her head lolled to one side, and thick, warm blood oozed over his fingers from the slash in her tiny neck.

At once, grief and anger flooded his veins like acid. Loath to leave Zoë alone, he forced himself to search the house for Leah, but she wasn't there. Anywhere.

It took every ounce of effort Jack had in him to not disturb the crime scene. With all his heart, he wanted to pull Zoë from her highchair and cradle her in his arms one last time, but he couldn't. She was dead. Those who would come needed a pristine crime scene.

When his colleagues arrived a short time later, they'd found him crouched in a corner of the living room and covered in blood, wailing as no man ever should.

The pounding started again. Jack rolled toward the sofa-back, folding his arm over his ear to block out the noise. As the knocking persisted, he realized it wasn't coming from inside his skull. Someone was at the door.

Ray was early.

Wait. That's not right. Jack had told him not to bother coming by after his shift, but Ray was a good friend and showed up anyway. Last night. As usual, their talk had been light and their drinking heavy, which was why Jack found himself still wearing the same clothes as yesterday.

He glanced at his watch through blurry eyes—8:50 a.m.— then at the door. Had Ray found something at the crime scene after all pointing to Leah? He launched himself off the sofa and was at the door in a handful of unsteady strides.

"You Jack Slaughter?" he thought he heard the man say through the sudden pounding in his head from standing too fast.

Jack recoiled and shielded his eyes from the shaft of light shooting through the open door. The shock of it after being in the darkened room for so long momentarily blinded him; the pain of it ricocheted through his eyes and into his brain. And the pungent scent of garlic from the neighboring Stinking Rose blended with the smell of greasy Chinese food from Wong's reminded him he hadn't eaten since yesterday morning's toast and coffee. Nausea flooded through him, as bile threatened to erupt from the back of his throat.

As his gaze adjusted to the morning light and the throbbing in his head and stomach ebbed, he gazed at the unremarkable man on the landing. If Jack were asked to ID him, he could only say the man was of average weight for his height, muted brown hair, receding hairline and graying temples, and rumpled casual clothes—tan cotton trousers, blue checked shirt, generic brown sneaker-type shoes. There were no dashing good looks about him, no penchant for jewelry, nor any brand name garments. He was what one could consider the 'Average Joe.' A very tired-looking Average Joe.

"Depends who's asking," Jack said.

"I was told he could be found at this address."

Jack glanced at the crude letters painted on the outside of his door—*Jack Slaughter, Private Investigations and Security*—then back to Average Joe. It didn't take a rocket scientist to see which of the two men was the private dick and which was just the dick.

Jack turned back into the room, leaving the door open. Average Joe could enter or leave. His choice. Shit! He chose to follow.

"My name's Carl Boyd."

"Good for you, Carl Boyd." Jack flopped down onto the sofa, putting his back to the man, and closed his eyes. If Boyd would just close the door on his way out, Jack could resume feeling sorry for himself, and hope the next time he slept it wasn't a nightmare he saw, but his family in happier times.

It wouldn't happen though. He hadn't had a good night's sleep, or good dreams, in three years.

"The police can't, or won't, do anything." When Jack only grunted, the man persisted. "I was told you're the best investigator in the city. Please. I need your help."

The best? He doubted it. He'd burned too many bridges before he left the force—left before they could fire him. "Sure. I'm the best, all right," he mumbled to himself. Then louder, so the man could hear him, "Who sent you?"

"Detective Ray Navarro."

Ray hadn't said anything last night.

"Why did Ray send you?"

He heard the man fidgeting. "It's my wife."

Oh, no. Did Ray think by sending him a cheating wife case it would keep him busy enough to stay away from crime scenes? Jack saw a lot of infidelity cases since he'd *changed careers*. Cheating wives or missing husbands—most turned up in one of the seedy motels around the city, caught in the act with a lover, or getting their freak on with a hooker. Or exploring their sexual options in other ways. This was San Francisco, after all. By the very nature of the city, her people tended to be either very open-minded, or very closed. By the looks of Carl Boyd, nothing about him screamed adventure.

"Sorry, I'm not taking cheating spouse cases at the moment."

"She's not cheating on me."

Jack scrubbed his palms over his tired eyes and rolled over to sit up, resting his elbows on his knees. Like it or not, he was fully awake now.

"Do you know for a fact she's not cheating? That's the number one reason a wife leaves her husband. She gets tired of—" He quickly took in Average Joe Carl Boyd again before forcing himself to be more tactful. "She gets tired and wants a change. At first, it's a fling in the afternoon while you're at work, and then she falls in love. She still loves you, but you can't give her what she needs, so she leaves. Takes her stuff, leaves a note, end of story."

Boyd shifted from one foot onto the other. "It's not like that. She's just . . . gone."

"What do you mean gone?"

"As in *gone*. There was no note. She didn't take anything. Her clothes are still in the closet. Her car is still in the driveway. When I got home from work, dinner was still in the oven, but she wasn't there, and no one had seen her."

That got his attention. Jack shot up from the sofa. "Be right back," he said before disappearing through the door into the backroom.

CHAPTER FOUR

A few minutes later, Jack reemerged into the front room, his damp hair curling at his neck and wearing a fresh change of clothes—a fitted white T-shirt, black jeans, and black socks. He rarely bothered with shoes when he was ho . . . here. He hadn't bothered shaving, letting his five o'clock shadow roll into a third day.

He carried a cup of dark coffee in each hand. Pulling the door closed with his toes, he proceeded to his desk between a pair of wide windows.

Setting down the cups, he waved to a chair in front of the desk. "Please, Mr. Boyd." The man moved from where he stood in front of one of the windows. While he'd waited, Boyd had slid open the curtain to look out, but now seated himself in front of the desk. Jack pushed a cup toward the man before turning to open the other curtain. Light flooded in, nearly bleaching out everything on the desktop with early morning light. Jack pulled a string at the side of the window and dropped down a blind from its recess until it blocked out most of the sun's glare while still brightening the room.

"Sorry about earlier," Jack said, rifling through the stacks of papers on the desk to find his notebook—the traditional little black notebook he, and all cops, always carried on the job. He spotted a pen under a folder and pulled it free, checking to make sure it still had ink in it. "You caught me on a bad day."

"It's okay. I understand. I imagine you must have a hard time finding good ones these days." Jack shot a glare at the man. "You were all over the news a few years ago. Sorry I didn't recognize you

17

before. You've changed."

"Let's talk about your wife." Jack looked around the desk for his cell phone, then remembered it was in his jacket pocket. He rose and went to where the jacket lay on the floor beside the sofa next to last night's bottle.

Even before he'd decided to set up his investigative business, he made sure to equip himself with the best his money could afford. For him, it was always the latest Samsung Note series. It always had extended video time with clear imagery, and the camera feature had better resolution than his traditional DSLR. Both features were essential for investigative work. Quick connectivity kept him online with the department, but especially with his family. And he would never complain about the added feature—the stylus. On the very rare occasion he'd been without his notebook, the note-taking feature kept him rolling.

He pulled out the Samsung from his jacket pocket and reseated himself at the desk.

"I hope you don't mind. I like to record my meetings."

"I don't know," Boyd said apprehensively. "Why?"

"It's just in case I miss something in my notes," he added, tapping the legal pad before him.

Boyd hesitated. "I suppose it's all right."

Jack pulled up the voice recording app on the menu and switched it on before placing the phone on the desk between himself and Boyd. Before beginning the interview, he made a verbal note of the date and time, Boyd's name, and the reason for the meeting.

"Let's begin."

Boyd kept the cup in his hands after taking the first sip. He didn't settle back in the chair, but nervously perched on the edge of it, as if waiting to launch himself off it. "Where do I start? I've never . . . I mean, this has never happened before. I don't know—"

"It's okay. Start at the beginning. Tell me about her. What's her name?"

Boyd set the cup on the desk and stood up, withdrawing his wallet from a back pocket. With shaking hands, he rifled through it then thrust a photograph onto the desk before reseating himself. "That's Bonnie. You can keep it if you need it."

Jack's gaze flicked between the beautiful woman in the photo and Boyd and back again. Bonnie could have been the Saint Pauli Girl with her long, wavy blonde hair, generous smile, and even more generous tits. "Wow!"

"I don't know how a guy like me scored a woman like her. She's amazing."

Setting the photo aside, he noted Boyd's lackluster response, despite his declaration. Jack said, "Tell me exactly what happened from the moment you got home. When did you first notice your wife was missing?"

"Night before last."

"What makes you think she's missing? Could she have just left? Did you two have a routine? If so, what broke it?"

He tried gauging Boyd's behavior. Everyone had *tells*. Boyd's would let Jack know if the man was serious or just jerking his chain at Ray's encouragement.

"We've only been married a couple years, but I guess that's long enough to settle into a routine. She's always there when I get home from work. She only works part time in a shop on Pier 39, so she's always home before me to start dinner." He grabbed the cup from the desk, lifted it to his mouth again and took a healthy gulp.

"When you first arrived, you said Bonnie's things were still in the closet, and her car was in the driveway?" As with any police investigation he'd ever conducted, he made sure to take thorough notes. Even if something didn't seem important now, it could be relevant later, which was why he backed up every interview with a recording.

Boyd nodded. "Yeah. Dinner was still in the oven. She always made our house very homey. You know, with the smell of food when I come through the door, everything in its place, the floors vacuumed . . ."

"Kids?"

Boyd shook his head. "We've been trying, but—"

Jack forced himself away from the familiarity of Boyd's story and let the man ramble. Sometimes, some of the best clues came from ramblings.

"Bonnie always has her hands in something; she can't just sit without doing something."

"Does she have any hobbies?"

"Like what?"

By the look on Boyd's face, the idea of his wife having her own interests hadn't been a consideration. Jack was sure Leah had hobbies. He didn't expect her to stay home alone all day while he worked. Even after Zoë was born, he'd encouraged her to have a life outside the home. For Boyd, the question seemed to confuse him.

"What do women like doing? Knitting . . . painting . . . reading group . . . gardening . . . or something more active like walking or jogging?"

Boyd thought for a moment. "Does spending my money count? She loved shopping."

Jack chuckled lightly. "Yeah, I suppose that's a hobby of sorts." He noted Boyd's serious gaze. He couldn't blame the man. This was an upsetting time. Jack knew that better than anyone. "What about friends? Does she have a close friend she goes with?"

"I don't know, Mr. Slaughter. When I'm at work, I'm at work and she does her thing. When I'm home, she's home. The only name I can think of is Lucy or Lucy-Anne . . . something like that. She only ever talked about one friend. I assume that's her."

Jack made a note of the names. "Do you have a last name for Lucy-Anne?"

Boyd just shook his head.

"Did you file a missing person's report?"

Boyd shook his head again. "Not right away. I knew they'd blow me off because she'd only been gone a few hours, regardless of her normal routine, but when she hadn't returned by midnight, I called anyway."

"It's a common misconception that you have to wait twenty-four hours to file a missing person's report—adults or kids. But they do prefer folks wait to be absolutely sure an adult is really missing, rather than just getting home late."

"That's pretty much what they told me. They took her description but said they'd wait to file a formal missing person's report in case she eventually decided to come home."

"And as far as you knew, by midnight, she'd only been gone, what . . .?" Jack trailed off, letting Boyd fill in the blank.

"A few hours. Like I said, I got home just before six and she wasn't there."

Jack continued making notes as he asked, "What about family? Does Bonnie have any family she could have gone to see, or relied on if she felt she needed help?"

He could tell by the narrowing of Boyd's eyes that the last question took the man aback. "N-no. She didn't have any family. Like me, she was an only child, and her parents died a long time ago. I think that's part of what drew us together—we were all alone." Boyd sat forward on the chair, set the now empty cup on the desk, and looked Jack in the eye. "I had a rough night. You of all people gotta understand that, right?"

Boyd wasn't wrong.

"I tried waiting twenty-four hours…just in case Bonnie really was just cooling off, from what I don't know, but just in case, ya know? They said give her time. I did. I really did. When she didn't come home by yesterday morning, I rang the police to see if there had been any news. They said they'd send someone out for a report. It had only been about twelve hours, but to be fair, they arrived pretty fast. And left just as fast, in my opinion."

"It can happen, especially if the scene is pristine…such as a lack of an obvious struggle." Jack tried assuring Boyd.

"I get it. I just don't know what to do with myself. She means everything to me. With her gone . . ." Boyd took a deep breath. "I got the same runaround from the officers as I had on the phone— She's an adult . . . blah blah blah . . . what could they do?"

Jack nodded. "It's an unfortunate fact, Mr. Boyd."

Boyd rubbed his palms down the length of his thighs and rocked slightly in his chair.

Ignoring the man's agitation, Jack continued taking notes. "Go on. When did Detective Navarro contact you?" he pressed.

"Late yesterday. I waited until normal business hours before coming here this morning. I didn't know you," Boyd quickly glanced over his shoulder, "lived in your office."

"Needs must, as they say." Jack hadn't intended on living here either, but why pay rent on two places when he spent all his time in the office anyway? "Go on."

Boyd nodded. "I kept calling the department to see if there had been any updates or leads. When I saw a report on the news yesterday about a woman's body being found out at Spreckels Lake, I had to know if it was her. I had to."

Boyd's gaze penetrated Jack. He knew all too well the anxiety the man must have felt when he saw the news report. It had been much the same when he'd received the text yesterday morning. His gaze flicked to his cell phone sitting on the corner of the desk beside him, and he suppressed a cold shiver threatening his spine.

Jack met the man's gaze again. "I understand, Mr. Boyd. Go on."

Boyd sat back slightly in the chair, sitting on his hands, Jack assumed, to keep from fidgeting. "In the afternoon, Detective Navarro said my information had been passed onto him. I got a new set of questions . . . *Did you have a fight?* No, we never argued. *Did you or she have any enemies?* No, everyone loved Bonnie. *Could either of you have had a falling out with a drug dealer?* Absolutely not; we don't do drugs. *Could Bonnie have been hiding something from you?* We tell each other everything . . . or at least I think so. Pretty sure."

"They're all valid questions. What did he say next?"

"He asked me for Bonnie's description. I'd given it to the officers at the house, but I guess he just needed to verify what I'd said. I don't care. I just want to get her home where she belongs." Boyd's voice trembled.

"I know you do. I'm sure the police will do everything they can."

"That's just it. Detective Navarro said he works Homicide. He'd only taken my call because I'd asked about that woman at the lake. He also said there weren't any Jane Does, I think he called them, with her description. And without a ransom note and the house not being disturbed, he said I was better off hiring a private investigator. He said he'd keep Bonnie's details, but unless a body turned up matching her description, or unless I received a ransom note or a call, she'd be treated like a disgruntled wife…that maybe she'd gone somewhere to cool off, like the other officers told me. I know he was only being honest with me, but I gotta know where she is. Will you help me?"

"You don't even know what my fee is yet."

"I don't care what it is. I just want Bonnie home."

Jack stared at Boyd for a long moment before swiveling his chair around to the filing cabinet behind his desk. He yanked open the top drawer and pulled some papers from a file before closing the drawer again. At the desk, he filled in the required details, then spun the documents around to face Boyd. "This is my contract. The fee is listed here." He tapped the amount with the tip of his pen. "Take a moment to read it over before signing." He tossed the pen down onto the contract and sat back.

Boyd immediately scrawled his signature at the bottom of the document. He pulled out his checkbook, tore out a slip and filled it in. He slid it under the pen's clip and pushed it and the contract back at Jack. "I don't need to read it. Detective Navarro said you were the best. After what *you've* been through, I know you won't let me down."

Ignoring the comment, Jack ran a copy of the contract on the printer-scanner on top of the filing cabinet before stuffing the original into a stained folder. And after snapping a picture of Bonnie's photo with his Samsung camera, he added the hard copy to the folder as well.

He looked at the documents in the folder to be sure he had everything he needed. "You mentioned Bonnie has a cell. I need the number. And if she has any credit cards she uses exclusively, I'll need that information as well."

"What for? She doesn't have it with her. Like I said, she left everything behind. Even her purse. Everything's in it. Including her phone."

Jack looked up. "It's routine. I want to check her call history. If she'd made any calls you weren't aware of, or if anyone called her, it would show up and could lead us to her. And she could have made purchases on her cards in the past that may give us some clues as to where she could have gone . . . a new apartment, a trip somewhere, a car . . . anything you might not have seen on a shared card."

"I don't have her card numbers with me. I can call you when I get home. Here's her cell number." Jack watched Boyd scrawl the cell number on a clean page in the notebook.

Jack stood and handed Boyd his copy of the contract. "I'd like to follow you back to your place, so I can do a walk-through. I can get the card info there."

"The officers who came to take my statement already did that."

Jack looked Boyd in the eye. "I know, but I'm no longer in the department. And I prefer doing my own investigation."

Boyd nodded, writing down his address in the notebook beside the phone number. "Whatever you need."

Jack threw on his black leather jacket, stuffed his notepad and a pen into the inside pocket, and zipped up. A few minutes later, helmet firmly in place, Jack straddled his black Harley Fatboy and followed Boyd out of the alley beside Tommy Wong's.

Maybe Carl Boyd wasn't such a dick after all.

CHAPTER FIVE

Carmelita Street was in the southernmost part of the Western Addition—an area at the heart of the peninsula that had once been a largely sandy region with some small-scale farming. It had eventually become a streetcar suburb with the arrival of the cable car. And with the area being more accessible, the city expanded westward to create more homes. Even with the continued growth and development, streets, like Carmelita, remained lined with Queen Anne Victorians—Victorian architecture in a Queen Anne revival style. Some of the more elaborately painted homes around the city were more affectionately known as Painted Ladies.

Because of the Western Addition's flatter aspect on the peninsula these houses had survived the Great Earthquake of 1906 and had become some of the most expensive homes in the city for their size.

Perhaps a hat-tip to farming times, these streets were lined with fruit trees, as was Dubose Park which butted up against Carmelita, with its sprawling, pet-friendly green, secured play areas for kids, and the arts center. The local elementary school was a block away. The location was the perfect place to raise a family.

Had Jack's salary been higher—much higher—he would have bought Leah a house in an area like this. As it was, the Sunset District—an area developed with smaller, affordable homes after the 1906 earthquake as a place for displaced San Franciscans to start over—was much more affordable at more than half the price. And he and Lead did—*had*—loved walking across the road most nights to the beach to watch the sunset . . . hence the name of that part of the city.

25

Jack forced himself to focus on Boyd, who had turned into the driveway of a pale-yellow house midway up Carmelita, parking beside a gray Nissan Altima that was so old, it could have been a Datsun. He pulled his bike in behind Boyd's newer Prius, partially blocking the sidewalk, and flipped down the kickstand. He swung his leg over the seat to stand, pulling off his helmet and stuffing his gloves inside it before hanging it from one of the handlebars.

On his way to meet Boyd at the front steps, Jack pulled out his phone, switched on video mode and slipped it into the top front pocket of his jacket with the lens pointing forward. He wanted to record his inspection of the house, so he could view the walk-through again later, in case he missed anything now. And since Boyd had already given him permission to record their interview, Jack took creative license with that permission to include video—technically, he hadn't concluded the interview. They'd only changed venues. He just wouldn't tell Boyd he was being video recorded.

Jack found that when people knew they were being recorded, they often played up for the camera or were on their best behavior. He saw the latter with Boyd back in the office but chalked it up to nerves. In his home, he should relax a little.

"Nice place," Jack said, following Boyd up the steps to the door. "This must have set you back a penny or two. What kind of work do you do?" He liked a little chit-chat. It put clients at ease and often revealed answers to unasked questions pertaining to the case.

"Property manager. I could never afford a place like this on my salary. My parents left me the house." Boyd fumbled with his keys until he found one for the door.

"Self-employed?" Jack pressed.

Boyd shook his head. "I work down on Market." He reached into his wallet and extracted his business card. "If you ever decide to upgrade your office space—" An odd thing to say just then, Jack raised the card as if making a mental note of the company but in reality, recording it on the video before slipping the card into the notebook. "It pays okay, but honestly, these days I can barely afford the property taxes and upkeep. Those fucking yuppies are driving out all of us city natives." Boyd swung open the door then hesitated, gazing inside.

"You all right?" Jack asked after a moment.

A noticeable shiver went through Boyd before he offered a weak smile. "Yes, just listening to see if Bonnie had come home. The place seems so quiet without her."

Jack nodded. "I understand. Shall we go in? The sooner I can look around, the sooner I can get on with my investigation."

Boyd stepped in and allowed Jack to enter before closing the door behind them.

From where he stood in the hallway, Jack saw the house was both exactly what he expected, yet not.

Boyd was right about the yuppies. In recent years, city officials recognized that people working in Silicon Valley were opting to live in the city where it was cheaper and commuting south for work. Traffic congestion meant commute times took hours to go just a few miles, increasing air pollution and road rage. More importantly, it took revenue out of the city.

So, officials came up with a plan. By offering Silicon Valley tech firms tax incentives to develop in low income and derelict inner-city areas, the city was able to regenerate without actually paying for it themselves. Unfortunately, it meant displacing low income and poor families, which led to the city's current homeless crisis. But for those who got in before the boom, they now saw property prices explode. And for those who could afford the cost of traditional homes, they were now gutting and upgrading with modern, high-tech gadgetry they'd come to Silicon Valley to create in the first place. A house that had cost a few hundred thousand dollars five years ago was now selling for a cool two or three million. He couldn't even guess at his own house's value, but then, who'd want to buy a house where two murders had occurred— he counted Trax's murder alongside his daughter's. Hell, even *he* didn't want to live there. And he couldn't sell. Not yet.

The city vibe was changing too, as yuppies filled the city. No longer was it commonplace to drive through residential areas and see kids playing on the sidewalks or old people sitting in chairs on their porches, shouting across the street to their neighbors as they conversed about the weather. Those streets were quickly filling with trendy cafes where techies sat all day over ten-dollar coffees and thirty-dollar sandwiches while developing the next app or writing code. Jack was saddened to see the city's traditional culture changing before his eyes. Kids and old people were rare sights these days, except for the few who ventured into the small parks, like Dubose.

What surprised Jack about Boyd's place was the lack of modern technology. He'd said he inherited the house from his parents. Jack believed it. The place retained all of its original architecture and Victorian features. And it appeared to have the same carpet and wallpaper too. The place was exceptionally clean, but it was also very dated. For a quick second, he wondered if Boyd had his parents stashed in an upstairs bedroom.

He would have laughed at the thought if the reality of it wasn't so possible. The news was full of stories about dead parents left in their beds and the doors shut on them, or love slaves locked in attics or basements, or worse.

Jack forced himself to walk through the first door and into the living room. Boyd followed close behind.

He crossed the worn, creaking timber floor that was covered with an equally worn rug at the center of the room to admire the original fireplace. "Great architecture." He envied the hand-carved fireplace mantel, original ceramic tiles and iron surround.

"I love these old houses too. My wife wants to modernize but I told her doing that will ruin the house."

He turned to face Boyd, so he could get the man's reaction on video. The man stood with his hands clasped behind him, his back stiff.

"Both have their merits," he suggested. "Leave the original architecture but upgrade appliances, such as an eco-friendly retro-style fire insert, reinsulate the walls, put in new windows with traditional sashes . . . you'd increase the value of your home while retaining the original architecture but also bring it into the 21st century."

Those were things he and Leah were doing to their little place—one of the few Victorian homes left in the Sunset District. When they'd bought the house, it needed a lot of work, as previous tenants hadn't been very kind over the years. But they'd been young and up for the challenge.

By the look on Boyd's face, he must have thought Jack was out of his mind to suggest changing *anything* in this house. "I don't think so," he said firmly, and walked through double sliding doors into the dining room. Jack followed.

Like the living room, the dining room retained its original purpose with the large dining table with matching chairs, and a china hutch against one wall. So far, if the last two rooms were any indication, the furniture in the rest of the house could also be nearly a century old. They were by no means antique collectables. Just well-cared-for hand-me-downs, some of which could be worth some money with a little restoration.

Jack remembered Boyd's earlier statement about barely being able to afford the property tax and upkeep. Was that why he seemed so defensive about spending money on upgrades?

He gazed around again. Clean. Very clean. But there was also a sense of newness—throw pillows and blankets, vases and fresh flowers, trinkets and what Leah called *tchotchkes* . . . little dust collectors as far as he was concerned, but nothing had any dust on it.

He spotted a couple bags on the floor near a wing-backed chair in the living room and casually walked in that direction. Looking down, hoping to see what was in the bags, he asked, "Some of your wife's *hobby?*" Boyd had seemed agitated in the office when he suggested Bonnie liked spending his money. Was this what he meant?

"Yes." Boyd turned through a side door from the dining room.

Jack's gaze flicked between the bags and the door Boyd had disappeared through, then back to the bags. He didn't see Bonnie's purse anywhere, but her wallet was inside one of the bags, on top of some clothes which Jack assumed were her purchases.

Something was off. Jack couldn't place it. Never mind. He'd

figure it out, but right now, he needed to see the rest of the house.

Using the same door Boyd had, Jack found himself in the kitchen, equally as dated as the rest of the house. He had to check himself before exclaiming his surprise. Clean but very old. No wonder Bonnie wanted to upgrade.

Jack went to the oven and checked for a timer. He didn't see anything. Given the age of the appliances in the kitchen, he wasn't even sure if timers were a feature back in the day.

He turned to Boyd, who still stood rigid with his hands behind him. He reminded Jack of a strict school teacher . . . or his commander at inspections. "You said dinner was in the oven when you came home. The oven is empty now. What did you do with it?"

"I threw it out and washed up. That was the night before last. I couldn't leave it in there to rot now, could I?" Boyd said, as if stating the obvious. Jack couldn't remember if he'd emptied Leah's pot of marinara, or if it were still rotting in the pot on their stove. The thought turned his stomach.

"Can I see the rest of the house?"

Boyd nodded and led him through another door back to the hallway where the stairs led to the next floor. Upstairs, there were three bedrooms and a bathroom, all in the same clean but old state as the rest of the house.

"Does this place have an attic?" he asked, just to satisfy his morbid thoughts, to be sure there weren't any old people hidden up there. Or Bonnie Boyd.

Shock crossed Boyd's otherwise composed features, the first real emotion Jack had seen since entering the house. "Why do you need to see that? There's nothing up there."

Why was the man getting so defensive? "It's just part of the normal inspection," he said calmly. "Didn't the investigating officers have a look last night?"

"They didn't ask."

"Well, I'm asking now. May I see the attic?"

The men stood looking at each other for a moment. Jack wasn't backing down. If Boyd didn't have anything to hide, why was the man stalling now?

Finally, Boyd said, "Sure, I just don't see the point." He led them to the end of the hall and into the smallest of the bedrooms located at the back of the house. Inside a small walk-in closet was a trap door in the ceiling. "I'll be right back. I'll get the ladder."

Jack stopped him. "No need. I can stand on this chair and just poke my head in." The look on Boyd's face at the thought of standing on the old chair beside the bed seemed to shock him. "I'll be careful."

Boyd nodded hesitantly.

Jack pulled over the chair and carefully stood up on the seat. He moved deliberately when he heard it squeak and groan under him.

He lifted the panel off the attic opening and pushed it aside, then pulled his phone from his pocket and pulled up the flashlight app. Tapping the icon to switch it on, he let the video record what it could see in the light.

The light shone a few feet into the space. Beyond that, the enveloping darkness smelled of decomposing boxes and whatever they contained. Large dust motes floated in the light beam. By the dust on the floorboards, no one had been up there in years. And no bodies of old people that he could see. Thank God.

He switched off the light and put the phone back in his pocket before replacing the panel. He stepped off the chair and returned it to where he'd found it. Boyd moved in beside Jack and replaced the chair directly into the divots in the carpet. "It goes here." Jack just nodded at the quirk. Maybe Boyd had OCD. The house did seem overly clean, and he had cleaned up the kitchen from Bonnie's cooking.

Back in the hallway, Jack asked, "Do you have a basement?"

Boyd shook his head. "These old houses barely have a crawl space under the floorboards."

"All right then, I think I've seen what I need to see here. Thanks for letting me look around."

"But you didn't take any notes," he said, worry tingeing his tone.

"I didn't see anything out of the ordinary so nothing to write down." He wasn't about to tell him about the video.

Nodding, Boyd asked, "What's next?"

"You were going to give me your wife's credit card numbers. Also, if you could lend me her phone, I'll see if anything's been deleted from her texts or emails. That stuff is usually recoverable," he added.

"Sure, whatever helps." Boyd's tone sounded tired.

Jack followed Boyd downstairs and back into the living room where the man retrieved the wallet he'd seen earlier in the bag. He moved out of view, but Jack heard a drawer open then close. A moment later, the man returned with Bonnie's wallet and phone in hand.

"Here's her phone. It's not password protected."

Jack took the old flip phone and switched it on to be sure it wasn't password protected. From the corner of his eye, he watched Boyd riffle through the wallet and pull out the plastic. "Here's her credit card."

"Just the one?" Jack asked, shocked. Leah had at least three, though she was very judicial over where and when she used them.

"Does a woman really need more than one?" Boyd asked. His smile didn't reach his eyes.

"I suppose not, Mr. Boyd." He opened the front door. While nothing screamed out at him, being in this house felt a little awkward, perhaps as if time was cloying at him and trying to drag him into the past. Suffocating him. Stepping onto the front porch, the fresh air caught him. He inhaled deeply to clear his lungs before facing Boyd and stretching out his hand. Boyd's grasp was damp and weak, and Jack nearly jerked his hand away. "Thanks for showing me around. I've got your details and will ring you as soon as I discover anything."

CHAPTER SIX

Ray Navarro rarely stood on ceremony, so Jack wasn't surprised when the apartment door swung open. He'd been only vaguely aware the sun had set. The motion sensor security light outside over the door shone down Ray's back, casting him in an imposing silhouette.

The only other light in the room came from the computer screen which spread a pale glow around the small space where Jack worked at his desk, inputting details from his new client, Carl Boyd.

After conducting his earlier inspection of the Boyd home, Jack had made a few stops at the closest women's shelters to Carmelita. If Carl was right—that Bonnie had just walked out, leaving behind her car and her belongings—it meant she had to have walked to wherever she'd gone. Women's shelters were always the first on his hit list—the list of the most common places disgruntled spouses go to in times of trouble, if they didn't have anywhere else to go, that is. In Bonnie Boyd's case, according to her husband, she didn't have family, so hitting the women's shelters first, then rape crisis centers and homeless shelters made sense.

Jack had been at this game long before he'd left the force, so he knew most of the people who helped those in need. While he could call them, he found he received a better response with a personal visit. Unfortunately, either no one had seen Bonnie, or they weren't talking. Jack had also learned over the years, when women—anyone—sought shelter, privacy was tantamount to their safety and getting the help they needed. While he understood this, there was still a missing woman to find. If nothing else, he could at least tell Boyd that Bonnie was alive and safe.

After the shelters, he went to some of the nearest cheap hotels and motels—since she didn't have her wallet, perhaps she had a little cash—and of course, hospitals and clinics. All had drawn a blank.

He reached up and flipped on the banker's lamp on the opposite side of a messy stack of files, and watched Ray push the door closed before striding over. He threw himself into the chair earlier occupied by Boyd and relaxed back into it, kicking his feet up onto the desk and crossing his legs at the ankles.

"Come on in, Ray. Make yourself at home." Jack purposefully laced his greeting with sarcasm. He reached into the bottom drawer for a clean glass and a mostly-full bottle of whiskey and pushed them toward Ray before refocusing on the computer screen again.

From the corner of his eye, he watched Ray pull the glass closer and uncap the bottle, pouring himself a single finger measure. "Don't mind if I do. You not drinking?"

Jack glanced up over the glasses he only wore at the computer— the second sign he was getting older; the first being the graying at his temples that he was forced to look at on those days he chose to shave, and today wasn't one of them.

"Do I look like I need a drink?"

Ray just chuckled as he sat back again. "Well, we hit it pretty hard last night."

Without looking at his friend, he said, "That was last night."

"No hair of the dog?"

Jack lifted a brow and scowled at him.

Thankfully, Ray let Jack work while he enjoyed his whiskey. The only sound came from the keys clicking as Jack typed. Jack had made a lot of mental notes at Boyd's house and wanted to be sure they were backed up in his files. That included the audio interview and the video from the home inspection.

He had never been overly tech-savvy while on the job, but now that he was . . . self-employed . . . an entrepreneur . . . *forced to do it* . . . he found tight recordkeeping an asset—for investigations and for his accountant.

A short time later, he leaned back in his chair, tossed the glasses onto the desk, and rubbed the bridge of his nose. This had been one long-ass day.

"Looks like you've had an attitude adjustment since last night." Ray was always great for pointing out the obvious.

"Yeah, and hey, thanks for the client."

Ray slowly swung his head. "Poor bastard. He must have really pissed her off for her to just up and leave like that."

Jack sat forward in his chair to see past the glow of the banker's lamp. The shadows falling across his friend defined his rich Hispanic heritage and revealed his exhaustion.

"Do you really think that's what happened to her?" He hated admitting it but . . . "She disappeared just like Leah did. I've been out to his place and did a thorough walk-through. Absolutely no clues—no struggle, nothing's missing, dinner had been in the oven. She's just gone. Just like—just like Leah." He barely got the words out.

Ray's focus shot to attention. "What do you mean *had been in the oven?*"

"I asked him the same question. He said he cleaned up. I think the guy's a bit obsessive. Everything had its place. I moved a chair to look up into the attic space, and when I put it back when I was done, he was immediately beside me, moving the chair back into those little divots in the rug. It must have been in that same position from when his parents owned the house."

"I've heard of people like that."

"I think this guy goes a little further out than others. He's got one of those houses up beside Dubose. Original inside and out. And I mean everything. Rugs, wallpaper, appliances . . . When I suggested upgrading with some modern retro fixtures designed to keep the original feel, he was absolutely against any of it. Looked at me like I was crazy."

"Damn! The place must have been a rat hole."

"That's just it. It wasn't. The place was immaculate. Just really old. It was like his parents, or maybe even grandparents, still lived in the place. For a minute, I was half expecting to find them stashed in an upstairs bedroom."

"What about the wife?" Ray sipped at his whiskey.

Jack shook his head. "Not there either, stashed or otherwise. That's why I wanted to check the attic." He tilted his head, trying to grasp that thing that had been niggling him since his inspection. "He seems genuine enough, but there's something weird about him too."

"Even weird guys need love." Ray chuckled.

"Remind me to ask Maria what she saw in you." Jack shot Ray a wide grin. It was good bantering with his friend. It reminded him of the old days. "By the way, I'd like to get a look at the missing person's report from Boyd's place."

"Why don't you just ask the cops yourself?" Ray suggested.

Jack gave a sideways nod. "I will, but I want to see the official report first."

Ray dropped his feet to the floor and sat up. "Do you think the beat cops fucked up? Missing person's cases can be subjective, and every cop has their way of getting the same result, if you know what I mean."

"You don't have to tell me that." Jack cringed. From the little he'd learned about Paul Travers since he became Ray's partner, he was always shortcutting investigations, so it was a surprise Ray put up with him. He'd gone through a few—Ray could be a real hard-ass—and Travers was just the most recent. Jack was sure he wouldn't last long either. "Speaking of fuck ups, remind yourself one day to tell me how you got tasked with Travers."

Ray chuffed under his breath. "I'm . . . difficult. Maybe the department is challenging me."

"Some challenge."

"He's been a pain in my ass since they saddled me with him last month." Ray downed the last of his whiskey and set the glass on the desk. "What's up with you two anyway? Ever since the department assigned him to me, he's like a dog with a bone with you."

Jack sat back and laced his fingers together over his stomach, elbows on the chair arms. "Do tell."

Ray shrugged. "Just talking shit."

"Like what *shit*?" He didn't like Travers—certainly no love was lost between them. There was nothing specific about Travers he didn't like, but everyone had intuition, and if they listened to it, sometimes trouble could be averted. Jack's intuition could never hone in on what it was about Travers he didn't like. The guy just brushed him the wrong way, and for no apparent reason. Until Travers had recently made detective, Jack hadn't thought about the guy since they left the academy.

Ray squirmed in his chair a little. "It's just shit, Jack. No big deal."

"You brought it up."

His friend gazed around the darkened room for a moment. "It's just stuff like yesterday morning at the scene. He keeps calling me *partner*, and *buddy* . . . like he's trying to prove something. He keeps asking me questions about working with you. And until you showed up yesterday, I've never heard him talk to another cop like he talked to you."

"I'm not a cop anymore," Jack said, his gut clenching at the reminder.

"You know what I mean. I was going to say something but figured he was just puffing his feathers. Or if it's something between you two, then you two can work it out."

"I don't know what's up his ass. I've rarely seen him since the academy, though rumors have gone around about his assholery. I was surprised when I heard you'd been tasked with him. I'm really sorry about that, man." Jack considered the whiskey then shot a glance at the file still open on the screen. "I need a favor."

Ray's head shot up. Jack just stared at him. "I can't do it."

"You've done it before."

"I'm sure I did, but I shouldn't have." After a short staring contest, Ray sank back in his chair. "What?"

"Carl Boyd. I got his wife's cell phone and credit card. I've made a copy of her phone's memory, so I can go through her messages and contacts, but it needs a deeper look—deleted files and such. And I need her purchase history on her card. Obviously," he stressed, "I can't get a warrant for it, but you have an open missing person's file, so *you* can."

"Maybe so, but I can't give you the information," Ray reminded him.

"Partner," Jack said overdramatically. Then, mimicking Travers, "*Buuuddy—*"

Ray shot up and stomped away from the desk. "Fuck you, Jack." He ran his fingers through his hair, putting his other hand on his hip as he paced.

Jack just laughed and reached into his desk drawer. "You're being a diva. Here, have a Snickers." He threw the candy at his friend who dodged it like it was a live grenade.

"*¡Jódete!* Fuck you!"

"Kiss me first."

Ray stopped where he was and glared at Jack. He didn't flinch. They stared at each other for a long minute before Ray finally broke down and started laughing. "*Tu esta un pendejo.* You know that, right?"

"So you keep telling me. You gonna help a friend out or do we have to take this to the next level?" Ray instantly stopped laughing, as if someone had flipped a switch. Jack sat back, crossed his arms and put on a shit-eating grin. "You know I will."

"Don't you dare," Ray warned. There was no mistaking the seriousness in his voice. Jack just lifted an eyebrow, like *dare me.* "Leave Maria out of this."

Maria Navarro was Jack's ultimate weapon, and Ray's kryptonite. Jack loved her like a sister, as he loved Ray like a brother, and going to her when Jack wanted something was playing dirty. Very dirty. He knew Ray would do anything his wife asked him to.

"Fuck you." Ray stomped over to the door. "Be right behind me?" he asked, glancing over his shoulder as he flung open the door.

"You bet."

"Bring the info with you."

Jack waited until he heard Ray's feet descend the stairs before laughing aloud. Sure, his friend had been through a lot of partners over the years, but Jack was the only one who didn't put up with his hard-assery. They had developed a great bond, and even now relied on each other as much as they could without still being partners on the force or getting Ray into trouble with the LT. Jack was still more of a partner to Ray than that fuckwit, Travers, would ever be. Or anyone else.

Jack shut down his computer but left on the banker's lamp before rising and heading into the bathroom for a piss.

Moments later, he grabbed his cell phone and the notebook off the desk and stuffed himself into his leather jacket. The notebook went into the inner pocket and phone into his side pocket. He grabbed his helmet and gloves, reaching for the door handle.

Dinner with the Navarros was something he looked forward to every week. Because Ray was a creature of habit, he would take the same route home he always did. But Jack knew a shortcut he could take on his bike and beat Ray home. Even with the ten-minute head start.

CHAPTER SEVEN

Friday

After listening to yesterday's interview with Boyd and watching the recording from the walk-through in his house, Jack was still no closer to figuring out where Bonnie Boyd might have gone.

He thrummed his fingers across the notes on the desk before him. Ray hadn't come back to him yet with Bonnie's credit card purchase history, or on anything buried on her phone. He checked the time; it was still early. He'd only given Ray the details last night. Until he heard from him, Jack still had other leads to chase.

He looked at the call logs, texts, and contacts list on Bonnie's phone, but it was almost as if she didn't have any friends, or a life. It appeared she used the phone just as a phone. There weren't any photos, no texts, and only a handful of numbers had been saved to her contacts list—house, work, Doctor Johanna Harvey, Julie Anne Sumner, Carl's work and cell numbers—and only one had regular and significant incoming and outgoing calls. Carl Boyd.

He checked the time again; 9 a.m. The office was open now, so Jack rang the doctor's number to make an appointment to interview the doctor after lunch.

Next, he focused on the name of Julie Anne Sumner.

Carl hadn't been sure about Bonnie's friend. He'd called her Lucy Anne. Could he have meant Julie Anne? Curiosity got the better of him, so he grabbed his phone and dialed.

When a man answered, Jack nearly hung up. Instead— "May I speak with Julie, please?"

"I think you have the wrong number." The man disconnected.

Jack redialed. "You still have the wrong number," the man said on greeting.

"I'm sorry to bother you, but maybe you can help me."

"Who is this?" the man asked.

"Jack Slaughter. I'm looking for Bonnie Boyd. This number is listed in her contacts as Julie Sumner."

There was a distinct pause on the line. "Who did you say you're with?"

"I'm a private investigator. Bonnie is missing, and I'm running down some leads and trying to find her." He waited a moment, but when the man didn't speak, nor hang up, he continued. "I'm wondering why this number—your number—is in her contacts list if there's no Julie there."

After another pause, the man asked, "Can we meet? Alone."

"Absolutely. Give me an address. I can be there in fifteen minutes."

Ten minutes later, Jack guided his bike off the Embarcadero and to the back of the Ferry Building, where people filled the large open space on the pier. He pulled the bike to the side and parked it, quickly scanning the area as he dismounted. He removed his gloves and helmet and, as always, ditched them on the handlebar. He left on his heavy leather jacket as a shield from the crisp morning breeze off the bay.

The bright sun cast long shadows around the dozens of people. Many were either busy taking selfies overlooking the Bay Bridge or had bought food inside the Ferry Building and were now eating it in the sunshine at one of the small café tables scattered around.

Sliding on his sunglasses, he strode toward the center of the pier, hoping to find the man he'd spoken with on the phone, though he only had a vague description to go by—dark hair and beard, white shirt, blue jeans. At least a dozen people matched that description.

Well, the guy could come to him. Jack checked the time on his phone. He'd arrived earlier than he'd said, so maybe the guy wasn't even here yet. Traffic on the Embarcadero was heavy at the best of times, just one more benefit of having a bike in the city, and Jack had no idea where the guy was coming from.

They'd agreed to meet by the Ghandi statue, so Jack chose one of the benches surrounding the plinth. He had a full view of the building in front of him, as well as people milling in that direction.

Even with the cool breeze, the sun beat down on him while he waited, his black jacket quickly absorbing the heat. He found himself relaxing and leaned back with his arms crossed and watched the crowd.

Curiosity was a strange thing. He had always been an inquisitive kid—some would say nosy—and had eventually grown into an adult who questioned everything. He supposed what made him a good cop was his ingrained sense of curiosity and wanting to know the whys of everything. He viewed everything like trying to solve puzzles. And when it came down to it, most cases were puzzles. He knew what the image would look like when it was completed—solving the case and locking up the bad guy—but it was his job to take the jumble of clues before him and put them together in the order to create that final image. Occasionally, some of those pieces wound up on the floor, and he'd have to go searching for them. Much like this mysterious man. Just another piece in the larger picture.

Jack was checking the time again when he heard the familiar voice behind him. He switched on the voice record app and slid the phone into his pocket and moved to stand. "Please, stay where you are." The man sat beside him on the bench and extended his left hand. He was just as he described, but Jack would never have pegged him as a hipster—short back and sides with a generous crop on top, full beard. His white shirt was buttoned to the top with a red and blue striped bowtie; the wrinkled shirt sleeves were buttoned at the wrist. He wore blue suspenders over tapered blue jeans, and on his feet, he wore pointed toe boots. "I'm Julian Sumner. Sorry I'm late. I got held up in the shop."

Jack's grasp halted for a moment before releasing the man's hand. "Julian." The puzzle was coming together.

"You sound surprised, Mr. Slaughter."

"Jack. And yeah, a little. Bonnie had you down as Julie Anne in her phone."

Julian responded with a quirk of his manicured eyebrow. "Clever woman."

"So, since you asked for this meeting, I can assume you know Bonnie Boyd."

"She works for me," Julian told him.

Jack pulled out his notebook and flipped a couple pages back. "Her husband said she works on Pier 39. I could have met you there."

Julian jerked his thumb toward the Ferry Building. "I've got a shop inside too. When I saw you arrive, I came out as soon as I could."

Jack made notes as they talked. "What do you sell?"

"Here, a little garden shop. Down on 39, souvenirs."

Flicking his gaze to the man's right hand, he asked, "Where did you hurt yourself?"

The man examined his right wrist, tightly wrapped with an elastic sports type bandage. "Here. One of the pots got away from me and I hurt myself trying to grab it before it hit the ground. We both lost the battle, I'm afraid." He chuckled lightly, gazing back up.

"And you said Bonnie sells souvenirs?"

"Well, I'd hired her to work in that shop, but she got bored. I brought her up here."

Jack's focus shot up. "Her husband says it's only a part time job."

"She loves it up here. There's a different buzz . . . not as many tourists. I give her all the hours she wants." Julian gazed away, as if contemplating what to say next. "What's going on with Bonnie?" he asked. "You said she's missing?" Obvious worry crossed his face.

Jack nodded. "Yes. When did you see her last?"

"Last Friday. She worked in the morning and went home after lunch. Do you know what happened to her?"

"That's what I'm hired to find out. I have to ask this. You seem a little more shaken up about this than I would expect from an

employer. Is there something else going on between you two?"
Julian turned away. Jack heard several deep inhales before the man
scrubbed at his eyes and turned back. "I guess that means yes."

Julian nodded. "I've never . . . I mean . . . It's not my style to
date married women. I swear. But Bonnie and I hit it off. She's an
amazing woman." He gazed directly at Jack, sincerity in his eyes.
"I love Bonnie. I want her to leave her husband and be with me."

Remembering the house and Boyd's quirks, it seemed
reasonable that Bonnie might consider it. "What did she say?"

"That she couldn't. Her husband's not a very nice man. Really
obsessive over her, I think. When she was working down on 39,
he'd call several times during her shift, asking where she was. Even
if she was with customers, he wanted to talk with her. Like he was
looking for proof she was really there or something." Julian shook
his head back and forth. "She's a really sweet lady, but when he
calls, it's like the light goes out of her."

Jack's spidey sense was tingling but he couldn't put his finger
on what was niggling him.

"When did you two start sleeping together?" No sense in
beating around the bush. He'd already admitted to seeing her.
That usually meant sex.

"Umm . . . Maybe three months ago? It just—"

"—happened," Jack finished the old cliché. Julian nodded.
"And you asked her to leave her husband and go with you." Julian
nodded again. "And she said she couldn't or wouldn't?"

"Can't. She's afraid of him."

"Afraid of him? Did she say she is?"

Julian shook his head. "I can tell. Like I said, he called the shop
repeatedly. Every time was like torture for her. Since she moved up
here, he doesn't seem to call as much, but—"

Rolling his hand in a hurry up motion, Jack asked, "But—?"

The man looked around them, perhaps thinking if he should
keep talking or not, or looking for Boyd? Then back at Jack, he
said, "A couple weeks ago, she was late for work. She's never late. If
anything, she comes in early. I don't know . . . maybe she loves the
job and can't stand to be away, or maybe she just loves *me* and can't

stay away. I like to think maybe the latter, but I also understand her reasons to get away from *him*."

"What was so special about two weeks ago?" Jack pressed.

"She had bruises." Julian motioned to a couple places on his body—his upper arm and his upper cheek. "She said they were nothing, that she fell, but I knew they weren't *nothing*. The bruise on her arm looked like he'd grabbed her. The eye . . . he probably hit her. It must have happened that morning because it got darker as the day went on. She tried covering it up with makeup, but couldn't put on enough to hide the bruising. I sent her to my place until the end of her shift—she couldn't work with a black eye, ya know? And he'd probably question why she was home early."

Yeah, Jack knew. Julian was in love with Bonnie, and it sounded like the feeling was mutual.

Julian shifted in his seat and pulled a cell phone out of his back pocket. He rifled through the apps then handed the device Jack's way. What he saw didn't require explanation. Julian had had the forethought to take several photos of Bonnie's bruises. Jack confirmed to himself that they did, indeed, look like a grab mark on her bicep, and a fist mark across her eye.

He scrolled through the collection of photos, suddenly feeling sorry for the woman. Then he scrolled onto other photos. Photos of a happy woman, smiling for the camera. Some of the photos were taken in the plant shop, but others from other places around the city, as if on a day out. And some in a bedroom. They weren't pornographic images—no nudes—but it was obvious there was peace between the couple, and love. The photos reminded Jack of the looks Leah gave him after making love. His breath caught for a moment before handing the phone back to Julian.

"Sorry, I scrolled too far," he said, clearing his voice.

The man gazed down at the last image Jack had seen. "It's okay," he said softly.

He saw Julian's distress and didn't want to add to it, but he had more questions. "Did you suggest she go to the hospital to get checked out? Or to file a police report?"

He nodded. "Oh yeah, but she wasn't having any of it. She said he'd done it before and if she just ignored it, he'd calm down and forget it ever happened. But that was the first time he'd hit her in the face."

"And you saw these bruises on her body when you were making love?" Jack looked at Julian over the top of his sunglasses.

Nodding, he said, "She told me she bruised easily, that she bumped into things a lot. I had my suspicions, but she had ways of shifting the subject." If they'd been in the bedroom, Jack was sure he understood what Sumner meant by distracting him away from the topic. "Honestly, I've never once seen her bump into anything in my shops. If anything, she's a sure and confident woman. Just don't bring up her husband. But when she came in with a black eye—"

The blatant claim hit Jack in the gut. Any man who hit a woman, for any reason, was a coward in his book, but in the face seemed more personal. "And she wouldn't file a report?"

Julian shook his head again. "Like I said, she was afraid of him. She could file a report, and they'd bring him in for questioning. But they'd eventually let him out—either with a warning or on bail—and he'd go right home to where she was, and probably beat the crap out of her. Or worse."

"You said the last time you saw her was this past Friday . . . three days ago." He looked at his notes. "She worked through lunch then went home." Then back up again. "How were things between her and her husband that day? Did she give you any reason to worry? And if you two are in love, wouldn't it be unusual for you not to see each other every day . . . wouldn't you have tried calling her since last Friday?"

Julian scrolled through his phone apps again. "Here's my call log. I call her from the shop line in case her husband answers. You know, like it's work, and we need her to come in or have a question or something."

The phone had several unanswered calls in the log. Julian had been worried. A lot. Why hadn't these numbers shown up on Bonnie's phone? Had Boyd wiped the phone in case he was asked for it later? Hopefully, Ray would be able to get his tech to find that deleted information. If Bonnie had actually answered one of those calls, then it would mean Julian was lying. If he lied about not speaking with her, what else could he be lying about? "Why wouldn't you have called the other number?"

"She had my personal number for emergencies. She never used it though, but she had it, just in case."

"And what about the last time you saw her? Anything I should know?" Jack asked.

Julian nodded. "She finally made the decision to leave him. She promised she was telling him that day. That's why she left after lunch. She'd bought a suitcase and was going home to pack while he was at work. She was just going to leave him a note to say goodbye. He didn't need a reason, or a note, as far as I was concerned. Just get the hell out." His eyes welled up again, but he didn't try hiding it. He gazed up at Jack. "You're going to find her, right?"

"That's my intention."

CHAPTER EIGHT

The black Harley Fatboy screamed up the Embarcadero, the mufflers rat-a-tat-tatting as he slowed at the junctions before accelerating again. Passing under the Bay Bridge, Jack wove through traffic toward the Giants' stadium. He winged left onto 3rd Street at Willie Mays Plaza and crossed Lefty O'Doul Bridge.

The new SFPD building—now called the San Francisco Public Safety Building and included the Mission Bay Fire Station—rose up before him with its multi-level glass façade. Public parking was scarce, so he swung into one of the reserved lots for the baseball stadium and made his way to a space directly across from the department. There wasn't a game on today, so the lot was virtually empty. Dismounting, he removed his helmet and gloves and hung them on the handlebar, then hopped the short fence and crossed Mission Rock Street.

It wasn't long after *that night* when Jack couldn't seem to get his shit together and had taken a sabbatical from the department. When he hadn't returned after a year, he was asked to turn in his badge. His commander left it open for his return when Jack was ready—and he *had* planned on going back to work—but after three years, he couldn't seem to find the same enthusiasm he'd once had for the work. He only tolerated investigative work because it gave him the funds he needed to continue his own investigation—finding his daughter's killer and his wife. But how could he return to work as a police detective when his family's case was still cold? He'd failed to protect them. He couldn't fail at finding the perpetrator.

Jack swung open one of the building's big glass doors and

quickly gazed around the wide, open foyer. To his left, he was immediately taken aback by the display that greeted him. *The Spiral of Gratitude* memorial to all fallen officers floored him every time he entered the building. The monument consisted of a long, glass tube that was suspended from a large skylight. It was big enough for a sizeable man like himself to comfortably stand inside with outstretched arms and not touch the sides. The inside of the glass was inscribed with an emotive poem by Margo Perin that spiraled in a single continuous line down from the skylight.

Somehow, the words *"Never do we have the gift of goodbye. The only choice is to carry on, make our peace"* always stood out to him. If his family's case was never solved, could he find the courage to one day make peace with the losses in his family and find his own peace?

He turned his attention back to the task at hand and strode across the foyer to the desk. Not being a cop anymore didn't mean he didn't still have a few friends on the force. Ray wasn't the only one he called on for favors.

Sgt. Bill Waters immediately snapped to attention. "Detective," he greeted with his baritone voice through the glass partition; his perfectly straight white teeth contrasted against the man's dark coffee-colored complexion.

"It's just Jack these days."

"What brings you all the way down here? Missing us yet?"

"Every day, Bill. Every damn day. How are the wife and kids?"

"Fine, fine. My eldest is off to college soon. Wants to be a cop."

Jack winced. Most cops, while they loved their jobs, didn't want their kids in the business. "Well, she had a great role model."

Waters just chuckled. "What can I do you for?"

Pulling out his notebook, he said, "I'm chasing up some details on a case."

"I'm glad to hear you're keeping busy." Waters pulled open a drawer and withdrew a visitor's pass and processed some details into his computer while they chatted.

Jack forced a chuckle. "Always have my hands in something. I'm heading up to Records before going in to see Ray. Is he in yet?"

Waters tapped a few keystrokes into his computer. "He's signed in, so he's somewhere in the building. Want me to page him?" he asked, sliding the pass under the partition window.

Clipping it on his jacket, Jack then patted the countertop as he stepped away. "Nah. Good enough for me. I'll find him. Great seeing you." Waters waved him off.

Jack opted for the stairs and made his way to Record Management. The SFPD website had a missing person's page, but it hadn't been updated in a while. The basic paperwork was easy enough to obtain since it was public information, as were the other reports he needed, including any other recent deaths, and after speaking with Julian Sumner, spousal abuse reports. Under normal circumstances, one would have to file a request for each one and wait up to two weeks to see if the department would send them. But as a former cop, and one with friends on the force who still treated him like family—Bill Waters for example—Jack sidestepped the rules and put on a flashy smile.

In Records, Jack riffled through the pages as Officer Amy Chin put them on the counter before him. "I don't see the missing person's report on Bonnie Boyd."

She eyed Jack with a coy smile. "Let me look her up." She tapped Bonnie's name into the system and waited for the information to come up, quickly glancing up at him.

"Thanks. I appreciate it."

"How you doing, Jack?" Sincerity filled her voice.

That was always a hard question to answer. Even he didn't know how he was doing. Not really. "Good, Amy," was all he could say. He didn't think she'd want to know his dark thoughts, or the depth of his despair.

Her gaze looked him up and down. "You sure? You look tired, and thin. Maybe you need some good Chinese home-cooking to fatten you up." She gave him a wink.

The thought of Chinese food made his stomach tighten, and not in a good way. Living over Tommy Wong's had its perks and its faults—like smelling Chinese food in his place twenty-four seven. It permeated everything so there was always a funk in the place. Over time, the perk of free meals had lost its appeal.

"Thanks, Amy, but I'm okay. Just working a case. I'll eat and sleep when I've found my client's wife."

Chin eyed him for a moment then nodded and turned back to her computer screen. "I see the report on Boyd has been logged in but it's still processing."

"Can you give me the names of the reporting officers?"

She wrote down the names and slid it toward him. "Give me your number and I'll call you when the full report is available."

Jack had known Chin from his time on the force, and even though he was married, she flirted with him anyway. He always took it as a friendly gesture. Since Leah had been missing for the last three years, did Chin assume Jack had accepted his wife was probably dead and at the bottom of the Bay? Getting hit on, even this subtly, wasn't new to Jack. But her flirtations seemed a bit sincerer this time. He wasn't interested—he wasn't interested in any woman but Leah—so he tried letting her down as nicely as possible. "If you could send the report to Ray, that would be perfect."

Then softly, she said, "I can cook something besides Chinese food, you know."

"I know. Thanks for the offer."

Chin noticeably pouted. "Are you sure?"

"I am. Thanks."

Jack's next stop was Ray's office . . . formerly known as *their office*. His stomach tightened again but this time it was the sight of seeing Travers sitting at what had once been Jack's own desk. He almost turned around and walked away, then considered the weight of the papers in his hand. The one file he'd come for was still out there, so he needed whatever information Ray had obtained on Bonnie's card and phone.

Taking a deep breath, he pushed open the door. Ray and Travers spun in his direction.

Ray opened his mouth to speak but it was Travers who had the first word. "Jackie," he exclaimed. "Love the visitor's pass. It suits you." Jack very nearly punched the guy in the face. Just because.

Ignoring the asshole, he looked at Ray. "Got a minute?" He cocked his head to follow him out of the office.

"*We're* partners now, Jack. You can't just waltz in here like this."

He shot Travers a look he hoped said *go ahead and test me, asshole*, but he kept his mouth shut. Bullies normally eventually left you alone if you ignored them or stood up to them.

Ray rose and followed Jack through the door. "Aw, come on, Ray!" Travers whined as Ray closed the door behind them.

"What's up?" he asked under his voice. From the corner of his eye, Jack saw Travers straining to hear what they were talking about.

"Jesus, how can you stand that guy?"

Ray laughed. "He's only like this when you're around. He says you like the needling . . . it takes your mind off your troubles."

Jack lifted an eyebrow at the comment. "And you believe that bullshit?"

Shaking his head, Ray said, "No, but like I said, if you two have a beef, you need to settle it. I'm not getting in the middle."

Jack cast a glance in Travers' direction then back to his friend. "Well, I hope when it comes down to it, you don't have me up on assault charges when I punch him in the face."

Ray laughed. "*No sé nada* . . . I know nothing."

Changing the subject, Jack said, "Well, I'm hoping you know something about Bonnie Boyd. Any news yet on the phone and card?"

"You only gave me the info last night. Do you expect me to work miracles here?" Jack just looked his friend in the eye. They both knew homicide detectives could usually get the information they needed quicker than other departments. "Yeah, okay, okay." Jack pulled out his notebook and pen. "I can't show you the reports. You know that." Jack used a hurry up motion with the fingers holding the pen. "On her phone, we didn't find much more than you did."

"Explain. Much more? That means you found something I didn't."

Ray nodded. "There were some deleted calls. Several from Julie

Anne Sumner, but they stopped on Friday."

This confirmed Jack's suspicion, that Boyd had tampered with his wife's phone. If he'd deleted missed calls, what else had he deleted?

"Is that it?" he prodded.

Ray shook his head. "There were also deleted calls to a medical clinic."

"You mean to her doctor—" Jack flipped through his notes to his appointment with Bonnie's doctor. "Doctor Johanna Harvey."

"No, a clinic over in the Inner Mission District called The Other Plan B."

Jack knew what Plan B was—the morning after pill. The other Plan B was when it was too late for that. "She had an abortion." It wasn't a question.

Ray nodded. "According the charges on her card, yeah."

"When?"

"About three months ago. According to her card statements from around the same time, she tried burying the cost between a few other larger charges."

The dates were starting to sync up. Three months ago, Bonnie had started seeing Julian Sumner. That wasn't long after he'd transferred her from the tourist shop up to the ferry building. The fetus had to have been her husband's. Had Boyd seen the charges on her statement and known what she'd done and beat her for it?

"What were the other charges?"

"They weren't significant items. What stood out was that the charge from the clinic was broken down over three months. The full charge would have stood out among the smaller purchases, but breaking it down, it was less noticeable. They looked like any other doctor's office fee, but one of the techs pointed out the same charge amount from the same clinic, and so close together, and well . . ."

"Right." Jack scribbled the details down on his notepad. Then, looking up, "Was there anything else?"

Shaking his head, he said, "That's about it. Do you need me to dig further back?"

"Nah, I think I have what I need. I just came from an interview with Bonnie's boss. Turns out Bonnie was leaving her husband for a hipster."

Ray's eyes widened. "I thought hipster was going out of style."

"No one told this guy."

CHAPTER NINE

"The doctor will see you now," said the nurse who appeared through a door signposted *Please wait to be seen* beside where Jack stood. The room was full of women and children waiting to see one of the doctors in what turned out to be a family clinic.

Jack had been to similar clinics with Leah before and after Zoë had been born, so he understood the tired looks on many of the women's faces, and why they let their toddlers cry or throw toys around the waiting room rather than try to instill manners in them. And why he'd stood along a wall to avoid some of those projectiles. He was grateful when the nurse appeared sooner than he'd expected. She led him down a short hallway and waved toward an open door before walking away.

The doctor rose from her cluttered desk—a slim woman with mousy brown hair and wearing a traditionally styled but pink lab coat. She extended a hand. "Mr. Slaughter. I'm Doctor Harvey. Please, have a seat." She closed the door then reseated herself, facing him.

Jack considered himself of average size and weight for a man of his height—an even six feet—but he felt considerably out of proportion sitting on the dainty chair in the feminine office. By the décor, it was clear Doctor Harvey catered to women, and why some of the women in the waiting room eyed him with curiosity. Not that a man in bike leathers in a women's clinic wasn't suspicious in the first place.

Being careful not to move around too much on the creaking chair, he extracted his notebook and pen. "Thanks for seeing me on short notice. I won't take much of your time."

55

"You have me curious, Mr. Slaughter. The receptionist only said this was regarding Bonnie Boyd." Jack nodded. "As she's my patient—"

"Yes, I know about doctor-patient confidentiality. I'm still hoping you can help."

Confusion crossed the doctor's face, her gray eyes narrowing.

"I'll get down to it. Bonnie Boyd was reported missing by her husband. I'm a private investigator hired to find her."

One of the doctor's hands lifted to her mouth to stifle her obvious shock. *Ohmygod* tumbled out as a single word.

"As you can appreciate, I'm covering as many angles as I can. Bonnie had few numbers in her cell phone, but one of them was yours. Obviously, I'm hoping you can fill in some blanks that will help me find her." Jack spoke softly but firmly. It was a delicate matter, and if the doctor did share anything confidential, anyone walking past in the hallway didn't need to hear it.

"Is she dead?" the doctor asked.

"I don't know, but evidence has revealed she saw you just before booking an appointment with The Other Plan B." He gazed at the doctor, anticipating her reply.

"Well . . . yes, but how did you know?"

"Did you refer her to the clinic?" When the doctor remained silent, Jack assumed she was weighing up what she could and couldn't reveal. He knew that until Bonnie was confirmed dead, doctor-patient confidentiality remained in place. "I'll assume you did, otherwise you would have offered alternatives to her situation." Like keeping the baby or adoption. "Were her other appointments routine?"

"If by routine you mean annual tests all women should have, yes."

"What about for other things?" He gazed directly into the doctor's eyes.

Suddenly the doctor shifted in her seat and started straightening files on her desk. "As I said, I can't discuss patient details with you."

"How about if I ask you some questions? If it's something you can't directly respond to, I'll make my own assumption. That way, you won't actually be discussing anything directly with me, or telling me something you shouldn't." He waited a moment while the doctor considered his suggestion. She then shrugged in a conciliatory fashion and faced him again. "Okay, great. I'll ask again, other than annual tests, did Bonnie come to you for anything else?"

"We're not just a family clinic. We cater to the complete well-being of women." A good neutral response, Jack noted.

"It's already been established she came to you about her pregnancy. Did she tell you why she didn't want to keep the baby?"

"We give all of our patients options."

"Did she tell you it was her lover's baby?" By the look on the doctor's face, it was possible she didn't know about Julian Sumner, so Jack assumed her reply was no, the baby wasn't his. Only Bonnie and her doctor knew exactly what they'd discussed. And by the timeline, it couldn't have been Sumner's anyway, but he had to ask the question to see what the doctor knew.

"So, it was her husband's baby, and she didn't want to keep it."

Doctor Harvey remained silent for a moment before repeating, "We give all of our patients options."

"Has Bonnie ever come to you for something other than annual tests and her pregnancy?"

"Like I said, we have a wide range of women's services."

"Did Bonnie ever come to you for treatment for any accidents?" Jack used his fingers indicating quotes around the word accidents, implying the accidents were *on purposes*. The doctor turned away. Jack took it as a yes. "We know her husband was beating her. Had he always?"

She hesitated, then shook her head *no*.

"Okay, so this was a recent thing. After the abortion?"

Yes, she nodded.

Jack continued making notes with each response. "Did he ever break any of her bones?"

"No," she blurted. Her hand went to her mouth, realizing her fumble. She'd just admitted to talking with Bonnie about her husband's mistreatment.

"Were any of her injuries life-threatening?"

No.

"Did you ever recommend she file a formal complaint?"

"Standard procedure for any patient who presents with suspicious injuries is to recommend going to the authorities." While it wasn't an outright admission that she'd told Bonnie to go to the cops, stating her office policy was as good as.

So far, everything he learned jived with what Julian had told him. "Did she ever say she was afraid for her life?"

She shook her head *no.*

"When was the last time you saw Bonnie?" he asked.

"Two weeks ago."

"I know she worked in the morning, so it must have been in the afternoon. I know you can't tell me what it was for, but I'm guessing it was because of her eye." Julian had told him it was the first time Carl had hit Bonnie in the face. "The socket is delicate."

The doctor nodded. "It's like an eggshell. Quite often when people are hit in the eye, or even the cheek, it can fracture the socket. Depending on the angle of the strike or severity, it can shatter. Of course, the largest worry is the loss of vision."

"And Bonnie had those concerns." It wasn't a question. He'd been struck in the eye a number of times while on the job. He always made sure to get checked out. Good eyesight was just part of what made him a keen observer.

The doctor nodded, confirming what he'd already thought.

"You said . . . rather you agreed that she didn't want to file a report against her husband, but did you ever talk with her about counseling? There are a number of therapists in the city who specialist in spousal abuse."

"We never got that far. She ran out of the exam room. I'd hoped she was all right, but there's nothing I can do to help her if she won't help herself," she said matter-of-factly.

"I hear you. I think I have everything I need. Thank you for your time," he said, rising and stowing his notepad and pen back in his jacket.

Doctor Harvey rose with him. "You'll let me know what

happened to her, won't you? I really hope she's all right. She's such a lovely woman."

"You'll probably be contacted by detectives from the department. I don't know if they'll come with a warrant, but you may want to have Bonnie's records ready in case they do. And," he added, "you don't need to let them know I was here. I was hired privately." Doctor Harvey nodded her agreement before turning to pull a tissue from the box on her desk. Jack let himself out.

It was late in the day by the time Jack pulled onto Scott Street, a block over from Carmelita. He hoped Boyd was still at work so he could interview his client's neighbors undisturbed.

Normally, neighborhood backyards backed up to each other. In the Boyds' case, their house had been built on a narrower strip of land, which meant the backyards of the houses on the west side of Carmelita backed up to a narrow green area on Scott Street near Harvey Milk Corner.

Jack backed his Harley into the first space beside the arts center's back driveway and used a narrow public walkway between the center and a house to access Carmelita on foot. He crossed to the other side of the street and looked down to see if Boyd's car was in the drive. It wasn't, and oddly, neither was Bonnie's beat-up Nissan.

Before he started knocking on doors, he withdrew his phone from his jacket pocket, brought up Boyd's home number, and let it ring while gazing at the residence. If he answered, Jack would use the excuse of updating him on the case. When the call diverted to the answering machine, he left his name and number, then keyed in Boyd's cell number and let it ring.

"Hello," Boyd answered, a sharp tone in his voice.

"Mr. Boyd, this is Jack Slaughter."

"Umm . . . I can't talk right now, Mr. Slaughter," he quickly said.

"Let me know when you'll be home this evening and I'll drop by for a chat," he suggested. There was a pause on the line. "Mr. Boyd?"

"Yes-yes, I'm here. I don't know when I'll be home. I'll call you when I'm free."

"I just thought you'd like an update on how things are going so far with finding your wife," Jack told him, feeling uneasy with how he was being put off.

"I'm assuming you haven't found her. Please, call me later. I have to go." With that, the phone went dead.

Jack stared at the phone as the screen automatically changed from the call app to his wallpaper—a family photo from Zoë's second birthday, a few months before her murder. He quickly clicked the screen to sleep mode, watching it go black before repocketing the device.

Well, that was odd. Boyd obviously wasn't home, but he didn't seem keen to know anything about the case either. What was he up to?

Pushing the man's odd behavior from his mind, there was no better time to start interviewing the neighbors.

At this hour of the day, Jack wasn't sure many people would be home, but as it turned out, most were elderly and retired. Unfortunately, that also meant many had hearing problems so never heard anything strange coming from the Boyd residence. That didn't mean he wasn't turning up anything juicy, but mostly about other neighbors than the Boyds. By the very nature of retirees, many bored people spent hours at a time looking from their front room windows. Some would call them voyeurs, others busybodies or just nosy. Jack was grateful no matter what their motives.

Mr. Walker lived directly across the street from Boyd and said he'd seen Bonnie return early the day she'd gone missing. He saw her go into the house but didn't remember her coming out. "That doesn't mean she didn't. My bladder isn't what it used to be," he'd told Jack.

A couple houses down, Mrs. O'Brien had been out front tending her roses when Bonnie rushed from the house toward her car, followed by Carl who quickly dragged her back inside. "That was two weeks ago . . . wait, maybe three. I remember that was the day my Surprise Roses started blooming." When Jack asked why they were called that, she said, "Because I bought white rootstock many years ago. When they finally bloomed, they were shocking pink. Surprise!" The woman's laugh made Jack smile. What he took away from that short conversation was that Carl and Bonnie had been fighting.

Mr. and Mrs. Wokowski lived on the left of the Boyds and had both been home the day the Nissan had been towed away. "That was yesterday. After you left, Mr. Slaughter," Mr. Wokowski said. Interesting. Boyd had never said he was removing her car.

"Are you sure Bonnie didn't drive her car away?" he asked.

Mrs. Wokowski shook her head quickly. "I know what a tow truck looks like, young man."

Jack chuckled. "Yes, ma'am. I only meant, it seems strange that Mr. Boyd would tow his wife's car away without her knowledge."

"We thought so too, so we went out to talk with Carl. Lovely man. He said it was time his wife had a newer car. He said she's at her sister's right now, and when she gets home, he'll surprise her with a new car." The old couple nodded in agreement that this was what they'd been told.

Interesting, he thought again. *Gone to see her sister? Is that what he's telling his neighbors to explain his wife's disappearance, rather than admit she might have left him?*

"How is his mother doing?" asked Mrs. Wokowski.

Jack was taken aback at the question. "What do you mean?"

She glanced at her husband before looking at Jack again. "Carl told us she'd taken to her bed after his father died a few years ago. We've tried to visit, but he won't let us see her."

"He said she was too fragile," said Mr. Wokowski.

Taken to her bed? Other than Boyd and himself, there had been no one else in the house when he was there. He'd told Jack his parents died. Well, not in so many words. He'd said he inherited the house from his parents. Now Jack was questioning that inheritance.

"I'm sorry. I didn't meet Mrs. Boyd, but I'll be sure to let Carl know you sent your regards to her."

Thanking the couple for their time, he briskly strolled back to his bike. He made a few notes before stuffing the notebook and pen back in his jacket pocket, geared up, and headed down the road, wondering what Boyd would say when Jack asked him about the sister. And his parents.

CHAPTER TEN

Saturday

Officers Gary Johnson and Phil Harris worked the Northern District Police Station, which serviced the Western Addition, so Jack couldn't ask the officers to swing by his place during their shift. He had to go to them. Since he wasn't a cop anymore, he didn't want to meet them in the department, so he asked them to meet him around the corner at the local fast food joint. He saw them as soon as they pulled into the parking lot. They stopped in front of the Harley where Jack had parked in the shade of a tree.

Without getting out of the car, Harris rolled down his passenger window. "Hey, Jack. Long time no see."

As Jack strolled toward the car carrying two small bags, he saw Johnson lean over so he could join the conversation. He shook both officers' hands then knelt beside the open window, setting the bags on the pavement beside him. "Hey, guys. They still have you in the car? I thought you'd applied for bike patrol."

"Harris got separation anxiety at the thought," said Johnson.

"You fucker." Harris showed his partner the finger. Then quietly said behind his hand, "*He* kept dumping the bike." By the look on Johnson's face, Harris was correct. "So fucking embarrassing. Rather than subject a new partner to . . . this," he waved his hand toward his partner, "I figured I better stay where I am for now."

Jack chuckled, envying the comradery of the men.

"So what's up, Jack?" Johnson asked from the driver's seat. "Why couldn't you meet at the department?"

"I'm on the job."

63

"Welcome back," the officers said in tandem.

Jack chuckled. "No-no. Not ready for that yet. I've been hired privately to investigate the disappearance of Bonnie Boyd. You two were called out to the Boyd residence to take the husband's report."

Johnson and Harris nodded, remembering. "Yeah, we were there. Weird dude."

"Right," Jack said. "I can't get my hands on your report yet and thought you could fill me in."

"What do you need to know?" Harrison asked.

"The usual . . . anything out of the ordinary? Did he do anything suspicious or give you any reason to think he had something to do with his wife's disappearance?" Jack suggested.

Both men shook their heads. "The only weird thing in my book," said Johnson, "was how old everything was, but the place didn't smell old."

Jack chuffed under his breath. "I suggested some retro upgrades and the look he gave me said he thought I was off my rocker." The men laughed. "Did you get a look at the kitchen . . . the dinner in the oven?"

Both men looked at each other, then back to Jack. "What dinner?" Harris asked.

"When I first interviewed him, he said dinner was still in the oven when he got home but she was gone."

Harris said, "The house smelled clean. Unless he's really good at cleaning up, I don't think anything had been cooked in that house for a few days."

"Hmm . . . Did you ask him about the bags in the living room? Why he hadn't put them away?"

"What bags?" Harris asked.

Things were unraveling even more for Carl Boyd. "When I did my walk-through, there were a couple bags in the living room that Boyd said Bonnie brought home from her shopping the day she disappeared. They were sitting beside the wing-back chair in the living room near the dining room door."

Both shook their heads again. "Nope. No bags anywhere," Harris said.

Remembering what the Wokowskis had told him, he added, "How was the mother?"

Again, the men looked at each other, then shook their heads. "No one was in the house, other than Boyd himself."

Curious.

Jack had only been taking mental notes, along with the audio recordings he always took when conducting interviews, but he would put them in his notebook as soon as the guys left. "You guys have been a big help. Thanks."

Johnson said, "I don't see how, but we're happy to help, Jack."

"Let us know if you need anything else," Harris said.

Jack retrieved the two bags at his feet and handed them into the car. "Thank *you*. Stay safe out there."

Harris took the offered bags, handing one to Johnson. Grins crossed both of their faces. "Donuts!" they exclaimed in unison.

Jack stood back with a grin of his own. "Don't let the coffee get cold."

He waved off the officers then strolled back to the bike and threw a leg over the seat. He pulled out the notebook and pen, writing down what Harris and Johnson had just told him.

When he finished, he looked at the time. It was getting late. He went into the restaurant, ordered a couple burgers and fries to go—he had beer at home.

Jack sat back in his chair and leaned away from the desk, popping the last of the cold second burger into his mouth. He grabbed his beer then rose to stand beside the window.

The sun had long set, and the city had turned on her nightlights. The Bay Bridge wore her string of pearls, the Trans-Am building looked like an electrified Egyptian monolith, and the three-story sign over the Condor Club entrance glowed with neon colors.

He missed the original Condor sign that had been hanging there in his youth—a sexy blonde woman wearing black panties and quarter-cup bra. Under the full-length figure: *Carol Doda Topless*. He and his friends used to run down there in the evenings, when the club turned on their lights. They'd point and laugh at the woman's flashing cherry-red nipples, and talk about the day they were old enough to go inside the club to see the famous stripper who danced fully nude. By the time he was old enough for that, she'd retired.

Now that he was back in Little Italy, it was easy for Jack to reminisce. These were the streets he'd grown up on. He'd lived and worked in the city through all her changes, rather than having moved away and come back years later to find the neighborhood had shrunk and everything different.

He looked left to the twin spires of Saint Frank's church—what the locals always called the Shrine of St Francis of Assisi, long before Father Nicholas Morrissey had been transferred there. Saint Frank's had been his family's church. He knew the place front to back, as any good Catholic boy would who spent time as an altar server.

He remembered the rivalry the local boys had with those whose families attended Saint Peter and Paul Catholic Church three blocks away. Peter and Paul had long been called the *Italian Cathedral of the West* as it looked more like a cathedral than a parish church like Saint Frank's. Jack and his pals spent endless hours defending Saint Frank's honor on the neutral ground of Washington Square Park that overlooked Peter and Paul's. There hadn't been a lot for growing boys to do in the city, but the park was a welcome playground. Over time, hide and seek grew into tag, which grew into football, or baseball depending on the season. Eventually the boys became young men and left, one by one, for jobs, or college. He didn't know anyone who'd returned. If they had, they probably wouldn't recognize the place. It was now teeming with restaurants and cafes, galleries, and trendy shops.

And of course, the erotic nightlife that had always been a staple of the area, had seen million-dollar upgrades to attract wealthier clients from the business districts. Even the seedy stores selling sex toys from behind the counter had rebranded into upscale clothing and adult toy shops. No longer was anything secreted away; it was all on display.

Yes, it was an all-new Little Italy.

He took a swig from his beer before turning away from the window and looked back at the papers on his desk. He needed to update his missing person's files, but first he needed to build a timeline for Bonnie Boyd.

His spidey sense tingled stronger than it had yesterday. Why would everything point back to Boyd? He was the one who'd filed the missing person's report.

Something wasn't right.

No one had ever been allowed into the backroom. Not even Ray.

Under normal circumstances, a renter was expected to use the front room as a living space, perhaps setting up a small cooking space, with a hotplate on top of a tiny fridge in the corner. The backroom would serve as a bedroom with its tiny bathroom. It was ideal for a single person.

But these weren't normal circumstances. For Jack, after that night, staying with the Navarros had only been meant as a temporary stopgap until he could get his shit together. The apartment was part of that. But with the department headquarters so close for work, and the familiarity of the place where he'd grown up giving him a certain amount of solace, he'd settled in. He hadn't anticipated that he'd still be here nearly three years later. In that time, he'd left the force and set up his own business, opting to run it from where he lived. All his public business was conducted in the front room. That left the backroom for private business.

He flipped on the light as he entered. It was a relatively small room, with the bathroom door directly opposite the bedroom door on the south facing wall, a single bed stacked with boxes and folders to the right of the door, and on the left was a small chest of drawers with a coffee pot on the top and a toaster oven.

To his left, the east facing wall was partially obscured by boxes from the Sunset house that he'd never unpacked.

On the west facing wall, a small window was covered in an equally worn and thin curtain as in the front room. Directly below that window outside were the steel stairs leading to his front door—the only door into the place— and the side alley where he parked his bike.

Rounding the door, he faced the north facing wall.

Not long after he got his investigator's license, Jack lined this wall on both sides of the door with thick corkboard to preserve the old plasterwork from any pins and tape he'd use while putting up evidence. The place might be a dive, but for now, it was his dive. And he respected other people's property.

He used this particular wall not because it was the largest section—that was the client wall on the right side of the door—but because if anyone was anywhere near the open door, they wouldn't see either evidence board.

While in the backroom, he was able to hear anyone walking up the external stairs through the small window. It gave him time to exit the backroom and close the door to maintain his privacy, and client confidentiality.

Even if the backroom had been meant to sleep in, it didn't mean he actually did. He'd tried. But even between the buildings, the city's glow forced its way through the thin curtains and shone on the second evidence wall—he still couldn't bring himself to call it his family's wall—keeping him awake. After the first few weeks of spending sleepless nights staring at the lack of evidence on the wall, he couldn't take it anymore and ended up sleeping on the front room sofa. It was more comfortable anyway, or so he'd convinced himself.

Every day, he spent time looking at the first wall, hoping to find the answers to what had changed his life so dramatically. And he was still no closer today than three years ago. By now, he'd expected to have piles of evidence, clues, leads . . . *something* to go on that would lead him to Leah, and find out who killed his precious little girl, and poor Trax.

It was a punch in the gut every time he thought about the innocent lives that had been so brutally taken. What had a two-year-old and her pet ever done to anyone? Yet the answers he searched for weren't just dangling out of reach. They were non-existent.

It had pissed him off, too, when Father Nick made the suggestion that Leah might have been responsible for what had happened. He'd spent the last three years keeping that thought out of his mind. He didn't want or need the priest forcing it back in.

His mind spun to Carl Boyd. The man had appeared genuinely distraught over his wife's disappearance. He gave Jack the impression he and Bonnie lived the perfect life as he thought he and Leah had. But the last few days severely skewed that first impression—the man's O.C.D., the cheating wife, the boyfriend, her terminated pregnancy, the beating . . . and the mystery of what happened to Boyd's mother.

Had the impression of his own tragedy been as skewed? Did Leah have secrets she hadn't shared with him? Did she have another life while he was at work? Had she been cheating on him? Had she had enough, slipped a few gears, and murdered their daughter and dog before just walking away, taking nothing with her to remind her of their life together?

Jack gulped in air until his body screamed at the lack of oxygen.

His eyes stung, blurring his vision. He scrubbed at them with the back of his fist until the city map on the wall came back into focus. The few notes and tags flashed at him like beacons, echoing his knowledge that he didn't have enough to go on, screaming at him that he'd failed. Failed everything—failed as a cop, failed as a husband and father, failed at protecting his family, and more importantly, was failing at finding out what had happened to them.

He took several deep breaths to try calming the pounding in his chest. Getting emotional wasn't going to help him do his job.

Realizing he hadn't added the tag yet, Jack grabbed a notepad and a pen and scrawled the date before pinning it in place over Spreckels Lake, where the texter had last sent him. That made twelve times he'd been called out on a wild goose chase.

He tossed down the notes and pen and forced himself to step back from the wall. He needed a piss and some sleep.

CHAPTER ELEVEN

Sunday

Jack stood back and looked at his handiwork.

He'd hung a big map of the city on the wall to the right of the door reserved for his cases.

The horizontal space above the map was for victims; he'd hung a print out of Bonnie Boyd. The vertical space on the left was reserved for suspects, which included a screen grab printout of Carl from the home inspection video, and the photos of Dr. Johanna Harvey and Julian Sumner, both of which he'd found with an internet search then copied to his printer.

Below each suspect's image, Jack added a white card with individual details, meeting notes and reference numbers to the video files on his computer—Carl Boyd's place of work, both of Bonnie Boyd's workplaces, Julian—aka Julie Anne—Sumner, Dr. Johanna Harvey, The Other Plan B clinic. Even Harris and Johnson got a card since he'd talked with them, as well as the Boyd neighbors. Everyone Jack had or would talk with would end up on a white card and stuck on the wall.

He used the green cards for questions and responses, taken from his written notes from the notepad and those he'd transcribed from the audio and video recordings.

Blue cards were used for evidence that had gone cold and may or may not warrant further investigation.

Yellow cards were for *notes to self.*

Next, he'd pinned a red flag on Carmelita Street, indicating the client's residence, then added various colored flags that pertained to the evidence he'd gathered so far, which until now just revolved around interviews he'd conducted.

He used colored index cards to write down individual evidence, clues, and other notes, and pinned those to the right side of the map in a vertical line, linking the cards with a piece of string to a location he'd pinned.

Red cards were reserved for inconsistencies in the investigation. There were a lot of red cards.

Now, Jack stood back and eyed his handiwork. It was a much fuller wall than his family's wall, as it should be with an active and ongoing case. And as he'd already surmised, seeing the details before him like this compounded everything leading back to the Boyd house.

The wall still missed one thing—the missing person's report Carl had filed. He filled that space with a yellow card, noting SFPD MP RPT—SFPD missing person's report—would go there when he was able to obtain a copy.

Even though the case seemed to be turning into something else, there was still no mistaking that dead or alive, Bonnie Boyd was still missing.

Just then, the notification bell sounded on his cell phone. He went out to his desk where the phone sat on the stack of missing person's files and picked it up. A text from Ray, with an attachment: *bboyd's mpr att hnj drpd off bwc rec from carmelita vst will brg by aft sft.*

Jack chuckled. Either Ray missed the memo that his texts were no longer restricted to the number of characters he could use, or he just couldn't bother typing out full messages. Either way, his message was welcome—Bonnie Boyd's missing person's report attached, Harris and Johnson dropped off body-worn-camera recording from Carmelita visit, will bring by after shift.

The attachment was a copy of that MPR. He emailed it to himself then set the printer to work so he could replace the yellow card on the wall.

He didn't think Bonnie's missing person report would say anything he didn't already know, but he was now kicking himself for not asking Harris and Johnson if they'd been wearing their body-worn-cameras the night they did their walk-through at the Boyd house. BWCs had become normal use as he was leaving the force, and where he'd got the idea to record his inspections as he'd done at the Boyds' with his cell phone camera. He chalked up the misstep with the guys to his being overly tired.

The printer's gears clicked and whirred as they spit out the pages. He read each page as it was deposited in the tray, then put them all in Bonnie's file. Nothing new, but he appreciated Chin getting Ray the file so quickly, and Ray for sending it right over.

He checked his watch. It would be several hours before Ray was off shift.

He went back to his desk and grabbed up a stack of papers Chin had printed out for him yesterday. He'd also made a point of asking for murder cases and Jane/John Doe files. Because the city was so densely populated, and there were so many district departments, sometimes things got missed. Over the course of other investigations, Jack had inadvertently stumbled upon a couple long-time missing people to unsolved murders and unidentified bodies.

He made himself a pot of coffee, then settled in for an afternoon of reading case files.

Warm breath whispered over his face. A low voice spoke softly, as if luring him. "Oh, Jack, you're such a foxy stud," she sighed against him. She blew in his ear. This certainly wasn't the kind of dream he was used to. He hadn't had a good dream in years. "Me love you long time," she continued. He turned toward her. Leah?

When he opened his eyes, Ray was practically sitting on top of him. His eyes were laughing while his lips puckered and made kissing noises.

Jack quickly pushed himself off the sofa, shoving Ray away from him. "You sick fucker."

Ray threw himself back on the sofa, holding his stomach while he laughed. "I knocked," he barely managed to get out.

"You never knock." Jack's heart pounded as he shoved his fingers through his hair. As he moved toward the desk, he looked up and noticed the backroom door was open. "I'm making coffee." He slammed the door behind him, so Ray wouldn't follow. He heard his friend laughing through the thin wall. He went in to take a piss while he waited for the coffee to make, and he couldn't help but chuckle a little too.

A short time later, Jack emerged from the backroom with two cups of coffee. He knew Ray took lots of sugar but gave it to him black to spite him.

Sitting at the desk, he asked, "Tell me about the video." Ray reached into his pocket and tossed something in Jack's direction. He caught it and spun it in his palm. Nodding, he inserted the thumb drive into his computer's USB port and waited for the system to recognize it.

Ray came around to stand beside Jack so they could both watch the video. He was sure Ray had already seen it, but having not actually walked through the house himself, seeing the recording would benefit his friend too.

The guys had been correct. There weren't any bags in the living room. Beside the chair or otherwise. Jack wondered why Boyd had lied to him. The rest of the video pretty much jived with the video he'd taken. He pulled up his file to show Ray. "This is my walk through the day after Harris and Johnson's."

When the video finished, Ray stood back. "Looks the same to me."

Jack spun in his friend's direction. "Really? What kind of investigator are you?" Back at the keyboard, he punched in the commands to open both videos side by side. He paused them both with the view of the chair. "This is from the BWC the night Harris and Johnson took the missing person's report and did their walk-through. This is from my walk-through."

Ray leaned in. "¡Carajo!" He cursed his favorite expletive under his breath. "The angles are different, but there are absolutely no bags anywhere in the room."

"Exactly. Why would he have put them there after the first walk-through, then tell me they'd been there since Bonnie put them there when she got home from shopping?" Jack asked, rhetorically.

"Did he actually tell you she put them there?"

Jack thought for a moment. Had Boyd told him or had Jack just assumed from the tone of the conversation? "The bags were there with her wallet inside on top of the clothes. I asked if it was her shopping and he agreed. I just assumed she'd dumped them there."

Stepping back around to the front of the desk, Ray sat in one of the chairs and crossed his ankle over his opposite thigh. Jack practically saw the gears in his friend's head working while he sipped the coffee. Then, "I think we need to have another word with Boyd."

Jack shook his head. "Not yet. I don't know what the department is doing in terms of investigation, but I've been doing one of my own. Things aren't stacking up. I want to be sure my speculation is correct before tossing this into Homicide's lap."

Ray set the cup on the desk. "What's going on? Anything I need to know?"

"Probably, and I think you and I should talk about this."

"Sounds sketchy. What's up?"

Jack sat back, stretching his elbows behind him and rolling his head to work out the tension in his neck. "I'm sorry, Ray, but I don't trust Travers. Anything I give you, I don't want it going back to him."

"He's my partner, Jack," Ray said, solemnly. "But this isn't a Homicide case. It's Missing Person's. Not in our wheelhouse, so why would it matter if he knows?"

There was no other way to put it than straight up. "Because I think Boyd killed his wife."

CHAPTER TWELVE

Silence ricocheted off the walls as the men stared at each other. Did Ray think he was kidding? Or was Jack waiting for his friend to start laughing again? But this wasn't a funny situation, and they both knew it.

"¡*Carajo!* Are you sure?" Jack nodded. "How—"

"The department works slower than I can," he said. "While it's taken four days to get the missing person's report filed on Bonnie Boyd, I've interviewed her doctor, employer, neighbors . . . even Harris and Johnson. There are too many inconsistencies. Everything keeps pointing back to Carl Boyd."

"I take it the shopping bags aren't the only clue things are *muy jodido*."

Jack nodded. "Not fucked up for us, but for Boyd. I'm just trying to figure out why he'd file a missing person's report if he killed her. And why he came to me to help find her. And," he stressed, "if he did kill her, where is she?"

"Chin said you asked for Jane Doe files and missing person's. I can help you go through them."

"Thanks, but like I said, I don't trust Travers. Besides, I already went through them before you . . . woke me up." He drew his brows together in mock anger, an effort to keep from laughing.

Ray thought for a moment. Then, "I can swing by after work to help you with this. I'll keep Travers out of it. God, I hate doing that to a partner," he exclaimed.

"Then don't do it. I'm good here on my own. I might need a favor or three though."

"Ha! Favors. Is that what you call them?" Ray asked, chuckling.

75

"Yeah, and you know I'll return the favors. I already am."

Ray crossed his arms before him and cocked his head to the side. "Do tell."

Jack waved a hand over his desk. "The department only just released the missing person's report, while I," he emphasized, "have already done the interviews and targeted a suspect. Until the case is investigated by the department, they won't kick it to Homicide until they've drawn the same conclusions I have. By the time that happens, Boyd could already be behind bars, waiting for arraignment."

"You sound pretty sure about yourself," Ray said. Jack nodded that he was. "All right, give me three reasons why you think the husband killed his wife, rather than her just walking away from the marriage."

Jack thought a moment. If he told Ray, would he escalate the internal investigation? "Is this between us, or are you taking this higher?"

Ray waved his hand between them. "*Hombre-a-hombre.*"

Jack nodded that he understood. He didn't speak fluent Spanish, but having been raised in an Italian family, and after years working with his friend, he understood enough to eavesdrop since both were Latin languages.

"One: The shopping bags."

"That's already been established."

"Yeah, but no one would have known if I hadn't gone out there. And why put them out and tell me that she'd left them there?" Ray nodded, capitulating. "Two: He started beating her recently when he found out she'd had an abortion."

"*¡Mierda!* How did you find that out?"

"I told you. I interviewed the boyfriend."

"We looked through her phone records. There wasn't any boyfriend listed."

Jack gave his friend a shit-eating smile. "Yes, he was. Julie Anne Sumner."

"That's a woman's name. Last I knew, women couldn't get each other knocked up."

Releasing a long groan, Jack said, "Julie Anne . . . Julian . . . get it? Julian Sumner. He owns the shops where Bonnie worked."

"*¡Carajo!* You need to get your shit together, man, and get back on the job."

"First things first, my friend."

Ray nodded his understanding. "Ok, number three?"

"Three: He had her car towed away after I spoke with him."

"And you learned this, how?" asked Ray.

"I went over to interview the neighbors. I didn't want to do it while Boyd was home, so I parked on Scott and walked over. His car was gone, and so was hers. One of the neighbors told me he'd had it towed right after I left the house after my walk-through."

"Nosy neighbors."

Jack chuckled. "Sure, but the street seems to be filled with retirees who've lived there most of their lives. You know how neighborhoods are. After a while, there's a routine everyone knows, even if they don't know you personally. And when something's off, it stands out. Such as when I was there. One of them heard my bike pull up so knew I was there. And later they saw the car being towed. When they asked Boyd, he told them Bonnie had gone to her sister's for a few days. When she got back, he would surprise her with a new car. Her sister's!" Jack's voice hitched up an octave with disbelief. "He just filed a missing person's report. And why would he not tell me he was having the car towed when I was there? Something's not right."

"Do you think the body was in the trunk?" Ray asked.

It was a simple question, and one asked calmly. But it sent a chill up Jack's back. "If you want to help, get on the phone and start calling wrecking yards." He pulled up a list of yards from the online Yellow Pages. "You take these. I'll take the others." Ray nodded and dialed the first number, walking to the other side of the room so they weren't talking over each other. Jack dialed the first on his list.

He was just dialing the second number when Ray shouted. "Got it! It's down at a place off 25th Street near the Muni Metro East facility. They've got it pulled aside with some other cars that are going for crushing. The transporter is coming in the morning. If we can get down there now, he'll wait before heading home."

Looking at his watch, he said, "He's working late tonight?" Businesses like these took in cars at all hours, from car wrecks to impounds and everything in between. Jack didn't think anyone would actually be on site on a Sunday, but on-call. He wasn't going to question it. He was grateful the guy agreed to wait.

"Apparently so. I don't care though. I told him we'd be right down. I'll drive."

Jack shook his head as he grabbed his leather jacket off the hook by the door. "The bike's faster. You gonna be warm enough with what you're wearing?" Ray looked down at his blue cotton hoodie and shrugged.

Jack disappeared into the backroom and returned with another leather jacket. A good biker didn't just have one set of leathers. He grabbed his helmet and gloves from the table under the coat hook and chucked a second set to Ray before heading out the door. Ray wasn't keen on the Harley, but right now, getting to the dismantlers' before Ray's contact left was more important than his friend's delicate constitution.

At this time of day on a late Sunday afternoon, and on the bike in light traffic, they were there in less than fifteen minutes. Jack maneuvered the Harley up to the yard's main gate and honked twice, then removed his helmet.

It hadn't slipped Jack's notice how Ray clung to him on their way over and grinned to himself. "We've stopped now, Ray. You can let go." He'd no sooner said that than Ray leapt off the bike, pulling at the helmet. "Chin strap, jock strap."

Ray fumbled with the buckle through padded gloves. It didn't take a rocket scientist to see he was rattled. Jack lifted a hand in the air for Ray to see and removed his glove with the other hand.

"*¡Culo!*" he heard from behind the shield as Ray threw off the gloves then unbuckled and removed the helmet. "In case you didn't hear me . . . *¡Culo!*"

Jack laughed. "I heard you the first time."

The gate rattled open just enough for a fat balding man to step through. His coveralls were caked with at least a decade's worth of grease and who knew what else.

"You here for the shitty Altima?" When Jack nodded, the man slid the gate open a little wider to get the bike through. There was no way in Hell he was leaving his Harley unattended in this part of town.

Inside, Jack dismounted and followed the fat man and Ray through the darkening yard. The lights surrounding the building barely made up for the quickly fading sun, but kept them from falling in one of the big potholes.

"There it is. What do you want with it anyway?" the man asked.

The Altima was parked in the shadows at the back gate that opened onto Illinois Street, where it would be easier to load onto the transport.

"Can you turn on more lights back here?"

"Naw, that's all I got. I'll give you a good price on the car," he pressed.

Ray pulled out his badge and clipped it on his belt. "Do you have the keys or did you just haul it away from the house?"

"Hauled it, but the keys are in it."

Jack pulled his phone from his pocket and tapped on the flashlight app he'd used to search Boyd's attic, then switched on the video. If there was anything in the car, he'd need a record of the discovery. He flung open the driver's side door on squeaky hinges and pulled the keys from the ignition. At the back of the car, the men looked at each other for a moment before Jack shone the light on the lock and stuck in the key.

Ray turned to the fat man, showing him his badge. "I'm sorry. This is part of an investigation, so I'm going to have to ask you to step away."

"Yeah, whatever," he mumbled as he waddled back toward the lot entrance.

"Ready?" asked Jack.

"No, but it's gotta be done."

Jack had to turn the key hard to get the mechanism to release.

When it popped, the lid sprang open like a jack-in-the-box, startling both men. In their scramble to jump back, they collided and nearly fell into a greasy puddle. Jack struggled to hold onto the phone.

"Jesus fuck goddamn H fucking Christ." Ray's exclamations were always creative, to say the least, even in English.

"Yeah, what you said." Jack's heart pounded in his throat and he took deep breaths to calm himself. When he saw the pale look on Ray's face, he nearly laughed. Instead, he stepped back to the rear of the car and looked into the trunk space.

It wasn't a body, but the shopping bags he'd seen in Boyd's living room were there, along with a small pile of women's clothes.

"What the fuck?"

Jack faced his friend. "Let's assume he knows she's dead. He's getting rid of her car, so why not her clothes too?"

"Are these the bags you saw in the house?"

"Looks like them." He pulled the bags closer and extracted the garments. What he'd thought were purchases looked like Bonnie's own clothes. There weren't any tags on them, so they definitely weren't the new things Boyd said his wife had bought that day. "He must have been in the process of clearing out her things before I got there. That would account for the bags not being there the night Harris and Johnson did their walk-through, but then they were the next day when I went over. He probably hadn't counted on me wanting to do a second walk-through when he hired me."

"¡Carajo!" Ray barked.

"What?"

"This means we're going to have to impound the car. How am I going to explain this to Haniford?"

Lt. Dick Haniford was Ray's boss and had been Jack's too when he was still on the force. He knew the guy played by the book. Ray was right. How were they going to explain Ray's involvement in discovering the car?

He couldn't help but echo his friend's own words. "Fuck."

CHAPTER THIRTEEN

Monday

In the years he'd known and worked with Ray Navarro, Jack didn't remember ever seeing his friend so worried about talking to Haniford. Finding Bonnie Boyd's car in the dismantler's yard, and her clothes in the trunk, had forced SFPD to open a homicide file. And because Jack had led Ray to the car, he'd been called in to account to his former boss as well.

Haniford didn't appreciate being called into work at 2 a.m. on a Monday morning, but he spent the rest of the day grilling Jack about his missing person's case and how it tied into the car and Ray's involvement. Jack didn't know exactly what Ray had told Haniford, but while waiting for backup to arrive to impound the car, they both agreed to keep the story as simple as possible.

The official report Jack gave the department was that Carl Boyd had hired him to find his wife, Bonnie. Jack supplied a copies of the contract his client had signed and the check. Jack told the LT he'd performed a walk-through of the residence on Carmelita Street the same day, noting Bonnie's car—a well-worn gray 1995 Nissan Altima—had been parked in the driveway.

When he'd returned on Friday to interview neighbors, he discovered that Bonnie's car was missing. Upon speaking with neighbors, those living directly beside the Boyds, Mr. and Mrs. Wokowski, had informed Jack that Carl Boyd had told them Bonnie had gone to her sister's for a visit, and that he intended on surprising her with a new car on her return. This struck Jack as odd, as he'd been hired to search for a missing woman—this fact being backed up by a formal missing person's report filed by Carl Boyd with the Northern District PD, made by officers Phil Harris and Gary Johnson.

Suspicious about the car removal, Jack rang around to various garages and wrecking yards until he found the car at the dismantlers across town. Suspecting foul play, he then called Ray to accompany him to the wrecking yard. Upon inspection of the vehicle, they discovered Bonnie's clothes in the trunk.

Detective Navarro agreed the case was suspicious and made the call to bring in backup to impound the car and open a formal case file for further investigation.

That was his story, and he was sticking to it.

If anyone retraced his steps, and he was sure someone would, absolutely nothing in his statement could be refuted.

However, Jack had made a point of leaving out the other evidence—Julian Sumner, Doctor Harvey, Bonnie's abortion, spousal abuse, inconsistent evidence . . .

Jack was in deep now and needed to solve this himself. And he still held out hope that something might lead him to Leah.

The only thing that really irked him—the one thing Jack had hoped to avoid—Paul Travers was now involved. Well, with the limited information in his sworn statement, Travers would have to start from the ground up. Ray had agreed to keep the details he knew to himself and let Travers spin his wheels. It would keep him out of Jack's hair. At least for a while.

Jack had started the job of sorting through the case files yesterday. He didn't sleep well at the best of times, and worse after he'd been texted about a new false lead to finding Leah. He'd been more tired than he'd thought and had fallen asleep on the sofa with the files in his lap.

After being rudely awakened by Ray, then finding Bonnie's car at the dismantler's yard, and subsequently spending most of last night and this morning giving his statement to Haniford and handing over the evidence relevant to his statement, it had been a busy couple of days and he hadn't had time to get back to the files.

And was why Jack still sat on the floor in the middle of the front room, wearing just a T-shirt and pair of sweatpants he'd long ago cut off just below the knee—missing person's, Jane Does, and murder files surrounding him in carefully laid-out piles, in order of importance.

The floor probably wasn't the most professional place to conduct business, but then, neither were a couple of cheap rooms over a Chinese restaurant. And frankly, his desk was too cluttered, and the narrow bed in the backroom had his family's case files spread out on it.

The floor was the biggest flat surface in the room for this kind of work. The reports were easier to see spread out in front of him. He still had interviews to get to, but the stack of murder files and Jane Does he'd put together would be instrumental when he went to the Medical Examiner's office this evening. He wasn't sure if it was a good thing or not that the ME was open twenty-four-seven, but he found the night shift was much quieter, and the staff was much more receptive to *upright* visitors.

Someone pounded at the door. It wasn't Ray. It was too early. Besides, he'd just let himself in. And he wasn't expecting anyone else. He looked at his watch. The date reminded him it wasn't time to pay Tommy the rent.

"Come in," he called, not bothering to get up.

He hadn't expected the gust of air to precede the visitor, but he did expect they'd quickly step in and close the door behind them. Whoever stood in the doorway was letting the wind scatter his carefully laid-out paperwork across the room.

"Goddamnit," he exclaimed, shooting to his knees to collect the pages. "Close the fucking door." He recognized the familiar laughter. Forcing himself to remain calm, he didn't have to look to see who it was. He squeezed his eyes shut for a moment and inhaled deeply before exhaling the man's name on a groan. "Travers."

"Jackie, *buddy*," Travers drawled in a condescending tone, still hovering in the open doorway.

Jack rose and collected the last of the scattering pages, trying to ignore just *two* of the words he disliked the most out of the guy's mouth—Jackie and buddy. Everything else he said was equally abhorrent. Basically, the guy just needed to shut the fuck up.

"I wish you wouldn't call me that."

"What? Buddy? Are you saying you're not my buddy?" Travers said, trying to sound disappointed.

"No. Jackie."

"Aww, but Jackie suits you."

"What do you want?" Jack glared at Travers, watching as he kicked the door closed before strolling into the center of the room, pushing his cocky attitude in front of him.

"You've come down in the world," he said in an arrogant tone, hands on his hips as he surveyed the space. He went to one of the windows and used the side of his pinky finger to pull back the thin curtain. "Nice view though, of the titty bar."

Oh, how easy it would be to push the asshole through that window. Could he justify doing the time? Nah, Travers wasn't worth it.

Jack straightened the papers then moved over to put them face down on his desk. He noticed Travers' gaze followed his movements. What game was he playing?

Jack paused for a moment, spotting his cell phone on the desk. Casually, he acted like he was checking messages as he switched on the record app, then slid the phone into the T-shirt pocket, just like he'd done at Boyd's house. If Travers was here to cause trouble, Jack wanted a record of it. Especially if he'd be forced to defend himself.

Moving to stand between the man and the desk, he saw in his peripheral vision that the backroom door was closed. Good. Travers was the very last person on the planet he wanted in that room. Hell, he didn't even want him in the apartment, let alone anywhere near Little Italy.

Jack leaned back on the desk and casually crossed his arms in front of him. "What do you want?" he asked again, staring directly into Travers' eyes.

"Just to talk, Jackie boy."

The tone of the man's voice dripped with sour sarcasm, but

Jack refused to rise to the bait. "Is this official business or are you just here to hassle me?"

Travers chuckled. "Maybe a little of both."

"Well, you weren't invited here, so say what you have to say then get the hell out. I don't have time for you." He crossed his legs at the ankles and waited. He hoped his overall body language told Travers he was shutting him out.

"All right then."

Travers stepped closer, until he stood directly in front of Jack. The tips of the man's shoes pressed against his bare toes, but he wouldn't give him the satisfaction of knowing it hurt. He stood so close, Jack felt the man's breath on his face. The mustache forming on his lip failed to block the odor. Travers' breath smelled like whatever crap he'd eaten for breakfast. "You need to brush your teeth, man," Jack said.

Travers' eyes widened. His ruddy features reddened. His fake smile vanished. Yeah, Jack had pissed him off.

"What did you say?" he asked with deliberation.

"I said your breath smells like shit."

"You better watch your mouth . . . Jackie."

"Step off, Travers," Jack calmly said.

Travers looked him up and down. "Or what? You gonna assault a *respected* member of the San Francisco Police Department?" He accentuated the word respected, making sure to exhale heavily over Jack's face.

"I'll do whatever it takes to protect myself. I didn't invite you here. There's no cause for you to be here. Legal or personal."

"Touch me and I'll haul you in for assault. Then how will you *ever* find your precious Leah?" The man laughed lightly.

Jack struggled to keep his cool. He turned his face slightly and slowly inhaled fresher air, trying to calm the pounding in his chest.

Bringing Leah into this was below the belt. What the fuck did Travers have against him anyway? He'd never done anything to the guy. So what if they hadn't clicked at the academy? He hadn't clicked with most of the people there. He just wanted to get in and get out and get on the job.

"My grandmother used to have a phrase for people like you—*spessa nella testa*. You're a little thick in the head, so I'll say it again slowly. Step . . . off. Now."

Travers didn't move, but the man's stinking breath quickened against Jack's face. What the hell was he eating? He heard the man's teeth squeak as he ground them together, saw his jaw muscles flex under the pressure. Travers' eyes darted quickly, as if daring Jack to take a swing at him, but he stood his ground. He wouldn't give the bastard satisfaction, nor his recording evidence of his own wrongdoing. If anything went down, it would all be on Travers.

He must have been weighing his options as a long moment later, Travers finally backed off. Not a lot, but enough that he took his stank breath with him and gave Jack back some of his personal space.

He inhaled low and deep for some fresh air but kept his gaze keen. He still didn't really know what the guy wanted. "Well?"

"I think you're holding out on us, Jackie," Travers finally said.

"On what?"

"Evidence, asshole. Bonnie Boyd. You've been on the case for a week and all you got is a missing car? Come on. I know you got more than that. Yeah, it's a little suspicious that the guy dumped the car, and some of her old clothes, but I know you. If you think there's enough here to impound the car for further investigation, you got more on this than you're telling us. I want to know what it is." Travers threw his hands on his hips again and put his weight on his toes.

Calmly, Jack said, "Like you said, I'm no longer on the force. It wasn't my call. Talk to your partner."

"Ray's a fucking traitor. He ain't talking."

It took great effort on Jack's part not to show any reaction. Ray didn't like Travers either, but as partners on the force, they were obliged to share intel. This told Jack that Ray was sticking to their agreement about the car and related evidence.

"Sounds like you have a problem."

"I'll deal with Ray later. Right now, I want what you got."

"You have a copy of the statement I gave yesterday, and all the evidence that pertains to it. I can't tell you anything more than that."

"You mean you *won't* tell me anything more."

Jack stared at him. "I don't know what you want me to tell you, Travers."

"Goddammit, Jack, tell me what you got!" Travers thrust his hands in Jack's direction, frustration scrawled all over him.

Still as calmly as he could, Jack said, "That's all I got. For you," he added, just to get under Travers' skin.

Travers pointed a threatening finger at him. "You're going to regret messing with me, Jackie." He threw open the door and stomped down the stairs. Jack heard Travers cursing as he moved through the alleyway and out onto the street.

Jack walked to the door and closed it, locking it. "Yep, I probably will."

CHAPTER FOURTEEN

Tuesday

The Medical Examiner's office was still located in a three-story extension at the back of the Hall of Justice building on Bryant Street, as the new building in the Bayview district remained in the last stages of construction.

The current autopsy suite hadn't changed much since its original construction in 1962. The same five white porcelain cadaver tables dominated the left side of the room, with the same stainless steel sinks at the feet end of each slab. The walls may have been repainted since the '60s, but it was the same pukey shade of avocado green that had been so popular back in the day; he doubted, though, that the cream-colored tiles bordering the ceiling had been replaced. And the original stainless steel spotlights hung from the same paneled ceiling.

From where Jack stood at the wide door, the expanse of the somber-colored floor between the head end of the slabs and the wall directly to his right should have remained clear for gurneys and mobile trolleys, but equipment lined the wall, making the space look more like a cluttered storage room than an autopsy suite.

He'd arrived just after midnight. The ME's was hardly the place Jack expected to hear music at any time of day, yet the acoustics reverberating off the dated tiles was, admittedly, perfect. From the moment he'd opened the facility doors, the woeful refrain of the guitar from the far end of the corridor lured him to where he now stood just outside the door, listening to the music. He didn't enter until the final note had been played.

A man sat between the last two slabs at the far end of the room in the dim light. The bright overhead ceiling lights hadn't been switched on, but one of the dated spotlights shone down on a white sheet covering a body on the last slab and causing a reflective brightness onto the lacquered guitar body and steel suite fixtures. From where Jack stood, the view at the end of the darkened room seemed more like a stage setting than what it really was.

The man rose and moved to the slab on his right where he slid the well-used but well-cared-for sunburst Fender Stratocaster back into its original hard case, carefully nestling it in the plush orange interior.

Jon Cutter wasn't just the city's most respected pathologist. He was also one hell of an accomplished guitarist. And probably the last of the city's original surfers.

"Dude," Cutter casually greeted, latching the case. He straightened his white lab coat and flipped over the collar on his vintage Kuu-Ipo Aloha shirt—a cream shirt with teal, red, and dark blue flowers and hula girls, and the names of the Hawaiian Islands printed all over it. He wore it over khaki-colored pants rolled at the ankles. He had on regulation rubber soled shoes with protective booties over them, but Jack knew if Cutter had been off duty, he'd be barefooted, or at the very least, wearing a cheap pair of flip-flops.

Cutter put money into one of only three things—his guitars, his Aloha shirts, and his sticks, including his collection of rare early surfboards—and not necessarily in that order.

Years back, Jack had asked his friend why he wore such pricey vintage shirts to work; wasn't he afraid of getting blood on them? Cutter had only smirked when he said the lifestyle wasn't about investments in frivolous things like the cost of clothes. Jack knew Cutter took care of the things he invested in, which meant the shirts had probably been bought new off rack back in the '60s, so he was careful of splatter.

Cutter wove his fingers through his thin, shoulder length, silvery-blond hair then tied it back with a similar type of small elastic band Jack had seen Leah use on Zoë's hair.

89

He strode through the room, extending his hand as he neared his friend. "Cutter." He nodded at the guitar case. "Albatross." Jack recognized the old surf-style tune by Fleetwood Mac . . . the original group before Stevie Nicks joined.

Cutter nodded.

The man played that tune when he was working on a particularly difficult postmortem, and glancing at the covered body on the slab beside them, Jack wondered if tonight was a good night to ask Cutter for his help. Jack had finally finished putting the Jane Doe and missing women's files back together after Travers' unexpected visit, and had some theories he wanted to discuss with his friend. But he knew he could be a hard reach when he was in the middle of something deeper.

"Maybe I'll come back."

"Nah, man, I need the distraction. What's up?" He grabbed his guitar case and jerked his head as an indication to follow him.

Cutter's office overlooked the I-80, otherwise known as the Dwight D. Eisenhower Highway, an elevated stretch of road connecting the SoMa district —South Market—of San Francisco to Berkley and Oakland across the Bay. At this hour, car headlights cast shafts of light through the darkened room as they sped by.

Cutter flipped on the light, revealing an office that leaned heavily on a surf theme. Jack suspected most people wouldn't expect such an unusual office, with several pictures of Cutter himself hanging ten, waxing his stick, and other related activities on surfing trips he'd taken around the world. Some of his many awards were pushed back against a shelf behind his desk. Jack had been here many times and understood Cutter needed a respite from the gruesomeness he worked with on a daily basis, even if it was something as simple as office décor and playing his guitar over dead bodies.

But that was the end of the personalization of the room, as every flat surface was piled high with case files, including being pushed into corners on the floor.

The Medical Examiner's office saw around fifteen hundred cases a year, and until recently, it could take months before the death certificate was completed and filed. In some cases, a couple years.

The department was still understaffed and overworked, but under current management, it was slowly climbing out from under mountains of files needing completion. At least they were able to get death certificates processed more quickly following a postmortem—families needed them to bury their loved ones, and for insurance purposes. The department still needed more staff, but at the same time, the city needed more money to afford the extra help. Right now, the funds were tied up in the construction of the new Bayview facility so the department had to do what they could to not get snowed under completely.

This was just part of the reason why Jack took on the missing person's reports and the Jane and John Doe files. It wasn't his job, but it gave him something to do between cases, and he hoped matching up what he could had helped Cutter close some of his backlog of work. And part of why he was here tonight.

Cutter cleared the chair in front of his desk then moved around it and plonked himself down in his old swivel chair that had probably also been here since '62.

Jack sat, extracting a set of papers from within his jacket pocket. "I think I've matched some files for you." He handed them to Cutter. "A Jane Doe and a couple John Does; they seem to match missing person's reports. Attached."

Cutter compared the files. The only indication that Jack could have found a correlation in the cases was a slight nod of the man's head and lifted eyebrow before setting aside the files.

Reclining back, Cutter stretched his shoulders before folding his hands behind his head, using them to support his head. "You didn't have to come all the way over here just for this."

Jack leaned back in the stiff chair and threw a booted foot over his knee. "Maybe I missed you."

Cutter chuffed lightly. "We could have met at the fire pits." He quickly glanced at his watch. "Grab your stick and I'll meet you at sunrise to catch some waves."

It had been three years since he'd waxed his board and met

Cutter at Ocean Beach, just two short blocks from his house, to go surfing. It had been that long since he'd done many things he used to enjoy. While Cutter was a great instructor, Jack wasn't very good, though the cold Pacific water was a great way to wash away the day's grit and grime . . . in a manner of speaking.

"One day." Silence settled between the men for a long moment before Jack pulled out another set of papers from his jacket, unfolded them, and considered it before handing it to his friend. "I'm working on a case and wanted to get your take." Cutter leaned over the desk and flipped through the paperwork as he continued listening. "A few days ago, a man came into my office and hired me to find his wife."

"You hate cheating spouse cases," Cutter reminded him.

"I told him as much, but then he told me about her disappearance; it was just like Leah's." Cutter noticeably winced but remained quiet. Jack explained the case and his investigation, including the abortion and the boyfriend. And his suspicions about the husband's involvement.

When he finished, Cutter set aside the file and spun toward the window, put his hands back behind his head, and gazed at the passing vehicles. If Jack hadn't been familiar with Cutter's reflective habits, he would have thought the guy hadn't listened to a thing he'd said. But Jack knew better, and let his friend think about what he'd just heard.

Turning back, his friend dropped his arms onto his desk and leaned forward. "How do you think I can help?"

Jack released a deep breath. "You know, I'm not sure. I guess I just need some assurance that you don't have a Saint Pauli Girl in your fridge." He pulled out his phone and opened his photo gallery app, scrolling to the photo he'd taken of Bonnie in his office, and showed it to Cutter.

"A couple bodies came in earlier in the day. Both are blonde women. I can show them to you." When Jack nodded, Cutter rose and led him back to the autopsy suite where he hauled open an oversized door and flipped on the room's light.

The cooler was an over-large room flanked by stainless steel walls. Bodies that had already been autopsied were enclosed in thin white body bags and occupied the dozens of shelving units. Those bodies in the heavier canvas bags were recent deliveries from crime scenes and rested on gurneys that had been pushed side-by-side and head-to-toe as far into the room as possible. He knew the city had storage for over four hundred bodies, but they couldn't all be kept on site. There were still more here than Jack expected.

"We get in an average of three or four bodies a day. These are all the new arrivals since the weekend." Cutter waved to the gurneys. "The blondes are over here."

Jack followed his friend over to one of the gurneys where he quickly unzipped the body bag. Cutter's brusque, matter-of-fact revelation of the body didn't faze Jack. It paid not to be squeamish about death when you made your living as a homicide detective. Except when it affected his family.

"Recognize her?"

The woman was beautiful, even in death, but she wasn't Bonnie Boyd. He shook his head.

Cutter rezipped the bag then moved to the next gurney and revealed the woman's face. Jack instantly knew she wasn't Bonnie either. "Sorry. Too young." He scratched his head, glancing at the remaining gurneys in the room. "I hate to ask, do you have any other blondes? I don't know how up-to-date the missing person's files are or how many Jane Does come through here, but if I have to grasp at straws to solve this case, I'll grasp."

Cutter glanced around at the room then back at Jack. He flicked his thumb in the direction of the autopsy suite and said, "The woman on the table is a blonde, but she's been here since before you took your case."

"At this point, when Bonnie Boyd really went missing is anyone's guess. I've been going on what the husband told me. He said she'd been missing about forty-eight hours before coming to my office. When I talked to the boyfriend two days ago, he said hadn't seen her since last Friday, which tells me she could have been missing a day earlier than what the husband told me." Running his fingers through his hair, he squeezed at his scalp where his head was starting to ache.

"Well, the one I'm working on could fit that timeline. She came in five days ago." Back in the autopsy suite, Jack stood beside the body, opposite his friend. "I understand you were at the scene where she was found."

Jack's head snapped up. "Me? What do you mean?"

"This is the one found at Spreckels Lake."

His heart leapt into his throat. "I was there, but I never saw her."

Cutter's brow lifted. "This might be a shock then."

"You've never been one for dramatics, Jon." His friend was one of the most laid-back people he knew and usually unflappable. Cutter just grunted then pulled back the sheet to reveal the woman's face. Blonde, but not Bonnie Boyd. "Okay, what gives? Nothing shocking here."

Cutter pulled back the sheet all the way.

Jack assumed the body had been laid out for the postmortem. However, when Cutter revealed the body, what had happened went far beyond a traditional dissection.

Jack had seen a lot of gruesome things from his time on the force. Humans were experts at torture and mayhem. But this . . . this looked like something he'd seen in images of the Spanish Inquisition.

From the neck down, the woman had been, for the lack of a better word, excarnated. In layman's terms, her skin had been flayed from her body and she had been completely defleshed. And what little remained looked like early morning carrion had been picking at exposed bone.

Jack swallowed hard and then swallowed again. He spun around and heaved into the nearest stainless steel basin.

CHAPTER FIFTEEN

With all the frenzy over the Boyd case, Jack had nearly forgotten about Spreckels Lake. Ray had promised the body wasn't Leah's and sent him away. After that, the last week seemed to have sped by in a blur with the Boyd investigation and all the interviews, and last night's marathon grilling from Haniford.

Back in the office, Cutter handed him the bottle of water he'd retrieved from the kitchen down the hall. Jack leaned back in the stiff chair, catching his breath, and nursing a sour gut. He hadn't been affected like that over a body since he'd attended his first postmortem as part of his academy training.

The taste of bile still flooded his mouth. "Thanks, Jon." He unscrewed the cap and guzzled half the water before recapping the bottle and setting it on the desk.

"You okay?"

"You could have warned me."

Cutter chuffed. "I did."

Jack cast his friend a glare that he hoped said the warning hadn't been good enough. "Yeah, but that was some fucked up shit, man."

"Tell me about it. It's not the first one either."

Cutter had his full attention now. "What . . . How many?"

Cutter threw himself into his swivel chair and leaned down behind his desk, hauling up from the floor a large file which he dropped onto the desk with a heavy thud. "This many."

"Jesus H.!"

"They come in regularly."

"What do you mean by regularly?"

95

Cutter tapped the page clipped to the top file with his finger. "See for yourself."

Jack pulled the stack of files closer and scanned the sheet. The actual dates were a little off, but sure as shit, Cutter was registering a body about every three months. Jack ran his finger down the list to the last known victim that had been found at Spreckels Lake. Then he went back to the top. This pattern had started nearly three years ago.

He noted the hand-written additional listing at the top of the printed ones. "What's this?"

"We think she's the first victim. Originally, this was treated as an unknown death, as the remains appeared to have been out in the elements long enough for the wildlife to contaminate the evidence. All we knew was she's female based on the bone structure, and probably in her '20s."

"And you added her to the list because . . ."

"Last year, I was shooting a curl when I remembered the case. It came to me so fast I nearly grubbed in the hollow." Jack had known Cutter for so long he understood the man's surfer lingo for being inside the curl of a wave and nearly falling off his board. "I immediately ordered an exhumation, and after a second autopsy, I compared the report to the ones we already had and was confident she was part of it. This is the oldest known victim so I'm calling her Victim Zero. The only difference between her and the one found at Spreckels Lake is that over time, each body's injuries have become more refined, as if the killer is perfecting his craft." Cutter found the folder at the bottom of the stack and opened it, scanning the detailed report. "The original police paperwork says you found her."

Jack's head spun toward his friend. "Me? Let me take a look at that." He reached over the desk and took the file Cutter handed him. In his time on the force, he'd investigated a lot of suspicious deaths around the city. Oddly, the Windmills had seen more than their fair share of them. Carefully scanning each line of this report, he noted the date was three months after Leah and Zoë— He'd been a mess by then. "I remember this one. A body was found at the Windmills. The CSIs said they thought the wildlife had caused the degradation to the body."

"Right. That's what we all thought."

"Were you able to determine a cause of death?"

Shaking his head, Cutter said, "No. There wasn't much to go on. Just like the others. What was there had been out in the elements too long—remember the ocean is just on the other side of the western tree boundary. We also accounted for the wildlife."

"How long do you estimate she was out there?"

"There's no way of telling. Without a liver, we couldn't estimate time of death. In the salty air, and with the animals feeding off the body, it could have been a day or a week. We just don't know."

Jack had seen decaying bodies before. It was the nature of being a homicide detective. With death came decay. But the image of this particular body had burned itself into his memory. And knowing there were twelve more just like it was unnerving, to say the least.

He looked back at the list, counting the cases to be sure his math was correct. Dumbfounded, he asked, "So that actually makes thirteen? And you're telling me they've all been eviscerated . . . exactly the same?"

Cutter nodded. "Same everything except dump location. They're being killed somewhere else, but they're being left around the city. Not quite posed, but not dumped either." He opened the top folder and pulled out some crime scene photos for the latest victim, the woman on the table. "See? If she was killed on site, there would be blood. A lot of it. And she wasn't just dumped here. You can see how she was placed. Not overtly posed, but not carelessly either."

Jack's stomach rolled as he looked at the images, but so far, the water was staying down. Apparently, his earlier shock was wearing off.

When the texter had sent Jack to Spreckels Lake, he'd only seen the back of the victim's head from behind the crime scene tape. The body appeared to be sitting on the ground on the lake side of one of the big logs delineating the parking area.

Now the photos showed the scene from its true angle and

revealed a completely different view—a woman completely devoid of most of her flesh and skin from the neck down to her feet. Her breasts hung from what little skin remained, her bowels fell across what had once been her lap, and the white of her bones glistened in places from where early morning birds had picked them clean.

His stomach rolled again, but he didn't look away.

Without looking up, Jack asked, "You said the cause of death was undetermined in all the cases?"

"Right."

"Were you able to determine if the women had been killed before they were excarnated, or"—swallowing hard—"were they still alive?"

"We have no idea."

Jack closed the folder and picked up the next one on the stack and went right to the photos. Another woman of similar description, her body in nearly the exact same condition and in an upright position. But something was different. He quickly shuffled back and forth through the images.

"See something?" Cutter asked.

"Where was this vic found? She's sitting up, but I don't see anything around her." The position of the body reminded him of a gruesome marionette that had been put into a sitting position as the strings went slack.

"Correct. She was found in the center of the rotunda at the Palace of Fine Arts. The body was sitting in a self-supporting position."

The victim in the next folder had been defleshed in an identical fashion to the previous two, only the location of the dump differed. He looked at the case notes, then at the site photos. "What the hell?"

Cutter leaned over the desk to look at the photo in Jack's hand. "That's an anomaly. That's the only body that appears posed."

Jack held up one of the photos toward the light and scowled. "She was placed in the arms of the Buddha at the Japanese Tea Garden." The woman's head was cradled in the statue's left hand. The scene looked like a parent holding a child. "How the hell did he crawl over the barrier with a body and put it up there?"

"This is the one that makes us wonder if maybe he has help." Cutter sat back in his chair again. "The rest of the victims are posed similar to the first two, but that one is the only one that appears to have needed help getting to the dump site."

"Or he's damn strong." Jack considered the other images he'd seen. "You don't think the one at the Palace was posed? What's the significance of propping a body up to support itself if not for a purpose?"

Cutter cocked his head, as if considering the idea. "The one at the Buddha is the only one that really stands out as being purposefully posed."

"Killers always have a purpose, Jon. Cradled in the Buddha's arms, propped up in the center of the rotunda . . . even just sitting against a log like at the lake . . . it all has to mean something."

"Maybe, but I don't see what it could mean. Then again, I'm not being paid to figure out that part of the investigation." He chuckled lightly.

Jack replaced the photos in the folder and tossed it back on the stack. "How is it that I didn't know anything about this until now?"

Cutter shrugged. "I don't think anyone was keeping anything from you specifically. But the department is keeping a tight lid on this. Only essential personnel are involved in the investigation. I'm sure I don't have to tell you, if the press got hold of this, there would be widespread panic."

"I bet. The city has a serial killer on the loose."

A serial killer.

Acid burned the back of his throat. This had been going on for at least three years.

Could the killer have taken Bonnie Boyd? He considered the bodies he'd seen and recalled the photo Carl had given him. She didn't seem to fit the profile, but until she was found, he couldn't be sure.

Then he considered Victim Zero. She'd been found three months after Leah had disappeared. Could *she* be the real Victim

Zero? The thought stole his breath; his heart leaped into his throat. If she was, why hadn't her body been found yet?

"I know you said this is being kept under wraps, but has the department assigned a name to this guy yet?"

"The Butcher, since they've all been excarnated the same way. The bodies are still here."

Jack's thoughts snapped to attention. "It looks like there's plenty of evidence in the folders. I'd have thought the bodies would have been buried by now," he said, glancing at the stack on the desk.

Nodding, Cutter said, "Normally we would, but given the situation, I requested we hang onto them a while longer. I've gone back a few times comparing notes, and since no one has claimed them, it's handy having them here. Storing the remains is actually cheaper than exhumation. If you think you can keep your puke to yourself, I can show you."

"No thanks," he said quickly. "I think the photos are more than enough, but I'd like to look through the rest of the files."

"Take your time. I'm going to make coffee. Want one?" As Cutter rose and walked toward the door, Jack gave a thumbs up over his shoulder while reaching for the stack of folders. "The usual?"

"Yeah, thanks," indicating his preferred black coffee, and the stronger the better.

By the time Cutter returned, Jack was on his knees in the center of the floor, with all the files fanned out around him and open to the postmortem reports. The stacks of photos centered on top of the folders, with the victim's face on top. He had his notebook in one hand and pen in the other. He'd scanned back and forth across each of the files in turn, making notes of the most important things.

So far, the killer didn't seem to stick to one race—he was an equal opportunity killer—but all the victims were female and of a similar age and build. Everything about them told Jack the killer had very specific tastes. Technically, Leah could have fit the profile he saw developing, but had to force his thoughts away from that direction. Bonnie Boyd didn't seem to fit the profile though as she was a strikingly beautiful woman where the victims had been more on the average side of looks. Could the killer be devolving?

The only thing that seemed to connect the victims to each other, other than age and build, was that they'd all been excarnated in the same way, as Cutter had said, then had been dumped in the location where they'd been discovered. None of them had been hidden. Otherwise, their connections ended there. Definitely though, the body at the Japanese Garden was the only one that stood out among the rest, and he wondered what had changed with that one.

Given Cutter's extensive notes and the additional police files, Jack was sure they—the investigating officers—knew they were only looking for one killer.

From his peripheral vision, he watched Cutter set a cup on the desk then move to the window where he sipped from his own cup while gazing over the city.

"Are all the vics the same—Jane Does, twenties, slim build . . . all defleshed?" Jack stated the facts as he'd read from the files.

"Yeah, so you can see why we haven't released anything to the press."

"There are thirteen files here, including Victim Zero. If they're all Jane Does, does this mean none of the vics have been identified?" Jack asked.

"From what we can tell, whoever is doing this is purposefully choosing unknown victims. No clothes or personal items have been found at the scenes, so no ID. There's no other DNA evidence leading us to a suspect. And no one has filed a missing person's report."

"I'm guessing that because the department is keeping this quiet is the reason I didn't get any of the Jane Doe files from Chin."

Cutter cocked his head. "Hmm . . . probably."

"I'm assuming you ran the victims' prints and DNA."

"One of the first things we did when they came in. Nothing in the system."

Thoughts tumbled around in Jack's head. How had these women avoided being in the system? California required everyone applying for a driver's permit or license, or even an ID card, to submit their fingerprints at the DMV. And DNA records were kept for anyone entering into the legal system.

"What about out-of-state databases?"

"Trust me, if a database has a print or DNA profile on file, we ran all these through it." Cutter put up his hand as Jack opened his mouth to speak. "And yes, we ran them through AFIS, IAFIS, INTERPOL, and EUROPOL, and I called in personal favors at EuroDac and SIRENE. It's like these women don't exist."

"None of them came up anywhere," Jack said under his breath. It wasn't a question, but Cutter shook his head anyway. "Whoever's doing this has to have some way of knowing these women couldn't be found. It can't be random. If it is, he's one lucky son of a bitch."

"Or she."

Jack scanned the files in front of him. "Do you think the perp is a woman?"

"Probably not, given the brutality of the defleshing, but at this point, we can't rule out anyone."

Scanning his notes and looking at a couple of the open reports, he then looked up at Cutter. "The reports said there weren't any defensive wounds on any of the vics. How did you account for that?"

"That's part of the mystery. What little blood remained went to toxicology, but it came back clean for narcotics, poisons, and prescription drugs, and there was only trace alcohol in nine of the victims. Either four of them didn't drink, or just hadn't had anything to drink the day they died," Cutter told him.

"I haven't looked through all the files, but did you do rape kits?" Jack asked.

Cutter nodded. "They'd all had sex prior to their deaths, but nothing indicates rape—there's no vaginal or anal tearing. However, the killer used the same brand condom in each instance."

"How can you tell?"

"The lube. Most companies who sell into the US use one of three formula lubricants on their condoms—water-based or silicone based, or a new hybrid that combines the two. But other brands make their way in from other countries. Those using oil-based lubricant are cheap so they're popular with people on limited incomes. Those are fine to use but not with condoms, as the oil breaks down the latex."

"And the killer's brand didn't use any of those."

Shaking his head, Cutter said, "No. His preferred brand is aloe based."

"I've seen aloe-based rubbers on the shelves. What makes this one unusual?"

"What makes it distinct is that it also uses *carageenan*, a type of seaweed."

Jack thought for a moment. "If *carageenan* is so unusual, it shouldn't be difficult to pin down the brand."

"You'd think, but the use of aloe and *carageenan* is even more unusual. Investigators haven't found any shops around the city selling condoms using lube with those ingredients, and so far, nothing has turned up on the black market."

"Are you sure the killer used a condom? Could he have just used the lube on its own? What if he came outside?"

Cutter shook his head. "Maybe he didn't come at all. No sperm was detected inside the vaginal canal or out, but as there is evidence of intercourse, it leads me to believe he did have sex with the women and used a condom."

Jack made additional notes in his notebook, then began closing the folders, being careful to keep the photos with the correct files.

He stopped at one image and held it up to the light for a better look.

"What's up?" asked Cutter.

He scanned the woman's face more carefully. "I dunno. Something. She looks familiar, but I don't know from where." He shrugged off the feeling. "Maybe I'm just projecting. I've looked at a lot of Jane Does and missing women files lately."

Cutter cocked his head to the side, lifting an eyebrow, indicating the possibility.

Closing the last of the folders, Jack restacked them in their original order. Then rising, he placed them back on Cutter's desk.

He took a sip of his now lukewarm coffee and stepped over to the window, opposite from his friend.

Even though the ME's office was a severely dated facility, there was no complaining about the view, once you looked past the highway. At this hour of the night, the city was awash in light. The black sky reflected the light with an orange halo.

The Financial District was full of historic buildings that had been the high rises of their day. But thousands of tons of stonework created by millions of hours of labor from master masons was being engulfed by modern steel and glass skyscrapers that were quickly changing the city skyline from the one he knew growing up in Little Italy, at the edge of the district. The lights were beautiful, but at what cost?

Jack considered downing the last of his coffee but decided to pass. He looked over to his friend. "I guess I better let you get back to work."

"Are you sure you don't want to take a look at the bodies?"

Jack cringed and waved his hand. "Very sure."

Cutter chuckled. "Did you get everything you need?"

Jack threw on his leather jacket, then folded the pen inside the notebook and pocketed them. "I think so."

"You know where to find me if you need anything else. I'll have the files copied and couriered to your office in the morning. Better to have it and not need it—"

Jack reached out a hand and met Cutter's. "—Than to need it and not have it." Jack finished the old saying. "Thanks. And thanks, too, for letting me take a look."

"Aloha 'oe."

CHAPTER SIXTEEN

Outside of prospective clients, Jack actually had few casual visitors—Tommy looking for rent and Ray who just let himself in. He had a lockbox downstairs for his mail. So he was leery about answering the knock on his door, especially after Travers' unannounced visit yesterday, though he didn't think the man dared coming back. At least, not so soon. And not on his own.

Drowsily, Jack threw caution to the wind and rose from where he'd been dozing on the sofa, wearing little more than a pair of sweatpants, and went to the door. If it *had* been Travers, Jack didn't have a pocket to stuff his phone into to record the meeting, not that his phone was even handy—he blearily eyed it across the room on his desk.

Cold air from the open door instantly prickled his exposed skin and ruffled the patch of dark hair across his chest, snapping him wide awake with a shiver. A quick glance up Columbus Avenue showed him the city's famous thick morning fog enveloping the buildings. Even the spires of Saint Frank's Church on the next block were obliterated.

"Good morning, Mr. Slaughter."

The young man at his door was one of Cutter's assistants. When he gave a questioning look at his meager five-dollar tip, Jack forced a smile, knowing Cutter paid his assistants well. "Thank Doctor Cutter for me." He closed the door and considered the thick packet now in his hands.

True to his word, Cutter sent the promised files. Jack had only left the ME's office around 2 a.m., which told Jack it must have been a slow night . . . not that Cutter had time for boredom . . . or had called in an assistant to do the work for him. Cutter didn't have to give Jack anything, or even let him look at the files last night, but he appreciated his friend putting him in the loop. Whatever Ray's excuse was for not confiding in him was something he'd get to later.

Grabbing his phone off the desk, he checked the time—9:07 a.m.—then collected the notebook off the table beside the sofa and strode into the backroom. He set the packet in the center of the floor, phone and notebook on top, then went to move aside the few boxes along the north wall. With thirteen victims, he needed all the space he could get.

He didn't bother removing the map and notes from the Boyd case wall. Technically, he was still working the investigation, even though it had been taken over by Homicide.

He also decided not to call Boyd, as a) that would tell him he was now under official investigation, and b) what if he didn't do it and Bonnie turned up as victim number fourteen? And c) Jack still felt obligated to see the case through. He wasn't sure Bonnie's disappearance had anything to do with the serial killings as she didn't fit the MO, and Jack was pretty sure Boyd had murdered his own wife. He just had to prove it.

There was also a strong chance he could solve this case long before Homicide, especially since the only other person who knew everything was Ray, and he wasn't saying anything, opting to just let Travers run with the limited information Jack had turned over to Haniford.

Instead, Jack pulled out a fresh, larger scale map from the box he kept under the table below the Boyd case wall and tacked it to his new murder wall, plaster be damned. He'd fix the holes he made later. Right now, this was more important.

After grabbing pens, sticky notes, and index cards, he sat on the floor in front of Cutter's packet and started pulling out the folders and fanning them in front of him.

Cutter had also included reprints of all the photos. "Good man," he murmured under his breath, grinning. He riffled through each stack, pulling out each vic's headshot, along with the photo of the position each woman had been discovered in, and laid them on the floor above the relevant folders.

The Butcher.

The last thing Jack had expected last night when he went to the ME's office was to find out the city had a serial killer on the loose. If that wasn't shocking enough, knowing he, or she, had been actively killing for three years blew Jack's mind. While he knew this wasn't his case, and Cutter had only been accommodating in sending copies of the files out of curiosity's sake, sorting through all the files and preparing the murder board made Jack feel like he was back on the force . . . like he had a purpose again. He wondered if he should consider going back. There was no doubt Ray could use a good partner. But was he ready to face the job again, day in and day out?

Not until I find Leah. Not until I find out who killed Zoë and Trax. Then there was the issue of the bullet with his name on it.

He refocused his mind on the task and lifted the folder for Victim Zero to refresh himself with the case. He hoped details in the files would reawaken some of those dormant memories. And he just hoped they were the right details. He didn't want to retrace everything from that time. It was too painful.

Hours later, his murder wall now intact, and having read through all thirteen folders, he looked at his handiwork.

In hindsight, with thirteen victims and related evidence, he could never have fit everything on the smaller wall. He needed the full expanse of the unobstructed north wall to display everything. And he'd practically filled it.

Jack straightened and stretched his taut back muscles. He had to admit, the murder wall looked like many others he'd created in the past. Victims' headshots lined the ceiling's edge at the top of the map. The photos with the positions the bodies had been found in were tacked to the right of the headshots; he'd written the date and location of discovery in black marker at the foot of each positional photo. He'd then used colored string to link each vic to the location where she'd been found around the city, until the map looked like a spider's web.

Finally, he'd attached his colored index cards and sticky notes around the wall, each with relevant notes and details from the folders.

He stepped back and leaned against the opposite wall beside the window and folded his arms. In the small room, the expansive murder wall was easy to see. He gazed up at each of the women's faces in turn.

About midway through tacking the photos up, Jack couldn't help but feel some emotional attachments to the women forming. Without being able to identify any of the women, it seemed like the only thing connecting them to each other was their anonymity. There were no families or friends claiming their remains, no one here championing them. No, this wasn't his case. He wasn't a cop anymore and no one had hired him to solve this. But knowing there was a killer in the city who was targeting the innocent made him angry, and at the same time, he empathized with the victims.

CHAPTER SEVENTEEN

He thought about the logic of his decision. All of these women couldn't be called Jane Doe. And by referring to them as Victim One, Two, or Three relegated them to little more than a case number or body count. Each of these women had been born and lived real lives. Their families and friends were out there. Somewhere. They just hadn't been found yet.

But until they could be located, they still needed to have some of their dignity restored. So Jack gave each one a name, based on where she'd been found. He'd written each name in black marker at the bottom of each headshot photo, and now, as he stood across the room, she would be more than just a number or anonymous corpse. His training had always told him never to get too personally involved or invested in victims, but until their families could be located, how could he not be *their* champion?

He gazed up at Eve—Victim Zero. Like Eve, the first woman, Cutter had determined she had been the first of the excarnations. The folder in Cutter's packet contained copies of Jack's original case files, though some he didn't remember. Even now, three years later, the fog clouded his brain, much like the fog up Columbus Avenue. Not even looking at her butchered body or gazing at her tortured expression shocked his memory awake. He'd been so fucked up at the time he only remembered odd details. Such as her location at the Dutch Windmill, her state of undress, and the exposed flesh and bones that looked like animals had ravaged her. At the time, she seemed to have been haphazardly dumped in one of the tulip beds. Anything more was lost in his foggy memory or missing from his official notes.

Given what Cutter had to work with, Eve had probably been in her twenties, Caucasian with brown hair, and with an estimated weight of around a hundred and twenty pounds. Her eye color was unknown as they were missing.

He turned his gaze to Janis. She had been the first *known* victim of excarnation. Her photo showed a young Caucasian woman with straight brown hair that was parted in the middle and hung past her shoulders. His notes had said she had brown eyes, was also in her early twenties and about a hundred and twenty pounds. She'd been found in the Panhandle—a one block wide and three-quarter mile strip of tree-filled green space on the eastern side of Golden Gate Park, and so named as, when looking at the park from the air, it looked like a rectangle pan with a handle.

Jack found it odd that Eve and Janis had been found on both extremes of the park. Unlike Eve, Janis' body had been propped against a tree, on the Oak Street side of the park, and facing up Ashbury Street. He'd named her Janis because the famous singer had lived just a couple blocks up on Ashbury during the famous Summer of Love.

He named the second known victim Violet—Caucasian, early twenties, about a hundred and twenty pounds, black hair, and green eyes—because she had been found at the Conservatory of Flowers. The conservatory was also in the park, and less than a mile away from where Janis had been found. There hadn't been any damage during the break-in, but the killer had somehow managed to avoid security guards and get into the greenhouse. Her body had been found propped up against the edge of the round picture window in the Potted Plants wing.

He'd named victim number three Kim—a petite blonde with blue eyes and similar physical attributes to the others—after the actress who'd starred in *Vertigo* which had been filmed at Fort Point where the victim had been discovered. Her body had been propped on a bench at the corner of the fort, facing the entrance into San Francisco Bay. The Golden Gate Bridge stretched out overhead, and on a clear day, Alcatraz Island was visible on the horizon in the center of the bay.

Kim was the first victim found outside Golden Gate Park, which meant the park wasn't The Butcher's focus for dumping his victims.

Victim four had been named Lillie, after the woman who bequeathed money for the construction of Coit Tower, also known as the Lillie Coit Tower. Lillie had been fascinated with firefighting from a young age, and when she settled in the city, she often chased fires with volunteer companies. The first fire she assisted in had been on Telegraph Hill, so it seemed appropriate her monument to firefighters should be placed on the hill. The woman who had been found at the foot of the Christopher Columbus monument was the first non-Caucasian victim. She had Hispanic features and dark brown eyes.

Victim five had been discovered by early morning walkers on China Beach. At first, they had thought the body was a homeless person camping on the beach, but as they got closer, they'd discovered the gruesome truth. Jack named this Asian woman Sandy.

Next was Madie, with green eyes and a head of brown curls, she had been found at the base of the one-hundred-three feet high cross at the peak of the highest of the city's forty-three hills— Mount Davidson. Early Spaniard explorers had placed crosses at landing points along California's coast, later establishing missions in those areas they settled. The faithful believed they were closest to God on the highest mountains and erected crosses for outdoor religious ceremonies. At the time of the official opening in 1934, Madie Brown had been instrumental in getting then President Roosevelt to San Francisco for the cross-lighting ceremony, putting aside the West Coast Longshoremen's Strike he'd been scheduled to attend in another part of the city.

Victim number seven was found at the San Francisco Zoo. She had been placed on one of the benches on the turn-of-the-century Eugene Friend Denzel Carousel. He named this woman Beatrix after Beatrix Potter. The two benches on the carousel sat beside the only rabbits in an otherwise equine-dominated ride. What made this victim stand out was her age was estimated as early forties. Until now, the victims had consistently been in their early to mid-twenties. Beatrix's hair was dark brown but starting to show some gray, and her green eyes were rimmed with laughter lines.

At Fort Funston, Sunny, a dark-haired and brown-eyed woman, had been found just off the Sunset Trail, a coastal pedestrian path along the cliff overlooking the Pacific Ocean. The fort had once been an active military reserve as part of the harbor defense system in the nineteenth century. Today, the cliffs were a popular jumping off place for hang gliders.

Luna had been found at the 16th Avenue Tiled Steps. Her body had been left on the moon mosaic section of the steps. A relatively new permanent art installation, the tiles on these steps were unique in that they absorbed sunlight during the day and illuminated at night. Luna had blonde hair and brown eyes.

Victim ten, a young Hispanic woman with dark hair and eyes, had been found at the center of Golden Gate Park in the Japanese Tea Garden. He named her Jasmine for the tea served in the tea house. Jack remembered this woman from last night's visit with Cutter. She seemed to have been posed with her body lying in the arms of the Buddha, her head cradled in his open left palm.

The woman found propped up in the center of the rotunda at the Palace of Fine Arts also seemed posed, in Jack's opinion. There had been nothing propping her up; she sat on her own in the center of the structure, as if she were a marionette whose strings had been cut. He named her Marion. She also stood out as an anomaly against the previous victims. Marion was black with short cut hair and almost black eyes.

Finally, the most recent victim. Number twelve, or thirteen including Eve and rounding out the baker's dozen, was found at Spreckels Lake just last week. He named her Alma, for the wife of one of the city's wealthiest magnates and philanthropist, Adolph Bernard Spreckels. Adolf had made his fortune in sugar production and breeding racehorses, and he'd donated the Palace of the Legion of Honor at the behest of Alma as reparations for having shot business partner Michael de Young who had accused Spreckels of defrauding shareholders. Alma became known as the Grandmother of San Francisco because of her philanthropy around the city until her death. While the victim was in no way the same six feet tall as Alma Spreckels, she did have the same black curling hair and green eyes.

As Jack gazed at the wall, each woman with a new, though he hoped temporary, identity, he scanned the map, trying to tie the locations together. Perhaps the killer had randomly dumped the women in order to throw off officials. He knew from years on the job that many serial killers dumped their victims in the same location, creating a field of burial sites. None of these women had been buried. They had all been left out in the open, and in specific locations, as if they were meant to be found. For what purpose? And what was The Butcher's motivation for choosing these particular places?

His stomach squelched just then, reminding him that he hadn't eaten since yesterday evening. He hadn't even stopped for coffee this morning before starting his task. And he had no idea what time it was.

Assuming his empty gut accounted for his sudden weariness, he turned and opened the window beside him. Looking through the dingy glass, he saw the morning fog had long ago burned off and the blue sky dominated the city skyline, telling him it had to be early afternoon. As the cooling bay breeze blew into the room, freshening the stale air, he inhaled deeply, his senses coming alert.

Gazing back at the wall, he scanned all the facts that he now knew and tried piecing them together.

One thing that stuck out was that, aside from the one middle-aged woman, each of the other victims was in her early to mid-twenties, all averaged between one hundred and one hundred and forty pounds, and all were around average height for her race. While the killer seemed to prefer Caucasian woman, there was a mix of Hispanic and Asian women, and one black woman.

His gaze shot back to Madie, the woman found at the cross on Mount Davidson. She was the one who seemed familiar to him, but he couldn't place her. Now that he was looking at the murder wall, his gaze kept going back to her and it started eating away at his brain.

Outside, he heard someone on the steel stairs but pushed it out of his mind. Maybe one of Tommy's employees was in the alley having a smoke or taking out the trash. He didn't care. Instead, he squeezed his eyes closed and deeply inhaled the fresh sea breeze filling the room, forcing his brain to come fully awake.

Who was Madie? Where did he recognize her from? She floated just on the edge of his memory.

The sound of gunfire snapped Jack's eyes open, his heart pounding in his chest.

No, it wasn't gunfire. It had been the backroom door slamming shut. With the open window beside him, the opening of the front door had created a strong enough draft that it slammed the backroom door shut. The only person he knew who'd just walk in was Ray.

He started toward the door when he saw movement to his left. Papers on the table below his family's case wall fluttered from the open window and a few scattered to the floor.

"Jack!" called Ray.

"Yeah. Be right there," he replied, bending to scoop up the papers. His vision grazed the map on the wall and he stopped in his tracks, gazing over it.

What the . . . ?

He looked back to the murder wall, then back to his family's map, then back and forth again.

Rage welled inside him along with sorrow.

"Goddammit! Fuckfuckfuck. Goddammit to fuck!" he yelled.

His heart pounded hard in his chest, making him fight for breath. His eyes burned with rage; his entire body flush from it. Before he could get control of himself, the fists now balled at his sides tightened, and he threw a punch. Right through the door. He pulled his fist out of the hole he'd made, prepared to strike it again, then saw Ray's concerned face staring back at him.

CHAPTER EIGHTEEN

Jack threw open the door and stomped toward Ray. The alarm on his friend's face was obvious. Ray stepped back as Jack neared, pinning him against the window. Jack stared hard into his eyes for a long moment, taking long and deep breaths, forcing himself to calm down. Did Ray think he was going to be the next thing his fist met? The way Jack felt, that was an option.

His friend had betrayed him, and along with discovering the city had a serial killer, and that his family was in some way tied to it, it was all he could do to keep his fists at his sides.

Ray wasn't afraid, but perhaps a bit intimidated from the way he stared back with equal determination. Ray's back stiffened, as if trying to gain some extra height to match Jack's more imposing stature.

"*Hola* to you too, *amigo.*" Ray's sarcastic tone matched the crease between his eyes.

Finally, Jack spoke between clenched teeth. "How could you keep this from me?" His blood pressure pulsed in his ears. "Why didn't you tell me? Goddammit, Ray, why didn't you tell me?"

"Tell you what?" Ray looked completely confused.

Without speaking, Jack grabbed Ray's jacket collar, feeling his friend flinch for the first time in all the years he'd known him, and practically dragged the man into the backroom. He faced Ray toward the murder wall and brusquely released him.

Ray had never been in the backroom before. He stood in the center of the room—the only clean spot where Jack had sat earlier—and watched while Ray spun, taking everything in. Ray's gaze lingered on Jack's family wall, and then the Boyds' before it

115

finally rested on the murder wall. It didn't take him long to realize what Jack had.

"What the fuck, Jack? Where did you get all this? It looks like you've got exact duplicates of our files." Ray's voice held an accusatory tone.

"It doesn't matter. What *does* matter is you didn't tell me the city is hunting a serial killer. And a sick fucker at that." When Ray opened his mouth to speak, Jack continued. "Yeah, I know about the excarnations. Don't lay it on me that it's because I'm no longer on the force. You tell me everything. Why keep *this* from me?"

Ray stepped toward the wall and looked over Jack's handiwork. "We didn't realize it ourselves until last year. The department agreed to keep it strictly in-house until we had a better handle on it."

"Yeah, I know. You didn't want a media frenzy or city-wide panic. I get it. But this has been going on for three years now. For fuck sake, Ray, I was at Spreckels Lake when the last victim was discovered. You could have told me that night when you were here. Why didn't you?"

Ray spun around, blurting out, "I couldn't, okay? Haniford has all of our *huevos* in a vice about this. You don't think I'm afraid for Maria? She fits the MO and I can't even tell *her*. I want to send her to her mother's until this guy is caught, but how long will that be? So, I tell her to be careful when she's out by herself, and now she's suspicious that I'm keeping something from her. She even asked me if I was cheating on her. Can you believe that? *Me?* Cheat on Maria?"

Jack knew Ray was like a besotted teenager with his wife. Even after all these years, they still loved each other like newlyweds. He remembered that feeling with Leah—

"I get it, Ray. I really do. But this . . . this has something directly to do with my family. You should have told me. *Goddammit*, you should have said something, man!"

"What do you mean it has something to do with your family?" Ray waved his hand toward the victims' headshots. "Leah isn't one of these women."

Jack moved around Ray and slammed the door, then again grabbed his friend by the collar and pulled him over to his family's case wall. "Look."

"What am I looking at, Jack? Another one of your PI cases?" Jack grunted with frustration. "Be a detective, damn you, and look."

Ray stepped closer to the smaller map and looked at each note Jack had pinned around the city. He looked over to the murder wall and back again. After several minutes, he turned around. "What's this all about?"

Pointing, Jack said, "*This* is the map I put up when I started getting texts about the body dumps around the city. See here?" He pointed to Spreckels Lake. "This was the last body dump. I had been texted that I'd find Leah there. Just like every other text. Look here." Jack pointed at various locations around his family's map. "The Panhandle. Janis is the first known victim. I had been sent to this location to find Leah, but instead, this woman was propped up against a tree, looking up Ashbury Street. Victim two, Violet, was found in the Conservatory of Flowers. I was texted to find Leah there too. And Kim at Fort Point, and all the rest."

"You discovered their identities? Where did you get their names?" Ray asked, his gaze now focusing on each victim's headshot.

"No, I gave them names based on where they were found, but that's not important. Just look."

Ray moved back and forth between the maps, comparing the dump locations to where Jack told him he'd been sent by the texter. By the look on his face, Jack knew Ray remembered the calls, and each and every time he'd had to send Jack away.

"What about Eve?" Ray finally asked. "You and I both were lead on that case."

"We determined she was Victim Zero. The first victim."

"We?" Ray's right eyebrow lifted. "Are you cheating on me?"

Ray's attempt at humor, suggesting Jack would work with anyone else, would have been funny at any other time. This was a serious matter and Jack didn't have time for levity. "I was at

Cutter's last night. He didn't know you hadn't told me about any of this. I told him I didn't know either. I still don't."

"I just told you."

Jack rolled his eyes with sarcasm. "Yeah, yeah, Haniford . . . your balls . . . Anyway, this was the last case we worked before I went on sabbatical."

With the pensive look on Ray's face, Jack reminded him of the case. "Yeah, yeah, I remember. *Jesus*," he exclaimed as Hey Zeus and crossing himself. "Why does Cutter think she's part of this?"

"She'd been cut up the same way. At the time, you and I agreed she'd been out there a while, and the wildlife had got to her before she'd been discovered. We had no other references to compare her to other than that. At the time, Cutter couldn't even determine her cause of death. When the next few bodies started turning up, he had her exhumed for a second autopsy and determined she had been the first. Over the years, the wounds have become more precise. Whoever is doing this has had three years to perfect his technique."

Ray noticeably shivered then swore under his breath in Spanish. "If all of these women are tied to the texter, where does this Eve fit in?"

Jack shook his head and tossed his hands in the air. "I dunno. But based on her condition, there's no doubt that she's tied to the rest. Somehow."

Gazing back and forth between the walls, Ray asked, "Have you come to any conclusions as to why these locations were chosen? If you were sent to each of these locations, they have to tie to something you can relate to."

Jack threw his hands onto his hips and shook his head again. "I have no idea, man."

"Let's think about this logically. Killers have a purpose. Especially serial killers. There is a reason for everything and everything has meaning. Even the smallest thing."

"Agreed."

"So there has to be a reason you were sent to all of these locations. Telling you Leah is there could just be the trigger that gets you out there."

"But why get me out there in the first place? I know this texter is just taunting me, but for what reason?"

"Let's find out. But first, I'm smelling egg rolls—"

"Are you sure you don't want some tacos or tamales? There's a taqueria just across the street." Jack tried keeping his expression neutral but the corner of his mouth twitched.

"Do you even know how racist you sound?" Ray's voice was filled with indignation. "Mexicans eat more than tacos, *cabrón!*"

CHAPTER NINETEEN

After more than two years of living above Wong's, Jack had grown tired of Chinese food and would've preferred something from the Mexican place, but to expedite his and Ray's task, he agreed to the egg rolls, and whatever else his friend wanted.

It seemed no sooner had he disconnected the call than the delivery boy was at his door with several traditional cartons swinging from his fingers. He pulled chopsticks from one pocket in his soiled apron and a fistful of foil-wrapped fortune cookies from the other. Jack tipped him then took the food into the backroom where he deposited the cartons, cookies, and chopsticks onto the center of the floor.

Ray started opening the cartons while Jack went to his mini fridge and grabbed a couple beers, and paper plates. "You gonna at least put on a shirt, or do I have to stare at your *tetas* while I'm eating?"

Gazing down, Jack realized he still only wore his cut-off sweatpants. "Tits my ass. Can you do this with your flabby man boobs?" Just to get on Ray's nerves, he tensed his shoulders and arms, then bunched his chest muscles, alternately bouncing each one up and down.

Without missing a beat, Ray replied, "Keep those away from my wife. Put on a shirt and let's eat."

Laughing, Jack grabbed a shirt out of the narrow closet and threw it on as he sat down. A few bites in, Jack put aside his lo mein and took a swig from his beer. "Where do you want to start?"

Ray pushed a mouthful of fried rice into one cheek like a chipmunk and muffled, "From the start. Let's put aside Eve for the moment and start with Janis. This asshole," he mumbled, spitting some of the rice as he talked, "sent you to the Panhandle for a reason. Why do you think he did this?"

He thought about it for a long moment. "I don't know. Cutter doesn't believe the women were posed in any way, but as you said, every killer has a reason for doing things. He didn't bury them like he was hiding them. He wanted them to be found. If he chose specific locations, what was his reasoning?"

Ray swallowed the rice and looked up at Janis' headshot and the photo showing the position of her body against the tree. "You said she was facing up Ashbury Street. Was this coincidence or could she have been posed to look in that direction? What's up that street besides the Hippies?"

The whole Haight-Ashbury District was one of the most iconic parts of the city. "Janis Joplin lived on Ashbury. That's why I named this victim Janis."

"What else?"

"The Grateful Dead had a house one block up, Hendrix was up on Haight—"

"I meant, is there a significance *to you* for this area? You said Janis was sitting up against the tree and looking up Ashbury. Was she looking up the street or was she facing anything specifically?" He stuffed his mouth with sweet and sour chicken next but kept his gaze on Jack who had to suppress himself from slapping his own forehead.

Nodding, he gazed up at Janis' pose photo and thought there was an angle to her body and tilt of her head that suggested she was staring in the direction of Leah's old apartment. "When I met Leah, she lived at the corner of Ashbury and Oak. It doesn't look like the victim is facing the building specifically, but maybe whoever placed the body here had trouble with the pose."

Ray quirked his head at the suggestion. "What about Violet? What does the Conservatory of Flowers mean to you?"

Jack didn't have to think twice. "Our first date. We walked over from her apartment."

Ray gazed up at the murder wall and rattled off names. "Kim?"

"Date. We sat on that bench watching the America's Cup yachting race."

"Lillie?"

"Date. I don't know what the Columbus statue has to do with it though, but I took Leah to see the wild parrots that live around Telegraph Hill."

"Think hard. Remember, this guy has a reason for doing these things."

Jack wracked his brain. What other time had he been to Coit Tower with Leah? "Well, there was one time we went up at night to . . . umm . . . look at the city lights," he said, not wanting to tell his friend the intimate nature of the visit. It had been the first time Leah had gone down on him. He'd definitely seen lights that night and they hadn't been over the city. "We may have parked under the statue."

"Uh-huh." Ray chuckled through another bite of his food. "What about Sandy?"

Memories flooded back into Jack's mind in a tidal wave of longing. He'd struggled for years to keep them at bay. But if something in his memory could help find the serial killer, and hopefully find Leah, and his daughter's killer, he'd search every cobweb-filled nook and cranny in his brain.

"Leah was house-sitting for the parents of a college friend. Their house overlooks China Beach. People and their money," he mumbled. "They have their own crazy golf in the yard. We went out to play and ended up down on the beach for a . . . umm . . . moonlight stroll."

Ray chuckled. "Is that what they call it these days?"

"Fuck you." Jack couldn't help but grin. If by stroll he meant fucking on the beach, then yeah, they were strolling. He loved strolling with Leah. Looking at the map, he said, "And we went strolling up on Mount Davidson where Madie was found."

"What about the zoo?" Ray continued. "Bee—Beet . . . how the hell do you pronounce her name? Couldn't you have picked an easier name for her?"

Ray grinned, knowing the X in Spanish had a few pronunciations. "Bee-a-tricks. As in Beatrix Potter. Leah and I went for a ride on the carousel at the zoo. We sat on one of the benches beside the Peter Rabbits."

"No strolling?"

"Don't sound so disappointed, *amigo*. Leah told me she was pregnant that day." Jack's heart leapt into his throat thinking about poor little Zoë and the last memory he had of her. It should have been on his own deathbed, preferably with her and Leah at his side and grandkids at his feet. Not her slumped in her highchair with warm blood oozing through his fingers. He pushed the memory away. Before Ray could ask about the next location, Jack said, "Yes, we had sex at Fort Funston."

"Amigo, you have a *fetiche* for the outdoors. *Bastardo pervertido*."

Thinking back, both he and Leah didn't seem too worried about where they had sex. As long as they had the place to themselves.

"What about the 16th Avenue Steps? You stroll there too, *chico amante?*"

Jack lifted an eyebrow. Loverboy. Funny. "She'd never seen the illuminated steps, so we went up one night to see them. By then, Leah was in her third trimester. No sex."

Ray's eye widened. "Nothing? Not even—"

"Move along, pal, nothing to see here."

"*¡Aguafiestas!* Okay, okay, killjoy, what about the Tea Garden?" Looking up at the photo of the body resting in the Buddha's arms, he asked, "What do you think this means?"

Jack shook his head, gazing at the image. "The body kind of looks like a babe in arms. See how the head is cradled in the hand? If we go by the timeline of the dumps, I'm going to guess this was when Zoë was born."

Ray nodded. "This *coño* has a sick mind. Clever, but sick." Jack agreed. "And the Palace?"

It hit Jack then what this posed body represented. "We took Zoë there for her first birthday. We stopped to watch the performer there with his marionettes. See how the body looks like one of those puppets, but collapsed, as if the strings were cut." Ray nodded again. "As for Spreckels Lake, the only thing I can think of is the boat races."

"Is that anything like the submarine races?" Ray winked.

"No, asshole. I took the girls there to see the Model Yacht Club racing their boats. That was a few weeks before—" He couldn't finish the thought.

From Eve to Alma, Jack's memories raced through his first date with Leah, Zoë's birth, and the last outing they'd taken together before he'd lost his girls.

"No wedding photos here," Ray noted. "I know you and Leah were married down in Carmel, but if this bastard knows you, he could have followed you. Do you suppose there's a body down there that could be tied to all of this?" Ray waved at the murder wall.

Jack thought for a moment then shook his head. "You should look into that, for sure, but I don't think so. If you look at all the discovery dates, they fall into the three-month pattern from the first victim."

Ray thought for a moment, stuffing an egg roll in his mouth. When he swallowed, he said, "If he knows you, I guess turning up uninvited would be suspicious, no?"

Jack nodded his agreement, trying his best to keep his emotions in check. Memories of his and Leah's wedding day flooded back as if it were yesterday. He fought to keep his breathing steady. A knot formed in the pit of his stomach, and he was pretty sure it wasn't Wong's food. He swallowed hard to keep the bile in his stomach where it belonged.

After a prolonged silence, Ray said, "Well, I don't want to be the one to say this, but I will anyway. Even if you don't know the killer, he knows you. He may or may not be killing because of you, but he *is* taunting you. The question is, why?"

"I have no idea. And we still haven't found a tie to Eve." He gazed back up at the sixth victim. "I keep going back to Madie. I know her face from somewhere but I can't place her. It's been driving me crazy since I first saw her at Cutter's last night."

Ray gazed up at the woman. "I can't help you there. I've never seen any of these women before, other than at the crime scenes. Perhaps if you put her out of your mind, it will come to you."

"Maybe." Jack looked at the debris in front of them. "I'll pack the rest of this stuff up and you can take it home."

"Are you sure? There's a lot of food here. You might get hungry later."

"Very sure. Living this close, the appeal of Chinese food wore off long ago." Both men rose from the floor. While Jack cleared away the food, he saw Ray walk back to the murder wall to study the information, hands on his hips. Jack found a handled bag and stuffed the containers into it. While he worked, he said, "You never did tell me why you dropped by."

Casually, over his shoulder, Ray said, "You never asked."

"Yeah, sorry about that. So, what gives? Do you have some news on Bonnie Boyd's case?" With today's new revelations—his texter was the serial killer—the Boyd case had gone right out of his mind.

Without turning around, Ray casually said, "How does *Tío Joaquín* sound?"

Jack stopped in his tracks. "*Tío* . . . isn't that uncle in Spanish?"

Just as casually, Ray reflected. "I think so."

Rushing over to his friend, Jack spun him around. "Are you telling me Maria is pregnant?" He could tell by the shit-eating grin on Ray's face that she was. He threw his arms around his friend in a bear hug. "Congratulations. Oh, man, this is wonderful news." Without missing a beat, he pushed Ray back and gave his friend a serious look. "Are you sure you're the daddy?"

CHAPTER TWENTY

He stared into his glass of whiskey as if it was a fortune teller's crystal ball and he was hoping to find an answer. But to what?

Would he only be allowed one answer to his many questions? And which question was most important?

Who was killing women in the city, and why was he doing it?

What made Carl Boyd snap and kill his wife, Bonnie? Where was she?

Who killed his Zoë?

Where was Leah?

Was he willing to sacrifice all the other answers just to find his wife, even if it meant never knowing who killed Zoë?

And what about all the innocent, butchered women? Did they not deserve to have their identities restored so they could finally be released to their families for proper burials?

His head spun with questions. His brain ached and put so much pressure against the inside of his skull that no amount of rubbing would ease it.

Perhaps another drink. He downed the glass' contents then held it in the air to get the bartender's attention.

The man limped down the length of the bar with a critical glare. He grabbed a bottle from the back bar and poured out another shot. "You're starting to look a little sloppy, Jack. This is the last one."

"Don't you think I should be the judge of sloppy, Max?" Okay, that didn't come out right, but dammit, that's exactly what he meant. The tone of his voice was gruff, but he was a paying customer, after all.

And wasn't that the purpose of drinking alone . . . to get sloppy? Or was it to loosen his mind so his thoughts would flow more easily? That's why the classic novelists had written so well, wasn't it? Hemingway, Chandler, Kerouac...all notorious alcoholics.

No, wait. Now he remembered. *He* drank to forget. Forget about his daughter's still-warm body oozing blood through his fingers. Forget about poor Trax. Forget about his missing wife and all the times the texter . . . no, The Butcher . . . had sent him on wild goose chases around the city. Forget about his ruined life and his lost career. Forget about *everything*.

Hell, he'd already forgotten about poor Madie. Who was she, dammit? He scrubbed at his eyes. Somehow, she was the key to solving this case.

Gazing up at Max, Jack downed the freshly-poured whiskey and indicated for another refill.

Max stepped back, bottle still in hand, a crease forming between his dark eyes.

"I know you're walking but I can't just keep serving you if one of us isn't setting limits. And what kind of friend would I be if I let you stagger out of here and you got hit by a car crossing the street to your place? I could lose my job. You wouldn't want that on your conscience, would you?"

Jack huffed. "You own the bar, now fill me up." Max's Bar was kitty-corner from Wong's. While the Condor was closer, Jack didn't need T&A in his face while he was trying to get drunk.

Max shook his head. "The city could shut me down, man. Tell me what's eating you first. I'll be the judge if you get one last drink or not."

"Father Nick is the only one who gets that confession. Now—" Jack waved the glass in Max's direction again.

Max was unrelenting. "Bartenders . . . priests . . . we're both in the job of hearing the confessions of our patrons. Spill."

Even after seven, or was it eight, shots of whiskey, Jack still knew he couldn't tell Max that a killer was stalking the city. But was that really why he was drinking?

No. He'd been handling. Handling the recent text to Spreckels

Lake. Handling the Boyd case, no matter how similar it was to his own. And handling the knowledge of what the city was up against. Apparently, he wasn't handling one thing though.

"Maria Navarro is pregnant." He didn't have to elaborate. Max was a retired cop who sustained a gunshot wound that took him off the force. Rather than suffer a desk job for the rest of his career, he opened a bar and suffered drunks. So, he knew Ray from his time on the force and as a result also knew Maria.

Max's face slightly softened. "That's great news, Jack."

Nodding, he said, "It is. They've been trying for a while."

"So why are you in here drinking? It's certainly not to celebrate their good fortune. Don't tell me you're holding it against them." Jack chuffed under his breath. "Oh, Jack." Max set down the bottle on the back bar with a thud.

"What? I'm not holding it against them. I couldn't be happier."

"Yeah, you could. But instead of bringing Ray in for a celebratory drink," Max leaned forward and slammed both hands on the bar, forcing Jack to look at him, "you're sitting in here alone and drinking yourself into a stupor. What gives?"

"I *am* happy for them," he repeated, but Max didn't seem to believe him. "Really, I am. It's just—"

"Just what?" Max waited, motionless.

Jack held his gaze for a long moment, then looked away. "Zoë's birthday is coming up. I know I shouldn't let Ray and Maria's news get to me." He gazed back at Max. "I really am thrilled for them. I just . . ."

Max stood up straight, a look of understanding crossing his face. "You just miss the hell out of your daughter." Jack shot the barman a look he hoped said *Leave my family out of this.* "I get it. But you can't lose sight of something good that's happening to you, man. Ray's kid will never replace Zoë, but you have a chance at watching your best friend's child grow up."

"I know. He called me *Tío Joaquín*. . . Uncle Jack." Just then, something pressed against his heart, making him remember the moment when Ray had said the word—uncle. Jack hadn't had family outside of the one he created for himself with Leah and

Zoë. While Ray was his best friend, and by extension Maria, it hadn't really settled on him that it also meant they were family. Which included their children.

Jack thought for a moment, then pushed the glass away from him. Max was right. He'd had enough. No matter how much he drank, he'd never forget the things that hurt the most. All it would do was dull the good things going on around him.

"Barkeep," called a man standing nearby. "A couple G&Ts for me and my special lady."

Jack slowly turned. Something in the man's tone when he said *special lady* was like a smack on the back of the head. The man held his left arm around the dark-haired woman, so when he extended his hand, she was forced against him. In his hand, the man held folded cash to pay for their drinks. They both appeared to have been drinking elsewhere so she either didn't notice the awkward move or didn't mind.

Jack did a double-take as memories flooded his mind. He squeezed his eyes shut as Madie's face flashed before him. Her living face. Memories awakened. He'd seen her in a similar embrace with another man. . . somewhere, but where?

He looked up at the couple again and saw the man cast Jack a cheeky wink. The same wink Madie's date had given him. He squeezed his eyes shut again.

Concentrate. Concentrate!

His hand, what was in her date's hand?

Jack saw the couple again—Madie under her date's arm, his cheeky wink. He'd said something. Jack had ignored it at the time, but why?

Then it hit him all at once, like an explosion going off in his brain. It was a similar feeling to the realization he'd felt earlier in the day when he discovered the serial killer was also his mysterious texter.

His heart pounded as anger welled inside him. He felt it rushing through his veins like fire. Like earlier, he wanted to put his fist through something, but the bar was no place to start throwing punches. He forced himself to bottle it up. The adrenaline racing through his body forced the effects of his inebriation to abate.

His mind seemed to overlay the image of Madie and her date over the couple down the bar. In the hand of her date, Jack saw the small, square packet—yellow with a smiling face. That shape was unmistakable. A condom.

The man's cheeky grin told Jack he was getting laid that night, as if driving home the fact that Jack wasn't and wouldn't be for a long time.

And the single word the man had uttered. It had always grated on Jack. He hadn't seen the man in a long time until that night, and not again until very recently.

Just as quickly as the moment had passed when he saw him with Madie, and uttered the single word in a manner he knew upset Jack—the drawn out "Jackie"—he let the memory slip from his mind. But there was no doubting it now. He remembered victim number six from that split-second meeting on the street nearly two years ago.

She'd been on Paul Travers' arm.

CHAPTER TWENTY-ONE

"Where's Tommy?"

Jack didn't have time for niceties. He'd taken just enough time to down a couple cups of strong coffee at Max's before crossing the road to Tommy Wong's. The wait staff already knew he wasn't one for chit-chat, so the waitress bobbed her head and motioned for him to follow.

Wong's was a small but clean establishment. All the chairs matched, as did the tables, but there were few frivolities; the décor didn't scream out Chinese. The only evidence it was a Chinese restaurant, other than the glowing sign over the door, were the uniforms—wait staff in a red Mandarin-collared shirt and buttoned black vest worn over pressed black pants and black shoes. Kitchen staff wore a more traditional Mandarin-collared white cook's jacket over black and white checked pants. The only difference with Tommy's uniform was that his cook's jacket was red.

Tommy was tall and lean, which made his loose-fitting jacket look like it was draped on a hanger. But the man was no wimp. Under his uniform, his slight form was tight with muscles he'd developed over the years from hours spent in a dojo, studying various forms of martial arts that brought him into the MMA scene. Jack knew all of this because he and Tommy had known each other from their school days. He was also a long-time local boy.

The waitress stopped at the foot of the three steps to a raised platform area and motioned for Jack to continue before returning to her work station. Tommy was seated at a table along the back wall. The position gave him a good view of the restaurant, from the comings and goings at the front door to the kitchen where he could watch the cooks churn out any number of more than fifty items on his menu.

Tommy didn't bother getting up when he saw Jack. Instead, just cocked his head to acknowledge his presence. When Jack extended his hand, Tommy said, "This is a first. Normally I have to come to you for the rent." He waved across the table where Jack seated himself, leaning back in the chair.

Chuffing, he said, "Not always."

Tommy lifted a thin brow that arched over his dark brown eyes. "Always. But hey, I'm not complaining. You got a lot on your plate. There's been a lot of traffic on your stairs recently. You must be on a new case."

"A couple."

He watched Tommy's long, thin fingers manipulate the chopsticks through the noodles then stuff them in his mouth. If not for all the hours in the dojo, Jack would have wondered where Tommy put all the food he ate. He wasn't quite as tall as Jack, but if he weighed more than a hundred and fifty pounds it was because he was soaking wet and carrying rolls of quarters in his pockets. "Want some?"

"Thanks, no. Still full from lunch."

A moment later, Tommy finished his meal and sat back, drawing those spiderlike fingers through his shiny black hair to move it out of his eyes. "So, you haven't come to give me the rent and you don't want to eat. What do you want?"

"Information." No point in beating around the old proverbial. That thin eyebrow arched again. "What kind of information?"

"Only one color and I can't find it over the counter."

A crease formed between Tommy's eyebrows. "Why do you think I know anything about the black market?"

"Because I know you, Tommy. You know how to get things."

"And you want me to get something for you. Is that it?"

"Possibly."

Tommy leaned forward. "If this is for one of your cases, Jack, I want my name left out of it."

Jack nodded. "Of course. You know how I operate."

Sitting back again, Tommy huffed. "Yeah, just on the edge of the law."

Jack wasn't sure if he should take umbrage to the comment or consider it a compliment. As a former cop, he knew his limits. Of course, he also knew how to cross those limits but still manipulate a situation to fit within the law. Like finding Bonnie Boyd's car. Even though it meant handing it over to Ray, Jack had withheld as much of the case details as possible since he knew Homicide was taking over.

"Always within the law."

Tommy chuckled this time. "What do you want?"

"Condoms."

Tommy's abrupt howls of laughter seemed to echo off the walls of the nearly empty restaurant. "Are you serious?"

"Deadly." Jack sat forward and lowered his voice. "Look, man, the city has a serious problem. Someone is out there raping women." Given that Cutter had said the women had had sex before being killed, nothing was ruling out rape. He couldn't tell Tommy there was a serial killer on the loose, so this seemed the lesser of the evils in order to get the information he needed.

Tommy quickly regained his composure, gazing directly at Jack. "You're telling me the city has a serial rapist on the loose?"

Jack nodded. "What do you need from me?"

"Like I said. Condoms. According to the ME's report, whoever is doing this is using a rubber. But it's not any of the over-the-counter brands. Whatever is being used has a special formulation of lubricant that's not sold in traditional brands. In fact, it's generally only used in Asian countries. Investigators have been into the shops in Chinatown to see if anyone's selling imported brands with this list of ingredients, but so far, they haven't found anything. So, I'm thinking—"

"Black market," Tommy finished for him.

Nodding, Jack continued. "I have reason to believe I know what the packaging looks like, but I don't know the brand. And if they're not readily available, then whoever is using this brand has to have either been to China, or wherever, and brought them back, or is buying them in the city, which means he's getting them *under* the counter."

Tommy thought for a moment. "If they're on the black market, it must mean they haven't got FDA approval or they're illegal for some reason."

Jack shrugged. "Probably. I really don't care. I just want to catch this bastard."

"Seems like a big case for an ex-cop."

"I took a case last week to find a missing woman. It's possible she could be the next victim." He wasn't lying. Bonnie Boyd still hadn't been found. He hated admitting it, but outside of her striking beauty, Bonnie could fit the profile. "Based on the evidence from the other victims, we're looking at one suspect and one brand of condoms." He left out the bit that the evidence had been obtained from dead women. He let Tommy assume they were alive.

"Cops have their snitches and lines to the underground market in the city. Why come to me?" Tommy asked.

"Come on. If a cop had unlimited access to the underground, would it still be the underground?"

"Point taken." A moment later, Tommy lowered his voice and gazed directly into Jack's eyes. "Do you know where the Terracotta Warriors are?" Jack nodded. "Then you know where Bruce Lee is." Jack nodded again. "Directly across the street, go into the shop and ask for *bìyùn tào* . . ."

"Bee yoon tow? Is that someone's name?"

Tommy chuckled. "No. *Bìyùn tào* is Chinese for condoms. Literally, a contraception jacket."

Jack sat back with a chuckle. "I just go in and ask for rubbers? How does this get me into the underground market?"

"When you see the shop, you'll know they don't stock them. It's a souvenir shop. When you ask for them by their Chinese name, anyone in the store will take you to someone who can help you—"

"Wait," Jack cut in. "Why can't I just ask for this person?"

"Trust me. This is how it's done."

Jack nodded and repeated the words to be sure he had the correct pronunciation. "Thanks, Tommy. I owe you one."

"I hope you find what you're looking for. As for owing me, maybe you can bring the rent to me next time." Tommy's smile reached his eyes.

Shaking hands, they pulled each other into a quick shoulder bump. "You got it."

CHAPTER TWENTY-TWO

He couldn't sleep.

Knowing he had a lead put him on edge. If he could just find the brand of condoms Travers had waved at him that night, it could mean there was a link between him and at least one of them. But what was it? Even though the condoms were only available on the black market, it didn't mean Travers was the only one using them. But two things pulled Jack closer to the truth . . . the condoms *and Madie*. And both had something to do with that asshole.

Jack tried keeping his perspective in check. He didn't hate Travers, but nor did he like him. Except for that one chance meeting on the street that night, and until Ray told him about his new partner, Jack had forgotten Travers even existed.

What was up Travers' ass anyway? Jack had never been close with the man. They hadn't grown up together and didn't run in the same circles. They'd only met at the academy; little more than ten years ago. Other than training, nothing put them together. So, what was his problem? Even Ray had told him Travers was like a dog with a bone whenever Jack's name came up. How was it that while he had almost no knowledge of the man, Travers approached him with some form of familiarity, like they were, he hated saying it, friends. The kind of friends who could throw insults at each other in a good-natured way, only Travers' invective behavior was anything but friendly.

Monday, when he turned up in the office, the man was in his face from the moment he walked through the door, taunting him, goading him . . . to what? Throw a punch at him? On duty or off, Travers was a cop. If Jack had been dumb enough to punch that asshole in the face, Jack would be the one going to jail, not Travers, the instigator. This was just one more reason why Jack recorded as much as possible.

Travers had been right to be suspicious that Jack was withholding information, but his attitude had been way over the top if he thought Jack would share anything with him.

And that breath. Damn! Was it always that rank? How had Madie tolerated it? Let alone had sex with him.

With so much adrenaline rushing through him, Jack tossed the blanket aside and got up. He paced his front room while thoughts screamed through him. Travers kept pushing through to the front of his mind. Jack needed to know more about him. Since the academy, what had the guy been up to?

Jack threw himself into the desk chair and switched on the computer. He clicked to open the browser and typed in Travers' name.

Unsurprisingly, several Paul Travers' came up in the search results, but only one was tied to the academy.

Following the few links, Jack was amazed to see so little was available on the guy. He didn't have any social media pages, no blogs, not even tags on photos from people he might know . . . there was almost nothing that gave him a web presence.

But one link did draw Jack's attention. A news piece from three years ago:

LONE SURVIVOR IN RED MOUNTAIN PLANE CRASH

[May – The Chronicle, San Francisco, CA] In early February, while en route to Las Vegas from San Francisco just after New Year's Day, Joe Patinkus made a judgment call to divert his four passenger, twin-engine Beechcraft Duchess airplane north of the scheduled route while crossing over the southern Sierra Nevada Mountains.

According to lone survivor, San Francisco Police Officer Paul W. Travers, Patinkus had just finished restoring his late father's plane and hoped to recoup some of the restoration costs at the roulette tables. But something malfunctioned, sending the plane into a tailspin in the inclement weather. Unable to control the aircraft, it crashed on Red Mountain, in an area of high mountains between the Sierra National Forest and Kings Canyon National Park, sending the wreck downhill to settle in a mostly-barren and remote area between Hell For Sure and Disappointment lakes.

When interviewed, Travers had this to say on how he managed to survive more than a month in life-threatening conditions: **"I used what remained of the plane's hull for shelter. I had to forage for wood, but it was so wet that I couldn't get a good fire going to raise the alarm. The electrics were gone, so I couldn't radio for help. We had clothes for the trip, so I layered up, and used an emergency blanket to block wind coming in through the hole in the side of the plane."** *When asked about food and water, he said,* **"I melted snow over the fire in a small piece of bent metal from the wreck. The emergency kit had a few rations, and I've always been an avid hunter. Really, it was a miracle from God that I woke up every morning."**

Travers survived on the mountain alone for nearly six weeks. Joe Patinkus' remains have never been found, assumed to have been lost on Red Mountain where the plane first impacted. A recovery mission will take place after the thaw.

This was news to Jack. Travers had been stranded on the mountain in winter. Every day, freezing and alone, wondering if he'd ever be found. Holy shit! That would take a lot out of anyone. No wonder he was an asshole. He'd kind of earned the right. Perhaps he needed a little understanding and sympathy too. But why hadn't he just started downhill to find help rather than waiting for them to find him?

Jack opened another tab on his browser and looked up Red Mountain and the lakes, the names ironic for the poor man's situation, for sure. Search results brought up more than sixty-two million results mostly having to do with the formerly-named Osdick Mountain in San Bernardino.

He then searched for Hell For Sure Lake. Certainly, there could be only one. Yep, only one, and it even had its own freaking zip code, which made Jack chuckle a little. By all accounts, no one lived up there, so what the fuck?

Over seven and a half million results came back, most of which revolved around personal hikes, treks, and spiritual journeys. But it was abundantly clear. While most summer trekkers started at Courtright Reservoir—as there was a good road for the nearly fourteen-mile trek on foot through the valley—no one ever went up in the winter.

From the other side, the small community of Aspendell was the nearest place with a road. The hike from there would have been three times as long as the only access was through the valleys and around the mountain, following marked trails. Red Mountain Pass could have been climbed by experienced mountaineers but was a much more dangerous option.

Looking at the elevation maps, Jack put himself at the top of Red Mountain. Had Travers even made it to the summit, all he would have seen in every direction was mountains. Any town, small or otherwise, would have been invisible. Had Jack been in the same situation, he probably would have also stayed with the wreck, and hoped to God that the transponder had been working and help would eventually find him.

Something didn't sit right with him though. He typed in *recovery Joe Patinkus*. Other than the few articles on the actual crash, there didn't seem to be much on the recovery mission. What he did read only said that Patinkus' remains could not be located.

Had Travers buried his friend? It didn't appear anyone had asked him.

Jack was weary but there was still something he needed to do. Update the murder wall. He went back to the article about the crash, which included two photos—one of Travers and one of Patinkus. Jack printed copies of both images. He also printed off a copy of the article, handwriting the accident and rescue date, and the dates referenced on the recovery articles for Patinkus.

Rising, he stretched, realizing he'd been sitting for more than two hours. He rubbed his eyes, gathered the printed pages and went into the backroom. He added Travers to the murder wall, placing his image under Madie's. On the side of the map, he tacked up the image of Patinkus along with the article, and used a bit of colored string to link Travers to the crash.

To Travers' image, Jack added a card that included his own memory of seeing Travers with Madie, approximate date, and the condom's yellow packet with the smiley face. Beside that, he added a big question mark. He hoped that mystery would be solved as soon as he went to the shop Tommy had directed him to.

He gazed at the time on his phone—2:23 a.m. If he went to bed now, rather to the sofa—*I really should buy a sofa-bed*—he could get at least six hours of sleep and still have time to walk up Grant Street in time for the store to open at 9 a.m.

CHAPTER TWENTY-THREE

Wednesday

No one ever said he was a patient man.

After tossing for a few hours on the sofa and playing through the new insight into Paul Travers, Jack finally got up to shower and get dressed. He downed a cup of coffee while looking over the murder wall to be sure he hadn't missed anything. It looked all right, but he still had a niggling sense something was missing . . . or just off in some way. He hoped he'd sort it out sooner rather than later.

A quick look at the time said it was 8:42 a.m., but he got moving anyway.

Grant Avenue was a busy one-way street running north from Mission Street to Broadway, directly across from Wong's. His destination was only four blocks away, so he walked. He could use the exercise. If the shop he was looking for wasn't open yet, he'd grab a coffee and moon cake at the bakery across the street and wait.

He easily found the Terracotta Warriors. Five statues of the iconic warriors stood on an overhang above some shops, behind them a mural depicting the faces of many other warriors. At the next junction was a portrait of Bruce Lee and a dragon painted on the Commercial Street side of the bakery. On the facing wall was another dragon.

Just as Tommy had promised, the shop Jack was looking for faced the bakery, and it was already open.

Jack's heart pounded in his chest. Not from the walk, but at the possibility that if this shop held the answers he looked for, it could very well launch him neck deep into the case.

Dodging between passing cars, he entered the shop, halting just inside the door to get his bearings. Before he could reach the sales counter, a pretty, young Chinese girl greeted him.

"Can I help you find something?" she asked, her voice sounding almost as fragile as she looked.

He swallowed hard. He wasn't one to mince words, and he rarely had trouble speaking his mind. But this young woman barely looked old enough to have sex herself, so asking her for condoms constricted his throat. "Just looking." He darted past her, moving deeper into the store. Perhaps there was a man working here he could ask. He moved past the front of the store which catered to tourists, with imitation ivory iconery and ceramic figurines, hand-painted fans and handmade baskets, traditional red paper lanterns and painted dragon kites, traditional costumes and I Love San Francisco T-shirts, and just about anything else a tourist would be looking for to commemorate their visit to Chinatown.

The back half of the store was full of wire bins of cheap household goods scattering the floor, along with dollar items like soap, plastic bowls, candles, and junk that wouldn't last long.

Overhead throughout the store, hundreds of chimes tinkled in the breeze coming through the open door. Paper lanterns, kites, flags and banners rustled together, sounding like wadding paper. Jack had to duck more than once to keep from hitting them.

Just when it seemed like no one else but the young girl at the front was in the store, a back door opened, and a young Asian man stepped through. Jack estimated he was between seventeen and twenty.

He stopped the man mid-aisle. "Excuse me." The young man stopped and looked up at Jack. Either it was too early in the morning for the man to be awake, or he was just bored with his job. He stared at Jack, neither willing to help or continue walking. "Can you help me find something?"

The young man kept looking at him. Jack didn't want to appear racist, but he wondered if the man even spoke English. It never surprised him that in the city, communities were still so tightly knit, many people never found it necessary to leave their safe enclaves their whole lives. To that end, one could grow up never learning English, only speaking Chinese, or whatever language, because that was all that was needed to live and work within that community.

Maybe that was why Tommy had told him the Chinese name of what Jack was looking for. If he remembered the correct pronunciation, he just might get what he needed. "I'm looking for *bìyùn tào*."

The young man's eyes focused a bit. "We don't sell those here."

So, he did speak English, and very well. "I was told you do."

"You a cop?"

Not anymore, he thought. "No, Tommy Wong sent me."

The young man's thin lips turned up slightly at the corners. "Tommy's an asshole."

Suppressing a chuckle, Jack said, "Maybe so, but he sent me here to get what I need." The young man didn't move. "Are you going to give me a hard time, or do I need to tell that pretty girl up front you got a hard on for her."

The young man's back noticeably straightened. "You're sick, old man. She's my sister."

"Stranger things have been known to happen."

"You're an asshole too. Wait here."

The young man returned through the door and a moment later, a pretty woman appeared.

"My son say you look for *bìyùn tào*." The tiny woman before him looked twenty, if she was a day. But if that cocky little bastard was her son, she was aging amazingly well. He nodded. "Not for sale here."

"Tommy Wong sent me."

The woman's gaze narrowed as she scrutinized him. Then, "Follow me."

She led him through the backroom door, down a narrow hallway and through another door to a small room. Jack didn't need to look hard to know that everything on the shelves was hot merchandise. "You're not going to ask me if I'm a cop?"

"You tell my son you aren't. Did you lie?"

She's a sharp woman.

"No, ma'am."

"Tell me what you looking for. Do you really need rubbers . . . or something else?"

"I'm looking for two things. Tommy said you can help with at least one of them. Perhaps both." She only nodded and waited for him to continue. "I'm looking for a brand of condoms that I'm pretty sure are black market—"

The woman put her hand up. "Black what? Never heard of it."

"Fair enough. Shall we say it's a specialty item. I can't find it anywhere else." He quickly gazed around the shelves. "I don't see it here, but maybe you can tell me where I can find it."

Shrugging, she said, "Maybe, maybe not. You tell me, and I let you know."

"Condoms, yellow packaging, smiley face. Have you seen them?"

The woman laughed. "Is that what all the fuss is about? For cry sake. Wait here." She disappeared through the door, and a few moments later, she reappeared with a plastic wrapped yellow box with a happy face on the top. "How many do you need? A big boy like you, maybe a case?" She gave him a wink.

Jack took the box in hand. The text on the box read:

HAPPY ENDINGS CONDOMS
12-pak
Have a nice lay!

He tore the protective plastic off the box and extracted a single, wrapped condom. Sure enough, it was exactly the same one he'd seen in Travers' hands that night.

"Just the one." He handed the box back to the woman.

"You buy whole box. Not sold separately." Under her breath she said, "Cry sake, who fuck only one time?" She grabbed the packet from Jack's hand and stuffed it back in the box, then thrust it back at him. "You buy whole box."

Jack would have laughed if he wasn't so nervous. He felt like the condoms were the first major piece of evidence to solving this case.

Cutter had said investigators hadn't gotten very far with their own underground search, but then, they didn't know exactly what they were looking for. Jack would have to get one of these condoms back to Cutter to analyze to be sure the lubricant was the same as that found on all the victims. Aside from the title on the box, the writing was in Chinese characters. He could ask the woman before him to translate but didn't want to involve her any more than he already had.

Jack knew without a doubt these were the ones Travers had on him the night he'd seen him with Madie. If Cutter confirmed these were the same condoms used on the other twelve victims, then it could mean Travers was tied to the case in at least two ways. Or at the very least, tying Travers to Madie. "Fair enough." He extracted a folded printout he'd remembered to bring with him. "Have you seen this man before?"

It only took a quick look for the woman to say, "What if I have?"

Jack put on his most charming smile. "Well, if you have, it would go a long way to helping me bring down a serial rapist in the city. He's buying these condoms from your little store." He cocked his head in the direction of the small but well-stocked room of illicit goods. "If you *have* seen him and are withholding information, the police could be visiting you very soon, and with a warrant to turn this place over. But if you cooperate, this will be the last time you see me, at least in an official capacity."

"You said you not cop."

"I'm not. But I am a private investigator with ties to the police."

A tiny crease appeared between her finely-shaped eyebrows. "You lied!"

"No, I didn't. You asked if I was a cop. I'm not. I just didn't elaborate, and you didn't ask. I was hired to find a missing woman. She fits the type the rapist is targeting. If the rapist is buying these in your store . . ." He left the rest to her imagination.

"You an asshole, just like Tommy." She snatched the printout of Travers from Jack and looked more closely. "Yes, I know him. He," she said, jabbing a thin finger on the paper, "is a cop."

This revelation surprised Jack. The image of Travers on the paper was in plain clothes. "Do you know his name?"

"On his uniform. Name tag say Travers."

"He usually comes in wearing his police uniform?" The woman nodded. "So he shops here a lot. Is this all he buys?"

"Once a month . . . maybe every six weeks. Every time he come, he walk out the door with a bag of candy . . . without paying, like a thief. Maybe he think if I don't say anything about *that*, he won't say anything about—" she nodded sharply toward the shelves.

Jack understood. Travers was passively blackmailing the woman. It made him wonder how many other shops around the city the asshole was shaking down. "I'm sorry for that. Tell me how much these are, and a bag of that candy he likes." He reached for his wallet and gave the woman what she asked for, and a twenty on top of it to make up for what had been taken from her. A dollar bag of candy wasn't a lot to steal, but it was the principle of the thing—Travers thought he could take what he wanted without question, using his position as a cop to intimidate shop owners into silence.

A few minutes later, Jack was walking back up Grant Avenue with a grin on his face. The box of Happy Endings Condoms was tucked in one pocket and a bag of candy in another. In his hands, he now carried a to-go cup of hot jasmine tea and the bunched-up end of a sack that contained a moon cake. In the other hand he held a baked pork bun he ate while walking back to his apartment. This was just one more reason why he loved the city. The food. While it was still Chinese food, they were things Tommy didn't sell in his restaurant, so Jack still considered them a treat.

And frankly, he needed to boost his energy for the next visit in his day. To see Travers.

First things first, his murder board needed updating, and he had to get the condoms to Cutter.

CHAPTER TWENTY-FOUR

"**I** need your help."

It was mid-afternoon by the time Jack made it to the department. At the front desk getting his visitor's pass, Waters had said Ray wasn't on site, but Travers was. That suited Jack fine. What he had to say to Travers didn't need Ray's involvement. However, if it turned out Travers was somehow involved in the killings, he'd immediately get Ray on board. And Haniford.

Travers spun his chair in Jack's direction, his gaze following him across the small office to where he sat in the chair beside the desk. "Jackie," Travers said, his voice sounding both surprised and wary. "What are you doing here? Ray's out."

Jack casually leaned back in the chair and crossed his legs, weaving his fingers together over his stomach. "I know. I'm here to see you." Travers' eyes widened with surprise. "Yeah, I know. Don't get your panties in a knot."

Travers leaned back and tried to look as casual as possible. Jack knew he'd thrown the man off balance by asking for his help and he didn't know what to do, so he reverted to his normal, cocky self. "What do you want? Or are you here to give me some of that evidence I know you're withholding on Bonnie Boyd?"

"You've got everything I do." *Except for my interviews, case notes, audio recordings, videos . . .* If Travers was even half the detective the man thought he was, he could do the same legwork Jack had done. Given how long he'd had the case, he should have at least already conducted some of the interviews with people on Bonnie's phone's contact list. By the looks of the screen on the desk which was open with the missing woman's photo, it didn't look like anything new had been added to the file. Maybe Ray was still withholding evidence, such as the BWC video.

Grumbling, Travers said, "Then I don't see any reason why you need to be here."

"Like I said, I need *your* help." He pulled out his notebook and pen. Before he'd entered the office, he'd switched on the video app on his phone and stuffed it in the top pocket of his black motorcycle jacket that he still wore. Part of what made Jack so good at his job was that he knew just how to stretch and bend the facts to get what he wanted. As a cop, he played as close to the letter of the law as necessary to get the results he needed. As a private detective, he had a little more leeway. "I'm tracking down a missing woman—"

"You handed over that case."

"This is another one. I get a lot of missing spouse cases." He hated admitting that, but that's part of what kept him in such luxurious digs over Wong's.

"This isn't Missing Person's, or have you been away so long you forgot?"

"Hear me out. I think you know her."

This made Travers' back stiffen. The subtle change on his face told Jack that the man was curious to know how he was involved, but at the same time, he looked leery of being scapegoated. "What makes you think I know who the woman is?"

"Because I saw you with her." Travers' eyes widened. "At least I think it was her. Dark, shoulder length hair, kinda curly. Green eyes. Around five and a half feet tall. The woman I saw you with came to about here." Travers flinched when Jack leaned forward and extended his hand with the pen in it to indicate the woman's height at around Travers' ear. Jack only grinned as he sat back in the chair. "Not too much shorter than you." He couldn't help but get a jab in at the man's ego.

Nervously, Travers asked, "When was this? I date a lot of women with that description."

He pretended to flip through his notebook to look for something, then said, "About two years ago? Give or take a couple months. I hadn't thought about it since then, but when her husband showed me her photo, it instantly came back to me. I'd recently moved in over Wong's. I still hadn't finished unpacking but I was hungry, so I went out to get something for dinner. You were taking your date into The Stinking Rose."

A crease formed between Travers' brows. "I've been there a few times with dates. What makes you think the woman you're looking for was the one I was with? I don't make a habit of dating married women."

If he hoped to get out of this with that comment, he was sadly mistaken. "They've only been married about eighteen months, so she was single when she was with you. Anyway, I distinctly remember that night because I hadn't seen you since, I think, the academy? You know how it is. You spend a lot of time with someone, but even though you haven't seen them for years, you still instantly recognize them." Travers said nothing but continued gazing at Jack, as if waiting for a shoe to drop. *Wait a minute, buddy,* Jack drawled the nickname out in his mind, *the shoe is coming and I'm going to stuff it right up your ass.* "I said hello, but you kept walking. Though you did turn around at the door and wink at me. And waved something in your hand."

"Yeah? What was it? If I had my arm around a woman, how could I have waved anything at you?"

First mistake. Jack never said Travers had his arm around the woman. "I don't know. Maybe you already had it in your hand, but at the time, I didn't know what it was . . . other than it was *really* small and yellow." Another subtle dig at his manhood.

"What was it?"

"Like I said, I hadn't seen you in a long time, and frankly, I didn't think about it afterward. I'd forgotten all about you until Ray said you finally made detective."

Travers folded his arms in front of him. "This all sounds inconsequential."

"Yeah, except now she's missing, and I know you dated her. So, I got to thinking what that little thing could have been . . . you know, as part of my investigation, following the leads and such . .

. which is why I'm here. Since you knew her, I'm wondering what you can tell me about her."

"I told you, I don't remember her."

"Maybe this will jog your memory. That little yellow thing in your hand started niggling the inside of my head. I made some inquiries and found this." Jack put the pen in his other hand with the notebook and dug into the jacket's inside pocket, pulling out the condom. Travers jerked back as the packet bounced onto the desk in front of him. The smiley face landed right side up, grinning at Travers. His face turned dark red and his eyes seemed to bulge, the crease between his brows deepened. Jack hit a nerve. A big one, apparently. "By the look on your face, I know you know her. Or at least now remember that you know her."

Travers' gaze shot up to Jack, his anger lingering. "So what if I dated her? It was only the one time."

"One time? She seemed like a nice woman. You certainly looked like you were having a good time."

"I always show my dates a good time. So what? What do I have to do with this? I dated her once. She disappeared after that. As you said, she got married and lived happily ever after."

The word *disappeared* was a curious thing to say. Jack marked that down as mistake number two. Calmly, Jack continued. "Happy . . . until she turned up missing. Why get so upset, Paul? I'm just here looking for some information on the woman you knew and dated two years ago. Did she have any friends she talked about? If she left her husband, maybe she could have gone to one of them."

"Ask her fucking husband," Travers snapped.

"I'm asking you. Wives don't always tell their husbands everything. Maybe she had friends back then she lost touch with . . . like us . . . but she reached out again after leaving her husband."

Confusion crossed Travers' face. Apparently, the suggestion of *friends like us* made his brain stumble as he fought through how he should be dealing with this. After a moment, he finally said, "We didn't talk much."

"Even over dinner? I know what it costs to eat at The Stinking

Rose. You certainly don't want to dine and dash there." The man had no reply. Either he couldn't think of something smug to say or decided to keep his mouth shut. "Okay, look. Something has obviously upset you. If you were closer with Madie Brown than you're letting on, you can tell me. I promise not to tell her husband."

Something changed on Travers' face. Some of it looked like relief to Jack. "Madie Brown?"

"Yeah, why?"

"Then it couldn't have been me. That wasn't the name of the woman I dated," he said.

Jack lifted an eyebrow. "Really? I was sure it had been her. I remember it so clearly . . . what she looked like, your wink, the little condom . . . all of it. I was sure it was Madie."

Travers chuckled lightly, some relief filling his voice now. "There are a lot of dark-haired women in the city, Jackie boy, but my date wasn't called Madie Brown. Her name was Georgina."

Jack wrote down the name. Could this be the victim's real name? "Georgina what?"

"Kearney, I think. I don't know. That was a long time ago."

Jack wrote that down too. "I really appreciate this, Paul, more than you know. The woman I'm looking for is called Madie, but if you say your date that night was Georgina Kearney, then we're talking about two separate women. Of course, I'll have to corroborate this with Ms. Kearney."

"You do that," flew out of Travers' mouth as he shot out of his chair and stomped to the office door, opening it. "If that's all you need . . ."

Jack took his time making obscure notes before putting the notepad and pen back into his jacket pocket. Rising, he stepped over to Travers and looked him in the eye. "I really appreciate you helping me, Paul. That was very nice of you. It doesn't do my investigation any good, but at least I don't have to spin my wheels in that direction anymore. Thanks."

Jack put his hand out as a friendly gesture of thanks, but Paul ignored it and glanced into the hall outside the office as if he didn't want to have to look Jack in the eye or touch him. "Yeah, whatever."

He spun his gaze back around to where Jack had placed his hand on Travers' shoulder and scowled again. "And hey, Paul. I'm really sorry about what happened."

"What the fuck are you talking about now?" He was obviously confused.

"You know . . . up on the mountain. I'm sorry. That must have been really rough on you." Jack was genuinely sorry for the man. Travers probably thought he was going to die in those brutal conditions.

Taken aback, he said, "Like you care. Why say something about it now? Because I gave you something you wanted?"

"No. Genuinely, I had no idea until I read about it online. The articles all said Joe was your best friend, and his body has never been found. I think I know how you must have felt. It's not easy losing someone you cared a lot about. Especially tragically. We have that in common," Jack suggested. "I don't know why you're so angry with me, Paul, but I'd like to find a way to put it behind us." Jack kept his cool, and his voice calm as he spoke.

"Whatever."

"Come on, man. I'm trying here," Jack said. He pushed his left hand into his pocket and clutched the bag of candy he'd bought earlier in the day with the condoms. He extended his right hand which Travers looked at for a moment before reluctantly grasping it. "Look. I even brought you a peace offering." Jack pulled his left hand out of his pocket and put the candy into the man's right hand. "The woman in the shop said you take a bag," emphasizing Travers was taking rather than buying them, "every time you come in to buy your rubbers." Trying to ignore how ashen the man's face went, Jack continued, "Look, I gotta run. Gotta see an ME about some tests he's running on the condom lube, but thanks for the talk. I really appreciate it."

"Wait, what do you mean about the condom lube?"

"I guess you're not on that investigation. You know, the serial killer case. Cutter said all the women had been sexually assaulted prior to death. One brand of condom comes back on each of them." Jack nodded toward the condom still on the desk. "Happy Endings." After a hearty clap on Travers' shoulder, Jack walked out the door.

From behind him, he heard the door slam and Travers start yelling. He couldn't hear what the man was saying as he continued walking away, but in that moment, Jack knew his suspicions were correct. Travers was deeply involved.

And now he had the name of victim number six.

CHAPTER TWENTY-FIVE

At the top of the stairs, he tossed the warm sack into his helmet which he held in one hand then slid the key into the lock with the other.

Jack had an immediate feeling something wasn't right. He swung open the door fully and let the overhead automatic sensor light cast a narrow beam into the room; his shadow stretched across the floor toward the desk. He slowly gazed around the room before entering. Reaching up, he flipped the light switch and used his foot to kick the door closed. He stood just inside the door, waiting. For what, he wasn't sure.

After depositing his helmet on the table beside the door, he grabbed the sack and strode to the desk. He set it on the table beside the sofa as he moved. As his eyes adjusted to the light, he honed his peripheral vision. Everything seemed normal but his spidey sense still tingled.

Taking a deep breath, he shed his jacket and slung it over the back of the desk chair. Maybe he was more exhausted than he thought. It put him on edge and made him jumpy for no reason. He just wanted to grab a beer, dig into his mildly warm burger, and crash in front of the TV, and hopefully not wake until morning. Late in the morning.

As he gazed across the desk—had he left it this messy?— something caught his eye, stopping him in his tracks. The backroom door was partially open. He always made sure to close it before he left in case of visitors. His heart rate clicked up. He waited. Listened.

Just now . . . was that rustling? He lifted his gaze a little more.

A shadow moved through the hole he'd punched in the door . . . from what? Probably a reflection from the small window in the room, he chided himself.

The door wavered slightly, or were his tired eyes playing tricks on him? He held his breath, hoping to pull in any other sounds from the apartment. Perhaps one of the people below him made the noise. They weren't always the quietest of tenants.

Straightening, he chuffed under his breath. What put him on edge? He stiffened his spine and strode toward the backroom for that beer. He really was more tired than he thought. The apartment door had been locked and the lights were off when he swung open the door. Maybe he did forget, on the very rare occasion, to close the backroom door all the way, but he couldn't remember the last time he had. Right now, everything was as he'd left it hours ago. He didn't understand the tingles running through him, but he was sure the long, busy day had something to do with it.

As he crossed the threshold, three things happened in rapid succession: a shadow appeared from behind the door, and before he could register a face, something blunt hit him in the solar plexus, robbing him of breath and doubling him over. The moment his knees hit the floor, he felt a sharp blow to the center of his upper back.

When he came to, the apartment was quiet, except for the pounding in his head. How long had he been out? His whole body seemed to throb with pain—his gut stung from the first strike, his spine from the second, and his skull from the third. He must have smacked it when he hit the floor.

Carefully sitting up to prevent a rush of blood to his head, he listened for the intruder, but Jack knew he was alone. The nervous feeling he'd had before the attack had also disappeared.

He used the door handle to brace himself as he stood and grabbed for the light switch with the other hand. The intruder had made short work of the room.

Jack slowly turned and looked around. Files he'd carefully stacked on the bed had been tossed. The contents of his boxes of personal things had been scattered. The walls with each of his cases had been stripped clean; evidence and notes covered every inch of floor space. As he moved, layers of papers crunched beneath his feet. When he gazed down, he noticed many of the victims' faces had been torn or crumpled. Directly under his left foot, half the face of one man glared up at him.

Travers.

He was the only one who could have done this. Jack had really riled him up in his office, and he'd made a point of telling Travers he was going to Cutter's office. Jack had only meant to plant the seed in the man's head that the test would confirm he was with the victim, Georgina Kearney, that night two years ago, around the time the woman's body had been discovered. There was no doubt in Jack's mind that she had been the one on Travers' arm. He may have confessed to having dated her, if only the once, but the forensic test would prove the Happy Endings condom had been the brand he'd waved at Jack.

Jack had no idea that he'd touched on such a serious nerve. Why would the man ransack his place?

Unless Travers was more involved in this case than Jack realized. The man couldn't have been this pissed off just because Jack tied him to Madie—no, Georgina Kearney. She had a name now. A real name.

Kneeling, he ruffled through the papers on the floor, trying to find her headshot. Travers had destroyed just about everything, but not all of it was torn up. If he was going to solve this case, and he was confident that he could, he'd need to put the murder board back together. But first, he needed to clean the room.

He wouldn't bother filing a break-in report. It would just waste the department's time, and his. He'd rather spend the rest of the night putting the room back to rights than filling out paperwork that would end up getting shuffled and forgotten since there weren't any witnesses and he couldn't prove it was Travers. He knew it but couldn't prove it without evidence. And he knew how cops stuck together. Even though Jack was an ex-cop, his former brothers and sisters would side with Travers because he was still in good standing within the department. Not a fallen wreck of a man like himself.

After swallowing a couple over-the-counter painkillers, he got busy. He worked in near silence through the night. His senses remained alert for any other strange noises, but the only sounds came from his moving around the backroom, shuffling of paper and boxes, and the squelch in his gut. He wasn't hungry. That bastard's sucker punch had left a lasting imprint there, as it had between his shoulder blades. But Jack worked through it all, his vision single-focused.

CHAPTER TWENTY-SIX

Thursday

The hairs on the back of his neck stood up against the warm, soft breeze coming through the backroom door. He braced himself but didn't turn around, trying not to let the person behind him know that Jack knew he was there. Either Travers had come back to see the damage he'd done, in which case, Jack would lay him out. Or it was Ray.

"Jack." Ray's voice was low and thready.

Jack dropped what was in his hands and went to his friend. "What's wrong?" He'd never seen Ray anything less than the macho bastard cop that he was. Now, it seemed life's rug had been pulled out from under his friend's feet.

He just repeated, "Jack." Ray's face was ashen and his chin quivered as he struggled with his composure.

Jack sat him on the edge of the bed, now partially covered in the folders he'd managed to sort out, and went to pour Ray a cup of coffee from the pot he'd kept brewing all night. Handing Ray the cup, he said, "Get this in you and tell me what's happened." He pulled over a chair and sat, waiting until his friend was ready to talk.

"Ha-have you seen Maria?" Ray finally asked.

Those four words instantly put Jack on edge. "What do you mean?"

"She's gone."

"What do you mean gone? Did she leave you?" Jack had to rein himself in and keep his voice calm. Ray was already upset and didn't need Jack's anger on top of it.

Ray shook his head. "She wasn't there when I got home after shift last night."

Jack sat forward in the chair and stared directly into his friend's eyes. "Tell me exactly what happened. Don't leave anything out. Anything!"

The cup in Ray's hands shook as he spoke, his voice little more than a whisper. "I came home, opened the door, and she wasn't there."

"Did you try her work? Maybe she worked late."

Ray nodded, "She wasn't there, but even if she had worked late, she's always home before me. I thought maybe she had gone to her mother's house to tell the family about the baby. We were going to do it together, but maybe there was some reason she wanted to do it on her own. I called everyone I could think of. No one has seen her." He slammed his fist down on his thigh, spilling some of the coffee from the cup in his other hand on his pants.

Jack took the cup and set it aside before Ray drenched himself. "When was the last time you talked with her?"

"Seven, maybe."

"And what time did you get home?"

"I don't know. It wasn't long after sunset."

It had been just around sunset last night when Jack got back to the apartment, making it about eight. This must have meant Maria went missing . . .

"Does nine sound about right?"

Ray thought then nodded.

Was it just a coincidence that his place had been broken into on the same night Maria went missing? Jack knew the Navarros were so in love they'd never leave each other. And now with a baby on the way—

Or had she been kidnapped? His heart skipped a beat. But why her? Did it have something to do with one of Ray's cases?

"What else, Ray? What haven't you told me?" He stared hard into Ray's eyes. He could tell his friend was struggling to hold it together, so he put a firm hand on the man's shoulder. "We'll find

Maria. I promise. But you gotta tell me everything."

Ray seemed to relax a little with Jack's promise. He'd do anything for the Navarros, even if it meant walking on hot coals or swimming through fire. He felt both coming.

"I knew she had been home. I smelled tamales before I even opened the back door. By the time I reached the kitchen, my mouth was watering. They were cooling on the counter, but she wasn't there. I heard voices in the living room and went to find her. She had been watching her *telenovela*, like she always does while waiting for me to get home, so we can eat together. The TV was still on." Jack had a feeling he knew where this was going. Could the person who took Maria also have taken Bonnie Boyd? If so, what tied the women together? "I looked everywhere but she wasn't in the house. I called everyone I could think of," he repeated.

"Why didn't you call me? Why wait so long to come to me, Ray? You know I'm always here for you." Jack tried keeping his anger and worry in check.

Anger crossed Ray's expression as he pulled his cell phone from his pocket. "I did," he said sharply. He brought up the calls log and thrust the phone into Jack's hand.

Rising, he went to find his phone in the other room. It was still in the pocket of his heavy leather jacket. He pulled it out and brought up his own call log. Sure enough, Ray had called him. A lot. The first calls came in while he'd been knocked out.

"Fuck!" He turned to find Ray had followed him out of the backroom. "Something fucked up is going on, Ray."

"I know. My Maria is missing. How fucked up is that, *vato*?" Ray spat.

"We'll find Maria. Listen to me a minute. Someone broke in here last night and tossed the backroom."

"Someone broke in?"

"He was here when I got home. He sucker-punched me. I don't know how long I was out, but when I came to, he was gone and everything in the room had been ransacked. I don't know if he was looking for something or just one seriously pissed off dude, but I spent most of the night getting it cleaned up."

"That's pretty fucked up, but how does that help me find Maria? Right now, that's all I care about."

"Hear me out." Jack gave his friend the rundown from the previous day, including his trip up Grant Avenue and the condoms, finding out about Travers' plane wreck, creating a fake missing person's case to get information from Travers about the woman he'd dated, and how pissed off the man had been by the time Jack left the office.

"I only meant to get under his skin, but something has clearly burrowed through to his brain. I'm pretty sure he's the one who broke in here. This was the only room he tossed. Why not the front room too if it had been a random break-in? Was he looking for something? Maybe it was to see what evidence I had tying him to the missing woman. If that was it, maybe he saw his name and photo on my murder board and went berserk. Who the fuck knows what goes on in that guy's head?"

"Do you think he could have taken Maria? I'll kill him if he did," Ray vowed.

"I can't figure out if he would be ballsy enough to take Maria, and if he did, what kind of fucked-up logic did he use to do it? She has nothing to do with any of my cases. And you're his partner. Why would he take *your* wife? Unless you pissed him off too."

"If he's not pissed off at me yet, he soon will be." Ray punched his fist into his palm with an audible slap.

"And something else isn't adding up," he continued. "Whoever took her did it when she was making dinner. That's also when Bonnie Boyd was taken. And—" He couldn't say his wife's name. "The similarity in all three disappearances is too coincidental. If there's a connection, what is it, and why had she been taken the same night this place had been tossed?" Jack's stomach roiled.

"What do I do, Jack? Tell me. I can't remember what the procedure is. My head— I'm all over the place."

Ray looked exhausted, but worse, defeat was etching its way across his face and echoing in his posture.

"I get it, Ray." Jack understood exactly where Ray was coming

161

from. He'd been there. He was still there—every damn day since that horrible night. "I hate to ask, but could she have left on her own?"

Rage reappeared in Ray's eyes; his spine noticeably straightened. Good. Jack got under his skin.

"Don't even go there."

Jack put up both palms in front of him. "I just wanted to be sure. If she didn't leave, then there's only one other possibility—someone took her."

Ray slammed a fist into his other palm. "I'll kill whoever it was."

"I believe you. I'll even hold him down while you do it. First, we need to find out who it was and where she is. If she was kidnapped, have you received any ransom calls?"

"You have my phone. See for yourself. Nothing."

As Jack scanned Ray's outgoing call log, he asked, "What about the house phone?"

"We got rid of that a long time ago. We both carry our cells around everywhere we go."

Looking up, Jack asked, "I know this is a stupid question, but you know I gotta ask it anyway. Did you try calling her phone?"

"Of course. I heard it ringing in the living room."

Okay, whoever took Maria didn't take her phone. If the kidnapper intended on calling Ray for a ransom, he had to know his number already. Jack's thoughts spun back to Travers. "Did you piss off Travers for any reason?"

Shrugging, he said, "No, but Waters said he saw Travers rush out the front door about fifteen minutes after you left. Maybe you pissed him off. Did he take Maria because he's mad at *you*?" Ray pushed a hard finger into Jack's chest.

"I'm asking myself the same question." Jack thought for a moment, ignoring his friend's poke. "Did you check the call log on Maria's phone?"

"Of course." Ray pulled another cell phone from his jacket pocket and brought up the call log. "Here. The last outgoing call was to me at—" He halted midsentence. Confusion etched his face. Every foul word in Ray's Spanish vocabulary spilled out just then. "I only checked the outgoing calls. She had called me earlier in the day to remind me about a doctor's appointment for the baby. That's where I was when you were in the office. I called her later to tell her I'd be home around nine." He pulled up the incoming calls and saw his call at 7:29 p.m. "What the hell?"

"What?"

He handed Jack the phone. Another call had come in at 8:36 p.m. The number was there but the caller was unknown. "Fuck." Jack pulled up the incoming call logs on his phone and scrolled back to last Wednesday. The number of his mysterious texter . . . The Butcher . . . was the same number that appeared on Maria's phone. "*Fuck!*" he said louder. Who the hell was it? And why was he calling Maria Navarro?

"What?" Ray repeated. Jack turned both phones to show Ray. "Fuck!" Then something else triggered in his head. "Does this mean what I think it means?"

Jack wasn't saying anything. Didn't mean he wasn't thinking it though. "What do you think it means?"

Ray sank into one of the chairs in front of the desk. "*¡Dios mio!* If the texter is The Butcher, and he called Maria before she disappeared—" The color drained from his face.

"Don't say it, Ray. We're both thinking it, but if you say it, it'll make it true." Thoughts flashed through his mind again that The Butcher had taken Leah. He went behind his desk and yanked open a drawer and pulled out Leah's phone. He kept it with him as part of the evidence from her disappearance and used it occasionally to make anonymous calls. He cursed again that the phone was dead; he hadn't turned it off since his call to Boyd earlier in the week. There was a very slim chance this same number appeared on his wife's incoming calls. He hadn't thought to check then because his life had been normal back then. Had the same person called Leah before taking her? He still couldn't figure out why her body had never turned up.

Get a grip, Jack.

"The texter might not be the serial killer. We only know

someone has been calling me when the bodies turn up. Whoever he is just happens to know Maria . . . or you. There could be any number of ways he got to her, and any number of reasons why he chose her. But we can't let our minds go down a dark path. Let's keep it together. We'll find her." He tried sounding positive, but if he couldn't convince himself, how was he going to convince Ray?

"What am I going to do, Jack? We're not even safe in our own homes."

Jack walked around the desk to stand beside Ray. "We've done what we can with what we have. Until or unless there's a ransom call, we need to examine everything else and see if something leads us in the kidnapper's direction. If the kidnapper is the killer, the evidence will link them together."

Ray looked up. "We should file a missing person's report. We should get the department involved—ask Haniford for an update on the killer. We can't just sit here and do nothing."

Jack clasped Ray's shoulder. "We won't be doing nothing. This all ties in somehow. We just need to put the pieces of the puzzle together."

"What if Travers has her? Let's find him and beat the truth out of him."

Beating the crap out of Travers sounded like a great idea. Jack would do it just because. But to do it legally, they needed proof that the bastard was involved. Even if it was just the man stalking him and misleading him for some reason about the identities of the bodies.

"There's no proof the number belongs to Travers. So far, all of this is just a lot of circumstance and gut feeling. We don't have proof of anything." His gut twisted. He felt like he was going to puke. He turned away from Ray in case he did and saw the greasy burger sack still sitting on the table beside the sofa. When did he eat last? "Let's get something to eat. Then you can help me finish putting the evidence back up on the walls. I'm pretty sure Travers was the one who ransacked the place and knocked me out. If we can confirm it was him—remember, we've already tied him to the sixth victim by his own admission—we'll have enough probable cause to get a search warrant to search his house."

"And find Maria."

"If Travers is the kidnapper, big if, we can only hope he's keeping her at his place."

Ray's face drained of color. "Do you think he'll kill her?"

"At this point, I don't know. Travers is a cop. He was trained to kill, if necessary. I would never have pegged him as a kidnapper, but right now, I'm not putting my money on any pony in this race. I don't know the man. I don't know what he's capable of. Kidnap? Maybe. Kill outside of his job? I don't know. I hope not."

"Do you think he's the . . . The Butcher?"

Ray asked the question so blatantly that it threw Jack off kilter for a moment. He shook his head, trying to clear it. "Let's focus on one thing at a time and do this the right way. Let the evidence lead us to the killer. Don't choose a suspect then make the evidence fit."

For a moment, both men gazed at each other. Jack was sure Ray was thinking the same thing he was. They'd find Maria, and whoever had taken her would get the shit beat out of him.

CHAPTER TWENTY-SEVEN

Jack ordered some deli sandwiches from a couple blocks away that were delivered half an hour later. They ate while getting to work on the walls. It took the rest of the afternoon, but they had restored the walls back to their former conditions. Nearly. They'd gone through a roll of tape, putting the murdered women's photos back together, as well as some of the notes and clues. And they'd gone through three rolls of different colored twine restringing the clues to the map locations.

In truth, the paper tacked to the walls looked like they'd been put through a washing machine, but everything was there that had been there before. At least it seemed to be. Jack kept looking. The walls seemed the same, but something felt off. Like something was missing. Or perhaps it was just the lingering feeling that his sanctuary had been violated.

Jack had turned on the overhead light a couple hours ago, meager as it was, but it enabled them to keep working until every scrap of paper found its rightful place.

He pulled up the time on his phone. 8:33 p.m.

Just as he was going to tell Ray they were done, his phone rang. Cutter's name came up on caller ID. Had he found something else having to do with the condoms? That moment, Ray's phone chirped. "Cutter," he greeted, watching Ray take his phone into the front room to answer.

"Jack. Got a minute?"

"Sure, what's up?"

"Man, you're gonna need to sit down for this shit." Jack wasn't sure if Cutter was laughing or a little high, but he sat on the edge

166

of the bed anyway. "I don't know how to say it so I'll just come out with it."

Jack was sure his heart stopped beating in that moment. Had Leah's body been found? He felt like he couldn't breathe. "What is it?" He barely got the question out.

"Early this morning, a jogger found what looked like paper lanterns floating in Spreckels Lake. A lot of them. He managed to grab one floating close to the path and opened it. What he saw inside made him call 9-1-1 immediately."

"So far I'm not sitting on the edge of my seat here, Jon," said Jack, his hand holding the phone shaking a little.

"It was meat, Jack, and still partially frozen. By my weights, it's about thirty-five pounds in total, all wrapped in butcher paper, and in packages ranging from one to five pounds each. Some ground up like hamburger."

Jack scratched his head, his attention pulled toward the murder wall. "Someone cleaned out their freezer? Maybe a local butcher hoped the wildlife would eat it."

Cutter chuffed. "It was a butcher all right. From the one who's been carving up our victims. These bundles were from the last victim."

Silence hung in the air as if the Earth had stopped spinning and everything hung in a sort of limbo. The sound of Ray's voice in the other room faded away. Cutter seemed to have disappeared on the end of the line. The permeated smells from Wong's and the Rose evaporated, along with any air remaining in the room. He tried breathing but there wasn't any oxygen in it. The dimly lighted space seemed to dim further.

And the murder wall looked like it started spinning away from him, but in the center of the vortex, one thing came clear.

Just as fast as the world had stopped, every sound, smell and vision rushed back as if he'd been hit with a bucket of ice water.

Nothing had been taken from his wall. Something had been *added!*

"Jack, are you there?" called Cutter.

'Yeah-yeah." He walked over to the wall and looked at the

printed copy in front of him.

"Did you hear what I said? The meat is the excarnated flesh from the last victim."

"I heard you. The killer dumped his stash. Hey, if I bring you something, how fast can you get it analyzed?" Jack pulled the paper off the wall and slid it into a legal-sized evidence envelope.

"Depends what it is, why?"

"I'll be right over."

Jack hit the end call icon and went into the front room where Ray was finishing his call. "You're never going to believe this," said Ray.

"That was Cutter. The last victim's flesh turned up in Spreckels Lake," Jack said.

Ray nodded, indicating he'd just heard the same news. "He must have called Haniford first. You're not part of the investigation, but I really think we need to tell Haniford what's going on so he can get you involved in case you need department back up."

Jack shook his head. "I'm not ready for that yet. I want to put my ducks in a row first. Did you tell him about Maria?"

"No. I trust you, Jack. Let's see this thing through. Like old times." Ray held out his fist and Jack fist bumped him.

Waving the envelope in his hand, Jack asked, "I don't suppose you wanna go for a bike ride?"

Ray stepped back. "Not really. Where do you need to go? I'll drive."

Shaking his head, he said, "Sorry. My bike will get us there faster. But if you'd rather, we need something from the department."

"You name it."

"I've got an itchy feeling all this stuff is tied in. What I need are copies of the surveillance videos taken at each of the dump sites. There's always someone there recording bystanders. If the texter is the killer, he will have been at each of the dump sites watching the investigation. He can't help himself. He might be standing in the background, but we should see him in the video or photos," Jack said.

"Great idea. Why didn't we do this a long time ago?"

Jack cocked his head and scratched the back of his neck. "The investigators probably did. They just didn't know what they were looking for. Can you get me copies of those files?"

"You bet. I'll get there and back as fast as I can. Where are you going?"

Jack waved the envelope again. "I found something on the wall. Ray, nothing was *taken*. Something was *added*. He cut himself while tearing the room apart. I'm going to have Cutter run it for DNA and see if we get a hit." Jack walked back behind his desk and pulled a key out of the top drawer and tossed it to Ray. "Let yourself in if I'm not here when you get back."

The journey to the ME's office on Bryant Street normally took about twenty minutes in good traffic. On his Harley, Jack got there in ten. He pulled up to the door, forgoing designated street parking, dismounted and hurried through the door, removing his helmet as he moved.

Cutter met him at the autopsy suite door. "What's up, Jack? You sounded distracted. I thought you would have appreciated the information."

"I did. More than you know." Jack gave him a quick rundown, much like he had with Ray, and included Maria's disappearance.

"Holy Christ. If anyone can find her, it'll be you."

Jack gave him a *yeah, right* look. He couldn't even find his own wife. "Ray helped me finish putting the murder wall back together. Everything was there but something wasn't sitting right with me. While you were on the phone, I found this." He pulled the envelope out of his jacket's inside pocket. "Don't worry. This is one of the evidence envelopes I keep at home. What's in here will be as pristine as when I pulled it off my wall."

Cutter leaned in to see what Jack pulled from the envelope—a copy of one of the postmortem reports. On the edge of the page was a red smear.

"Blood."

"How soon can you get this analyzed?" Jack asked.

Cutter led him into the forensics suite where he put on a pair of gloves before taking the paper from Jack. "Give me a couple of hours. The city finally sprung for the new Rapid DNA machine."

"Sweet."

Before getting to work, Cutter said, "Oh, Jack, in my office on the desk is a folder with your name on it. Results from the condom tests. I was going to email it to you, but since you're here—"

"Thanks."

"Come back in a couple hours and I'll have your results."

"I'll wait in your office. Maybe looking over your shoulder will make you work faster," Jack said with a grin.

"You'll get it when you get it, man." Cutter threw him a *shaka* hand wave and disappeared into the lab.

Jack took a seat behind Cutter's desk and opened the folder. He spread out the paperwork in front of him and studied the results. Cutter had seen fit to include the results from the thirteen swabs so they could all be compared to the Happy Endings results. There was no doubt. The killer had used Happy Endings condoms while having sex with all the victims.

The only victim that couldn't be verified was Eve, victim zero. Her body had been too mutilated and ravaged by the weather and wildlife. But they had the other twelve dead to rights.

CHAPTER TWENTY-EIGHT

H is phone rang. He pulled it out of his pocket and checked the time before answering—he'd been going over the reports for more than an hour. His gaze flicked to the open door. He knew it was still early but hoped Cutter had come up with something already.

"Yeah, Ray," Jack said on answering.

"I really think we need to get Haniford involved in this, Jack." The worry in Ray's voice was audible. "What did you find?"

"I got the videos and photos from each of the dump sites and started with the photos since they go faster. At first, no one popped up."

"At first? What did you find?" he repeated. Something inside Jack began reverberating in his gut.

Ray chuffed lightly. "I'm guessing here, but it looks like investigators were looking for someone who didn't belong there. But who *does?*"

"Detectives, ME, CSI . . . Who else?"

"Cops, Jack. Cops. They control the perimeter line to keep out curious bystanders."

"And?" Jack's hands shook.

"And," Ray emphasized, "until recently, one cop stood out at every scene, either on duty or in plain clothes, but he was there."

"What do you mean until recently?" The remnants of his earlier deli sandwich pushed its way up. The bile burned the back of his throat. He inhaled deeply in an effort to stay calm. "Jesus, just tell me."

"I mean that until recently he was a cop. He's now a detective."

171

"Travers." He let it sink in for a moment.

There was a short silence on the phone, then under his breath, Ray said, "There's something else."

There it was, the other shoe dropping. "What?"

"I remembered what you said about the plane crash and looked up those reports. Remember, Joe Patinkus' body had never been found. They had assumed it had been lost in a snow drift or something. They went back after the thaw to do a second search."

"Did they find the body?" Of course they did or Ray wouldn't have brought it up.

"Yes. The body appeared to have been partially buried under some rocks, well away from the crash site. At the time, the heavy snow probably made it appear like a drift, but after the thaw when investigators went back up, they found Patinkus' body. The report suggests that it had been up there for so long that it had to have been mauled by animals. There are bobcat and fox up there." Jack heard Ray inhale deeply before continuing. "I have a copy of the autopsy report which says parts of the corpse had been completely defleshed, and by the marks on the exposed bone, the ME assumed animal teeth."

Jack swallowed hard. "I don't think I like where this is going."

"There's more. I also have copies of the postmortem photos. They're suggesting the teeth marks look a lot like the ones on the victims' bones. Those have already been defined as cut marks, probably a butcher style knife. Even though bobcat and fox usually move to lower grounds in the winter where it's easier to find food, the ME assumed something was still living up there and feeding off the remains."

"Something . . . or someone?" The last word hung like a weight around Jack's neck while his thoughts spiraled. He remembered reading about Flight 571 that crashed in the Andes in 1972. He hadn't even been born then, but years later after seeing the movie, *Alive*, he bought a book penned by one of the survivors. There had been forty-five people on board, passengers and crew, when the plane crashed in October of that year. Only sixteen survived. There had been a lot of speculation on how they'd survived for two months in the stark and frozen conditions, but later one of the survivors confessed to having eaten victim remains. Investigators had then assumed that was the only way so many could have survived.

Jack swallowed hard again. Had Travers cannibalized his friend in order to survive in the mountains until his own rescue?

Thoughts and emotions whirled through him. If he'd been in Travers' position, up there on the mountain with his best friend lying dead, would he resort to eating him in order to survive? The thought turned his stomach. But what if the tables were reversed and he died and Ray lived? Would he want Ray to take the forbidden step so that he could survive? Absolutely. It would be the ultimate gift to his friend—nourishment so that Ray would live.

Jack recalled his days in parochial school and studying for his Confirmation. John 6:54-56—*Whoever eats my flesh, and drinks my blood, has eternal life; and I will raise him up at the last day. For my flesh is meat indeed, and my blood is drink indeed. He that eats my flesh, and drinks my blood, dwells in me, and I in him.*

Shaking off the acceptance that was beginning to settle inside him, Jack asked, "What about the videos? Do they also confirm Travers was at all the body dump locations?"

"I haven't had the chance to go through them. I only sat down with the files an hour ago. That's why I started with the photos. Now that I have my suspicions, I gave the videos to one of the officers on the late shift to go through."

"Can you trust this person not to run to Travers and give him a heads up he's now our prime suspect?" The last thing they needed was for Travers to disappear.

"Absolutely. She hates Travers as much as you do," Ray said with a slight chuckle.

Just then, Cutter walked into the office, carrying two sheets of paper. "Hang on, Ray. I'm going to put you on speaker. Cutter's here. What have you got, Jon? Tell me you got a hit." Jack moved around the desk to stand before Cutter.

Cutter looked bewildered. "You're never going to believe this."

"Whatever it is, you need to give it to us."

"I'm not sure whether I should cry or laugh, man." A grin crossed Cutter's lips. Gone was the normally passive surfer dude Jack was most familiar with. By the look on his face, Jack thought he'd just won the lottery.

Jack grabbed the paper out of Cutter's left hand and quickly scanned it. He was familiar with the form so his gaze shot over the results, including the hit that came up. Paul Travers.

Over the phone's speaker, Ray said, "Don't hold me in suspense. What are the results?"

In the pit of his stomach, Jack had already known it was Travers. This only confirmed it. "Ray, it's Travers." To Cutter he asked, "How did you get a hit so quickly? I thought Rapid DNA only brought up strings of DNA coding. Only a direct hit through CODIS brings up names."

"I ran it through local known subjects. Cops have their DNA on file already, so I can rule them out in case of cross contamination at a crime scene. Travers is on file, just as you are."

"Ray, this confirms Travers is the one who destroyed my backroom. But is he involved in the serial killings? I'm afraid to guess," Jack said.

"We can get a warrant now to search his place, and find Maria," Ray said. "We have the photos proving Travers was at all the crime scenes where the women were found—on and off duty. Why would he show up if he was off duty? And if the victims were found around the city, why would he be there while on duty? His precinct isn't even near where most of the women were found."

"He's also admitted he dated victim number six, Georgina Kearney," Jack said. "And the condom brands match. We also have a very strong suspicion about how he survived the plane crash. And now the blood from my office raid matches him." Jack muddled over everything rumbling around in his head.

"We have more than enough for a search warrant. Let me call Haniford."

"Why get a search warrant when you can get an arrest warrant?" Cutter chimed in.

Jack swung his head up to gaze into Cutter's eyes. "We have a lot of circumstantial evidence but none of it will justify just going in for an arrest. We have enough just to search his properties and detain him for questioning."

Cutter waved the second sheet of paper he held in Jack's face.

"What's that? It looks like another test result. Was there a second bloodstain on the paper I gave you?"

Cutter shook his head. "Remember all the half-frozen bundles fished out of the lake? We didn't just sample one to determine the contents and who it belonged to."

Before Jack could ask, Ray said, "Don't tell me they were samples from all the women."

"No, they were all from just the last victim. But we had to go through each package to look for evidence. We've never had remains like this to examine before, so we had to be thorough and go through them all. They may be from the same victim, but every cut the killer made could have left something behind."

Cutter stood with his hands behind him now, and rocking on the balls of his feet. A knowing grin crossed his smug face.

"Out with it, damn it!" Jack rarely raised his voice in such a solemn place like this but he did now. "What the hell did you find?"

"The evidence was remarkably clean, but we did find a single hair in one of the packages. I thought it might have been from the victim herself, but the color was wrong. We ran it for DNA—"

"Fuck this," Jack said, reaching behind Cutter and ripping the paper out of his hands. He quickly scanned the report. "This is the same report you just gave me. What gives?"

"This is the test results from the hair. The DNA exactly matches—"

"Travers," the three men said in unison.

"*Now* do we get Haniford involved?" Ray asked through his exasperation.

It hadn't taken much convincing to get Haniford to agree to ask for a full arrest warrant. Jack and Ray, along with Cutter's help, had uncovered more evidence in the last few days than the investigators managing the case had collected in three years.

Haniford was so impressed by their work he forgave the call he'd received in the middle of the night. The judge Haniford called to sign the Ramey warrant had been equally forgiving. All agreed with so much evidence before them that they couldn't afford to waste time waiting for the D.A.'s office to open and go through all the usual red tape, only to have the request land on the same judge's desk in two or three days.

Jack grinned, but his gut was still in knots. He loved the thought that by the end of the day, the District Attorney could be filing charges against Paul Travers for thirteen murders. The more minor charge of vandalism, and possibly kidnapping if they found Maria with him, and anything else they could make stick would be icing on the cake. The murders alone would mean he'd get the death penalty.

The only thing Jack and Ray had yet to prove was Travers' involvement in Maria's disappearance. There was still no motive and no evidence to go by, but Jack felt it in his gut Travers had something to do with it.

And the question that kept pushing all others aside—had Travers also been the one who'd killed Zoë and taken Leah?

He starred at the small, black security box sitting in front of him on the desktop, his heart pounding the inside of his chest.

When he'd left the force, he'd been required to turn in his badge and department issued firearm—a SIG Sauer P226. The SIG had been his shadow through his career, from beat cop to detective. As it was meant to be, the weapon had been like an extension of his arm. Whether on the range or being forced to use it on the job, he was as familiar with the weapon as he was with his own body.

Yet, as proficient as he was with the SIG, he preferred the Beretta. He'd owned a few in his life as personal weapons, and when he'd decided to get his private investigator's license, he chose the Beretta Px4 Storm as his weapon of choice. In order to obtain a carry concealed weapon permit, he'd qualified with the Beretta, as the weight of it in his hands was more comfortable. And a decidedly better fit in his shoulder holster.

As a private investigator, he had never needed to carry a weapon. As proficient as he was with a gun, he was equally as lethal with his fists. Fortunately, he also had rare cause to use them. Physical violence was rarely called for when he was searching for missing spouses and lost pets. And when he worked security jobs, he opted for a baton and pepper spray over a gun every time. Less paperwork that way when taking down assailants.

Inhaling deeply to steady his nerves, Jack pulled the box toward him. The small dial built into the lid glared up, as if taunting him. Beside it were two small lights. The red shone now, telling Jack the box was securely locked.

Could he remember the combination? Of course, he could. How could he ever forget the date his life had changed forever?

He held his breath as he spun the dial one way, then the other, and back again until the red light turned green, telling him he'd got it right.

He hesitated before lifting the lid. He'd only ever planned on using the weapon three times—the first for the range qualification in order to keep his CCW permit up-to-date, the second when he found the person who'd killed his daughter and taken his wife. The third and last time he would make the ultimate sacrifice to be with his family again. Without Leah and Zoë, he had nothing to live for.

His eyes stung, thinking about his lost family. As much as he prayed Leah was still alive, the Devil sat on his shoulder and continually whispered the opposite was true.

With his permit renewed last year, and now taking down Travers, Jack only had to solve his family's case before he could join his family.

He couldn't think about that now. He had responsibilities, which included finding Maria Navarro.

He lifted the lid and stared into the box. The black Beretta was nestled on the gray foam insert. Beside it were two empty magazines and a box of 9x19mm Parabellum rounds. He wrung his hands to steady them before lifting the weapon, turning it one way then the other, testing the balance. He wrapped both hands around the grip and aimed the weapon at the hole he'd punched in the backroom door. He slowly inhaled and held his breath, steadying his aim. Muscle memory was a great thing. The weapon never wavered. It fit perfectly.

CHAPTER TWENTY-NINE

It galled him to have to stand on the sidelines and watch the arresting team enter Paul Travers' residence—a small, rundown house on 48th Street, just two blocks from Jack's own family home.

Since he wasn't a cop anymore, he had no right to enter Travers' residence with them. He was lucky Haniford had agreed to let him into the house once it had been secured. He could go in and look around but he wouldn't be allowed to touch anything or question the suspect, assuming the asshole was here.

Seemingly, it had taken forever to get to this point. Though, to Haniford's credit, everything was playing out exceptionally fast. The search and Ramey warrants had been signed while Jack had gone back to the apartment for his Beretta. He'd then met Ray, Haniford and the team at Travers'. Haniford had hoped to take Travers at the department, but he'd failed to show up for work. Another box ticked in the guilty column.

Restlessness filled Jack where he stood beside his bike under the amber glow of the street lamp. His feet were planted on the pavement, his arms crossed, and his fingers nervously aware of his holstered weapon beneath them.

He watched the team swarm the residence like bees in a hive. As soon as it had been breached, the interior and exterior lights came on.

It would take some time for the team to secure the residence, but he didn't feel any less useless just waiting on the sidelines. Team member or not, his trained instincts kept him alert. In his mind, he followed Ray room to room, as they'd done so many other times when they were partners. He knew Ray searched for Maria—it had now been twenty-four hours since her disappearance—while the rest of the team combed the place for Travers.

Had that asshole lived this close to Jack before his family had been destroyed? Bile rose in his throat. He had to swallow hard to keep it down. Glancing up the road, he could practically see his own house from where he stood.

Ray finally emerged through the front door and strode purposefully toward Jack, forcing him to refocus. He uncrossed his arms and let them fall to his sides, feeling the weight in his shoulder holster move against him. He'd grown used to the feeling while on the job, but now it jabbed at him like a constant reminder of everything he'd lost.

He tried gauging the look on Ray's face as he approached. Was he reading disappointment, or was it frustration?

"She's not there," Jack said before Ray could open his mouth. "Travers?"

Ray shook his head. "No, but there's a shitload of evidence in his basement."

"What kind of evidence?"

"You gotta see it to believe it, Jack." Ray turned and led Jack to the house. As they neared, the garage door swung up and open. "The place looks like Cutter's autopsy suite. Here, you'll need to put these on." Ray handed Jack a pair of booties and gloves. "Follow me."

"I know how the game is played. Just get me inside." He slid on the gloves as he stepped into the garage, but nothing in the space screamed out autopsy suite. "What gives?"

Ray signaled Jack to keep following him. At the back of the garage that extended the length of the small house, Jack saw a long chest freezer, and opposite was a door he assumed was a closet until Ray opened it.

He slid on his booties and followed Ray down the stairs to where a basement space about half the length of the garage above opened up. The room was filled with tools and equipment any respectable autopsy suite would contain.

"Holy Mother of God," Jack cursed under his breath.

"We just found it so be careful where you walk," Ray said. "Follow me."

In the center of the room was an autopsy table that was overhung by a table-length light. While the table was clean, it was evident it had been recently used, as duct tape still clung to some of the edges, strands of black hair in the adhesive. *Maria's hair is black.* Under the table, a grille-covered drain opened in the center of a highly-polished concrete floor. Everything appeared clean, so he prayed Maria was still alive. Somewhere.

A long counter with cabinets below and above stretched along the far wall. Under-cabinet lighting shone off canisters and boxes filled with swabs, gauze, rubber gloves and some items Jack couldn't see without opening.

On the top of a rolling cart lay a selection of surgical tools—knives, scissors and hand saws. His stomach rolled thinking Travers had been using those tools to kill women down here. The space took on a suffocating feeling, as if the ghosts of all the murdered women were pressing down on him, begging him to release them from the horror of what had happened to them.

Ray opened cabinets and drawers as he moved through the room. Jack saw cases of Tyvek coveralls, heavy-duty yard waste bags, rolls of duct tape, industrial size boxes of plastic wrap, commercial quantities of spools of butcher paper, more boxes of rubber gloves . . . everything an enterprising serial killer needed to kill and butcher his victims.

Moving to a narrower wall, cabinets revealed dozens of heavy-duty paper towels, gallons of industrial cleaner and bleach, boxes of scouring pads and sponges, rolls of general waste trash bags . . .

On the next wall, several small monitors were mounted over the desk, each still live and showing the perimeter of the house in real time. For a moment Jack watched Haniford's team search the property.

"Hey, what's this?" Ray motioned to the desk, which held a computer, printer, and files and folders. Folders with a woman's name on each tab.

"Looks like files on our victims," Ray said.

As Jack turned to ask him a question, he spotted the wall behind the door and it stopped him in his tracks. "Fuck me," Jack exclaimed.

"Me too!"

Dozens of what looked like home printer photos hung on the wall. They weren't randomly placed but hung in order, one of whom was what Jack now realized was Victim Zero—Eve. But these were not postmortem photos. These were of the living victims, all of which looked like surveillance photos—all taken from afar with a long-range zoom lens. Jack shivered.

Travers had been stalking his victims.

Jack's body tensed as he examined all the photos—there weren't any of Leah or Zoë. But what disturbed him was that there were more victims displayed in the wall photos than had been discovered.

"Shit, Ray. Are you seeing what I'm seeing?"

"Yeah, he was stalking the victims."

"No, man, look. We have thirteen victims in the morgue. There has to be..." Jack counted under his breath ". . . twenty women on this wall. Where are the other seven?" The men could only gape at each other with the revelation.

"Navarro. Slaughter. Get up here," Haniford hollered. They spun toward the door.

"What have you got, Lieutenant?" Ray asked as they reached the top step. Haniford led them through a door at the back of the garage and into an overgrown back yard. Forensics had arrived and there was some commotion behind some poorly-tended Manzanita shrubs at the far end of the property.

Haniford cocked his head then followed the broken pavers in the weedy grass to the back of the yard where a crew had pulled back the shrub's limbs to expose the soil below. The white bones of a human hand stretched out, as if reaching for a limb to help pull its body free.

Was this Leah?

Jack spun and went to the farthest corner of the yard and

puked. He now knew where the other seven victims were.

Once his already sore gut calmed, Jack righted himself, spitting the last of the bile from his mouth.

"You okay, Jack?" Haniford asked. "Maybe you've been away from the job too long."

Jack knew his former boss was just razzing him, but he wondered if the man had seen the wall downstairs.

He opened his mouth to ask the question when his phone buzzed with an incoming text. He pulled the phone from his jacket pocket, realizing it had probably caught him puking his guts out. "Great," he muttered.

Letting the phone continue recording, he tapped the text icon and watched the message come up.

You need a better housekeeper, Jack.

"What the *fuck*?" he exclaimed. Ray and Haniford spun in unison as Jack started running. He called over his shoulder, "He's at my house."

He ran the two blocks to his house, hoping to God Travers was still there, and that Maria was safe.

Jack now knew that Travers had been his texter and the man who'd been killing women all over the city for the last three years. What he didn't know was why.

Nor did he know why Travers had targeted him for the texts, or why the man wanted some women found and not the others. While he didn't see Leah's image on the wall, could there be more women? Could Leah be one of the bodies buried in the back yard?

He nearly stopped to puke again at the thought that Leah might have been just two blocks away, cast into a black hole like trash, but he pushed on.

It seemed like forever to reach his house, but it only took a moment before he was skidding to a halt at the corner of the short fence that enclosed the front of the property. Leah's old Mustang still sat in its parking space just behind the short timber fence rails. The tires were flat and rust had appeared through the paint around the windows and the bottom of the door. The windscreen had been cracked. The little punk's rock still sat on the hood where it had come to a rest after it hit the glass.

But he didn't have time to get angry about this. He quickly gazed around him. At this late hour of the night, most of the lights were off in the surrounding houses. Only the dim street lights shone in narrow arcs around their poles. Looking up, he saw a faint glow coming from his living room window above the garage.

The garage door had been left ajar. Had Travers set a trap, expecting him to just race through it without thinking? That wasn't an option, nor was the front door; he'd be heard on the steps. He opted for the back.

Staying in the shadows, he passed his house then stole along his neighbor's breezeway and hopped the fence into his own backyard. He crouched in the dark and listened, watching for any signs of movement from the back of the house. A dog barked a few blocks away but all was calm here.

Safe to move, he quickly crossed the tiny garden, making sure not to trip on the overgrowth and stopped at the steps leading up to the back door. Keeping to the far edge of each step, where he knew there would be minimal creaking, he took them by twos.

At the back door, he looked through the dirty glass and past the thin lace curtain that hung partially open. The house was in the shotgun style. He forced his gaze past the still-bloody crime scene in the kitchen, through the dining area and into the living room. At the time, it seemed as though the rooms had been covered in blood, but now, the evidence was only concentrated in a small, dried pool where Trax had lost his life on the pale kitchen linoleum, and beneath the highchair where he'd found Zoë.

A single candle was set on the coffee table and just barely illuminated Maria who had been tied to a chair Travers had pulled away from the dining area. Her mouth was duct taped to keep her quiet but there was obvious terror on her tired face. Travers sat on the edge of Jack's own recliner opposite Maria, elbows on his knees, his pistol on the table in front of him. He was talking to her, but Jack couldn't hear what he was saying. It was obvious he was angry by his drawn eyebrows and pinched lips that spit as he spoke. Maria's body jerked through her tears.

Reaching above the door, he hoped the spare key was still there. It was. He brushed off the dust and cobwebs and carefully slid it into the old lock. At first, the key refused to move past the first couple pins, but with gentle persuasion, the key drove home with a sharp click. Jack kept his eye on Travers as he carefully turned the key to unlock the door. Travers gave no indication he'd heard anything, so Jack continued.

He turned the knob and pushed on the door. Disused for so long, the rubber weather proofing was stuck on the painted door jamb. It made a sound like peeling off duct tape.

Travers stopped talking and tilted his head, listening. Jack stopped too, his pounding heart in his throat.

CHAPTER THIRTY

Something out front had drawn Travers' attention and he turned to the front window. Jack heard it too—screeching tires and commotion. He saw the whirling red and blue lights through the living room windows bouncing off surrounding houses. They turned the front window into a multi-color strobe light and dully illuminated the small room.

Drawing his Beretta, Jack took advantage of the distraction and pushed open the kitchen door. He wrapped both hands around the gun's grip, flipping off the safety, and indexed his finger along the barrel. As he moved sideways through the kitchen, he kept the weapon level with his line of sight.

Travers still seemed unaware of his presence as he rose and moved to the side of the window, staying in the shadows behind the drawn curtains. Jack remembered closing all the curtains in the house when he left, to preserve the evidence. Travers must have opened the living room curtains to watch for his arrival. No doubt, the asshole had expected him to race through the open garage door, or at the very least use the front door. He was going to get the surprise of his life when he turned around.

Careful to step around Trax's blood that still stained the old kitchen linoleum and making sure not to touch any of the surfaces, Jack stopped short at the dining area. The highchair was still in place where he'd found Zoë, and for a moment, the image of her lifeless body flashed in his mind and shone against the empty chair. Even now, he swore he could almost feel her warm blood oozing over his hands, and he very nearly dropped the Beretta.

Focus, asshole. This is about Travers, and getting Maria safe.

When Maria spotted him, Jack gave a quick shake of his head. She was a cop's wife and knew to stay quiet. She forced her glance away from him and focused on Travers at the window.

"Well, it looks like your husband has come to the rescue. And he brought the posse. But I wonder where old Jackie boy is." He checked his watch. "I would have thought he'd be here by now. I only texted him . . ." Travers leaned a little closer to the window and looked around, then stepped back, "five minutes ago."

Jack stood with his feet planted, the Beretta in his outstretched hands, his gaze never wavering from Travers. He had the perfect shot to take off the man's head. Or at least aerate it a little.

Just then, Travers' back stiffened and he turned his head slightly. It was then Jack saw his reflection in the dirty window pane. Travers had seen it too. "Ah, speak of the Devil and he shall appear."

Jack jerked his head at Maria, indicating she needed to look away. She squeezed her eyes shut and faced the window.

Jack didn't move or relax his stance but watched as Travers slowly turned. Jack now saw the man had his service weapon in hand. The same department issue SIG he'd once used.

As if reading his mind, Travers slowly turned his hand forward and gazed down at the palmed weapon and then back to Jack. "I wonder what the department does when issued weapons are handed in. Do you suppose they're destroyed, or passed onto the next cop in line like hand-me-downs?"

"Why don't you slide it this way and I'll ask Haniford about it?"

Travers chuckled. "Nice try, Jackie boy."

Jack glanced at Maria then back to Travers. "Why did you take Maria? She has nothing to do with this."

Travers glanced at Maria then back at Jack. "To get your attention."

"You have it now, so what do you say we let Maria go."

"I don't think so. While I have her, I control the situation."

Jack looked up at the window that was now awash in swirling red and blue lights that echoed around the room. Even from the back of the living room, Jack could see the street was flooded with light and activity. "Doesn't seem like it to me. You're a cop. You know how this will play out for you—alive or not, it makes no difference to me."

"I guess we'll see. But you can be sure of one thing. If they take me down," Travers said, motioning toward Maria, "she's going with me." His statement hung in the musty air. Only Maria's sudden whimpering broke the silence.

"You gonna kill a pregnant woman, Paul?" Travers' eyes widened. "You've killed a lot of women over the years but I'm guessing none of them were carrying a child. Please, tell me you have *some* humanity, man. Let's both put down our weapons and I'll untie her. She can walk out now, and it'll be just you and me."

"Let me think. No." Travers shot Jack a cocky glare, but he still made no effort to raise his weapon or move from where he stood.

"Then let's talk. Why are you doing this . . . any of this? Twenty women, Paul? Or are there more?" Jack hoped that by keeping Travers talking he could get as much information out of him before he was forced to shoot the bastard. And he hoped to keep his attention away from whatever was going on down on the street. So far, it was working.

Travers thought for a moment then said, "Honestly, I haven't been counting. I guess this means you've been gardening? Or you've found my little room. I had wondered how long it would take. Did you enjoy my game with you, Jackie boy?"

Jack chuffed. "You think that was a game? You killed twenty women, Paul. You dumped thirteen of them around the city. Why?"

Only then did Travers lean forward and raise his voice. "Because of you, Jackie. It's always been about you."

"What do you mean it's always been about me? I barely even know you."

"Oh, don't be coy with me. Ever since the academy, you've always been one-upping me. I'm every bit as smart as you, but at every turn, Jackie's always been the golden boy. Always the teacher's pet."

"The academy wasn't high school. We weren't there to make friends or join the glee club. We were there for training and to learn the law. Period. I'm sorry if you took anything I did personal, but believe me, I didn't know who you were. I barely knew who any of the cadets were. I wanted in and out as fast as possible, so I could get to work helping keep this city safe." Jack was going to add *from people like you* but thought better of it. He wanted to keep the situation as calm as possible and hoped he could talk the gun out of Travers' hands.

Gesturing now with his free hand, Travers' body became more animated as his agitation rose. "And you don't think I could do that job? I *have* been doing that job. While you kissed asses all the way up the ladder, I was still on the street. For years, I sweated and bled the job while you sat in your tower . . . with Ray and being everyone's buddy." His voice rose again and became sarcastic in tone. "Everyone *loveslovesloves* Jack Slaughter. Jack Slaughter can do no wrong. I did *everything* by the book—I worked hard, took overtime without complaint, made sure the paperwork was perfect before I turned it in. And I still couldn't get off the street."

"It must have paid off because you earned your detective shield."

"Fuck you! Do you know how many partners Ray went through before me? I'm the last person Haniford wants in his office."

"I doubt that. Haniford only wants the best in his department."

"I heard him!"

"Somehow I doubt the LT said he didn't want you there." Haniford was one of the fairest lieutenants Jack had ever known.

"He as good as said it, Jackie: *Why the fuck doesn't Slaughter just get his ass back behind his desk? I'm sick of Ray running new partners out of the department* . . . Blah, blah, blah. No one wants me there. They all want Jack Slaughter. Jack Fucking Slaughter," he screamed, now spitting as he talked.

It was becoming more difficult, but Jack forced his voice to remain as neutral and calm as possible. Travers was obviously on the edge of a breakdown, but he still needed to give up his secrets. Jack prayed his phone was still recording. He'd switched it on when he arrived at Travers' house but hadn't switched it off before running here. He didn't know how long it would run. At least he had Maria as a witness to all this madness. If it came to that. *Please, God, let her make it through this.*

"I'm sorry, Paul. I had no idea any of that was going on. Really. But what does killing all those women have to do with me? Why dump those bodies around the city?"

With a maniacal laugh, Travers asked, "It was part of the game. I'm disappointed you didn't get why I dumped them where I did."

"What game? I don't understand." Jack's arms started aching holding the Beretta but there was no way in Hell he was lowering his weapon just to get a little comfort.

For a moment, Travers didn't seem to understand. "They were important places to you. I wanted to ruin the memories of you and Leah in all those places."

"It worked, man. Good job. But how did you know any of them were important to me?"

Travers leaned over the coffee table, his gaze boring into Jack. He lowered his voice but his insanity was becoming more evident.

"Because I was there, Jackie boy," he nearly whispered. "And Jesus H., you do love to fuck outside." He straightened and laughed outright.

"So I've been told." Jack tried keeping his anger inside as something squeezed his gut. Travers had been in all those locations? He'd been following Jack all these years? How could he have done it? He supposed as a cop, Travers would have known how to blend into the crowd, but . . . "You do know how crazy you sound, right?"

Travers instantly stopped laughing and just as quickly turned serious again. "You have no idea what I've gone through. While you have been riding high on your white stallion, I've been beat down and pushed around, always forced to prove myself, over and over and over again," he stressed. "Everything comes so easily for you. But me . . .? My hands are bloody from the struggle." Travers thrust both hands forward, palm up, the gun still in one hand.

Keeping his gaze focused between the weapon and Travers' eyes,

Jack said, "Life is what you make it, Paul. You're right. You are a smart man. Whether Haniford wanted you in the department or not, you're there now. Why not focus your energy on showing him you're worth every bit as much as I was? And more. I haven't been in the department for nearly three years. I'm not going back. But you're there. Prove to everyone you deserve to be there. Don't do. . . this." He cocked his head toward Maria who continued looking away but was clearly now paying attention to the conversation.

For anyone else, Jack's advice would be sound—take the situation and make it work for you. He'd always worked that way. Don't fight it; just make the best of it. For Travers though, there was no way he was keeping his job after this. Jack prayed Travers wouldn't realize it.

"I'm tired of proving myself. That one at Spreckels Lake was going to be the last. I wasn't going to text you again after her. I had your job, your desk, and your partner. I was supposed to have that partner relationship too. But that faggoty Mexican is still so in love with you that no one can get close to him. Why do you think he keeps blowing though partners?"

"Ray's just a hard-ass. It takes a while for him to warm to anyone." Jack was going to add *just ask Maria* but thought better of that one too. He wanted to keep Travers focused away from her—get him to forget she was in the room. Jack had to keep her safe, had to get her out of this.

Ray was probably going crazy down on the street. But he'd keep his distance until or unless the situation got out of control. Jack didn't have much time before Haniford grew impatient and sent in a takedown team.

"Well, he won't warm to anyone until you're out of the picture," Travers said.

"I'm not in the department anymore. You know that."

"You're still in it. You just don't know it. You sit there in your high tower playing Private Dick, but you're still all over the department. I see how everyone still bows to the Almighty Jack Slaughter. It's disgusting. Not even killing your family can get rid of you."

Jack didn't think it was possible to lose his cool, but the mention of his family shot a fiery arrow through his chest. He very nearly put a bullet in Travers' head there and then. Through clenched teeth, he said, "Don't mention my family, asshole."

Travers chuckled again. "Did I get under your skin, Jackie boy? You said we had something in common. We both lost someone we loved."

He didn't want to talk about his family, so he focused on Travers. "What happened up there on the mountain was something no one should have to go through. The decisions you were forced to make were out of desperation. Joe was your friend—"

"Joe was my *lover!*"

CHAPTER THIRTY-ONE

J ack nearly dropped his weapon.

The phrase *being blindsided* was usually bandied about in jest, but Travers' confession came from out of nowhere. Nothing about the man hinted he was gay. This was San Francisco and homosexuality was part of the city's make-up. He knew there were gay officers on the force, but no one cared. All anyone was concerned about was that everyone did their job to the best of their ability. Who anyone chose to sleep with was no one else's business. The only reason Travers' words startled him was because of all the women he had killed.

Jack wasn't sure how to respond so he just blurted, "You're gay. So what?"

Travers' eyes widened. "*I am not gay!*"

"You just said you and Joe were lovers. You must have loved him. How does that not make you gay? Bi at the very least." Jack shrugged.

"I'm not gay, goddamn you!" Spit flew across the space between them.

Still trying not to let this escalate, Jack said, "Okay then, explain it to me. You're obviously smarter than I am." He pandered to Travers' ego. "Talk to me like I'm a rookie. Tell me how it is."

Travers straightened. "We were just friends. Joe was married, but we liked spending time together. After a while . . ." he trailed off.

Jack finished for him. "It just happened." Travers hesitantly nodded. "It wasn't your fault. We can't control who we give our hearts to. But what about the women, Paul?"

193

"Gay men don't date women. I like fucking women. But . . ."

"There's nothing wrong with bisexuality, Paul. Especially in this city. But why kill them?"

"You don't get it. I don't *want* to be gay, or bi, or any of it."

"I don't think we have a choice in the matter."

"It's my life. I have a choice, and I don't want to be a fag. I want . . . I—"

"What, Paul? What do you want?" Jack had to steel himself from feeling sorry for the man. Whether Travers accepted his sexuality or he didn't, there was no reason to make others suffer.

"I—I wanted what you had. All of it. The perfect job, the perfect wife, the perfect family . . . everything being handed to me on a silver plate. Like you," Travers said. Whatever breakdown Jack thought the man was going to have moments ago, it now looked like Travers was close to tears.

Taking a deep breath, he said, "Nothing has been easy for me, Paul. It may look like it from where you're standing, but I've had my own struggles."

"Yeah? Like what? What do you struggle with, Jackie?" Travers' tone was almost accusatory.

Jack really didn't want to go down this path. This wasn't about him. It was about Travers. But according to Travers, at least in his mind, what he was going through, what he'd done, had everything do to with Jack. The paradox muddled his mind.

As much as he didn't want to get personal with Travers, the only way to get through this was to give him what he wanted. "Self-doubt. That's what I struggle with."

Travers laughed. "The mighty Jack Slaughter doubts himself? I don't believe it."

"Believe it, man. You're not the only one who doesn't think they're good enough. Or smart enough, or strong enough."

"But you had it all, Jackie."

"Had is right. And I struggled for it all, Paul. It wasn't given to me. I had to take it. My old man's voice is always in the back of my head, telling me I'm not good enough. It just made me want to work harder and do better, to prove him wrong. But even when I graduated from the academy, and at the top of the class, he refused to attend the ceremony. He brushed off my achievement and told me schooling wasn't anything to be proud of. It was the job that mattered. By the time I made detective, he was gone. All those years, he made me feel like I was never good enough, like he didn't care. It was only when he died that I found the box of newspaper clippings. He'd been following my career and had obviously cared enough to save each of my achievements, but when it came to talking with him face-to-face, the *atta boys* and *well done, sons* I never received were the usual emotional slaps in my face."

By the softening look on Travers' face, it was apparent he didn't know as much about Jack as he thought he did. "So what? You still got all the accolades in the department." Travers glanced around the room. "And this house." His tone suggested the house also included Leah and Zoë.

"That wasn't easy either. Sometimes I think Leah only agreed to marry me to shut me up. She never accepted my other proposals." He had to admit she was right though. He often proposed to her while they were making love. They fit together so perfectly. He never wanted those moments to end and by marrying her, he guaranteed it would always feel the same.

"But in the end, you got the girl."

"It wasn't always rosy, Paul. I loved her, yeah, and still do. With everything that I am. As much as I miss my daughter, Leah could walk through that door right now and I'd welcome her home. And together we'd find Zoë's killer. We'd never get her back, but we'd have each other." He didn't want to do this. He didn't want to open his wounds. Not to this man. But as his gaze flicked to Maria, knowing everything he said would get back to Ray, he wondered if his friend would think less of him. Or worse, feel sorry for him? "You think I don't struggle," he said, forcing himself to focus back on Travers. "I blame myself every goddamn day for what I put her through."

"Through what? The perfect house, the perfect family, the perfect life?"

"I'm trying to tell you, it wasn't perfect, Paul. What you think you saw wasn't the reality of it. Not only did I . . . *do I* struggle with feeling like I forced Leah to marry me, when she got pregnant with Zoë, we should have been a happy couple and looking forward to starting a family. Instead, there were complications through the whole pregnancy. At one point, we nearly lost Zoë. When she was born, the doctors warned Leah not to get pregnant again because it could kill her."

Maria gasped at the revelation, but Jack kept his gaze riveted on Travers. He continued. "It wasn't that we were keeping secrets. Leah didn't want anyone feeling sorry for her. I thought it was the post-partum talking, but I actually understood. We kept it from everyone, including our closest friends. We were both too emotional to think beyond ourselves, but now—" he hoped Maria listened more than ever, "—I understand that we needed the support of friends. I can't get my family back and it haunts me every day, Paul. Which is why I'll do anything, give everything, to protect Maria and keep her baby safe."

Travers gazed at Maria. She sat quiet and still in the chair, still looking away from the situation, and still very much paying attention to what was going on around her.

"I live in a very dark place, Paul. My life isn't what you think you see. But even through everything Leah and I experienced together, I wouldn't trade any of it because we loved each other and it brought us closer together. The guilt of what happened that night will always haunt me—what if I'd been home five, ten . . . thirty minutes sooner, could I have saved them? And every goddamn day, I wonder if I know the bastard who did these horrible things."

"Like me," Travers volunteered.

"I'm still trying to wrap my head around this, Paul. Genuinely. You are the last person I would have ever suspected to do something so heinous . . . all those killings." That was the truth.

Both were quiet for a moment as they gazed at each other. Jack wasn't sure what he read in Travers' gaze or his posture, but after his recent revelations, Jack wondered if he'd ever read any suspect correctly. Then, almost under his breath, Travers asked, "Do you think I killed your family?"

Jack had no idea. "Did you?"

"Would you believe me if I said no?"

Jack shrugged slightly. "Honestly, Paul, I don't know. But if you tell me no, I'll try making that my new reality, and pray to God one of the bodies they pull out of your back yard isn't Leah's."

"She won't be."

Jack just nodded, indicating he'd take Travers at his word. Of course, the proof would come when the entire property had been excavated. And that still didn't mean he hadn't killed his wife. "What about the other women? Why'd you do it? I understand trying to convince yourself that you aren't gay— you dated them, had sex with them. But why kill them? You could have just let them go and found another way to deal with your feelings. Why did they have to die?"

To Jack, it seemed like the steam was quickly going out of Travers. His moment of manic anger seemed to be gone, as was any care that he wanted anything Jack had. The man before him seemed . . . beaten, for the lack of a better word. The heaviness in the room was also evaporating.

"None of them made me feel like a man. A proper man. Having sex with them should have proved I was a man. I am a man. So, it had to be their fault. If I was gay, I wouldn't be able to get it up for them, right?"

Jack shrugged again, more to stretch his tired shoulders than agree. "I don't know, Paul. I've never been in your situation. Sexuality isn't cut and dried, but I get what you're saying." Feeling like he had defused the situation, the next task was getting the gun off Travers. "I think we've made some headway here, Paul."

"You think?" Paul raised the gun up in his palm to look at it, then back to Jack.

"I really do. I'll help you through this . . . help you get the counseling you need. You've obviously struggled too long on your own. You need help, and a friend to support you."

"And you'll be that friend?" No, but to get him to give up the gun, Jack would tell Travers whatever he needed to hear, so he nodded that he would. Travers chuckled lightly, quickly flicking his gaze from the gun back to Jack again. "You know, I almost believe you."

CHAPTER THIRTY-TWO

Before Jack's eyes, Travers lifted the SIG toward Maria's temple. "Whoa, Paul!" Jack released one hand from the Beretta, palm forward in a halting gesture he hoped would stop Travers. "Don't do this. I told you I'd help you. Give me the gun and let me help you. Give me a chance, Paul."

"I can't do that, Jack."

It didn't escape Jack's notice that Paul stopped calling him Jackie. Had he got through to this maniac? Probably not, if he was still intent on killing an innocent woman. "Sure you can. Life is about choices. Everything we do is a choice. You said so yourself."

"I've made a lot of bad choices."

"And now you have the chance to make a lot of good choices. The first will be to hand me the gun. The next will be to let Maria walk out of here."

"And then?" Travers asked.

"And then I'll put my weapon away, and you and I can talk about getting you that help."

Travers seemed to consider Jack's words then looked him straight in the eye. "You do realize I know I'm going to prison. There's no turning back from this."

"Of course, you know it. Like I said, you're a smart guy. That doesn't mean I can't still help you. There are some great counselors in prison, programs you can join," Jack suggested.

"Little good it'll do me. California has the death penalty for situations like this."

Lying, Jack said, "It never occurred to me that it would be an option. I just want to see you get the help you need."

"That's very generous of you, Jack. But I'm not cut out for prison. Think of all the people I helped put away. How long do you think I'd last?"

"Maybe Haniford can arrange for you to go to an out-of-county facility."

Travers waved the gun as he talked with that hand now. "Do you think after all this there'll still be a place in California where no one will know me? Let alone the country. Hell, once this breaks on the news, I'll be infamous." He chuckled.

"Is that what you want, fame?"

"No. I just want . . . wanted to be . . . Hell, I don't know now. I just wanted more than I had and I couldn't seem to get it. Not from anyone, anywhere. But every time I looked up, you were always in the limelight." The weapon in his hand shook as Travers continued aiming at Maria. "After my rescue, I looked in the old papers. Even when I was up on that mountain, any news about the crash or that I was still missing was shuffled into the back pages, while the front-page news was all about you and what happened to your family. Not even with my rescue and having nearly lost my life did I rate front page news. But you did. You always did."

Jack knew then that Travers had nothing to do with what happened to his family. He'd been stuck on the mountain. And whoever had destroyed his family was still out there. Jack's chest squeezed at both the horrible memories that lived in the front of his mind and the thought of what Travers had gone through after the crash and once he got home.

"Paul, I'm so sorry. I had no idea. You know as well as I do that we can't control the media. You can't blame that on me. But it's over. It's in the past. Look at me." Travers gazed up again, his attention diverted. If Jack allowed him to kill Maria, Ray would never forgive him. Hell, he'd never forgive himself. "You got your shit together and you went right back to work and made detective. You don't know what else is possible until you try. I told you I'd help you. Let's let Maria go, then you and I can talk about your options. We can bring in Haniford for his help. I know he'll pull some strings for you." As much as it galled him to say it, "You're one of us. A brother. We stick by each other. I know you don't want to do this, not to a pregnant woman. Come on, man, you gotta give that little baby a chance in the world . . . to be better than you or me."

Something seemed to click in Travers' head. He hesitated for a moment and stood back, lowering his weapon. "All right. She can go."

"Thank you, Paul. Will you hand me your weapon first?"

"I don't think so. I only agreed to let Maria go."

"Fair enough. Step back so I can help her. She's already scared enough." As Jack moved closer to Maria, Travers backed up to stand on the other side of the coffee table.

With Maria seated on Jack's dominant side, he kept the Beretta aimed at Travers in his other hand and used his now free hand to pull at the duct tape from around one of Maria's wrists that bound her to the chair arms. When he managed to get one wrist free, she quickly removed the tape from her other wrist. Once free, she tore the tape from her lips with little more than a deep gasp for air.

Jack helped her stand and pushed her behind him, using his body to shield her in case Travers changed his mind. He shifted the Beretta into his dominant hand as he ushered Maria to the front door, all the time, keeping his gaze on Travers. He heard her unlock the door then felt the night breeze ruffling through his whiskers. Until then, he hadn't realized how stifling the house had become. The fresh, briny breeze coming off the Pacific just two blocks away invigorated him.

"Thank you, Jack," Maria said through her tears. "Come with me now and let the cops take care of that piece of shit."

"I can't," he said softly. "Just tell Ray and Haniford what happened here." Maria kissed the back of his hand before pushing her through the door. Before closing it, Jack heard commotion on the street as she descended the steps. "Okay, Paul. It's just the two of us." He moved back to where he'd stood near the dining area door, gripped the Beretta in both hands again and planted his legs as he had before, keeping Travers in his sights, who now stood directly between him and the window.

"Now what?" Travers spread his arms with a shrug.

"Now, I'd like you to give me your weapon so we can talk."

Travers shook his head. "We've talked enough."

"I still have some questions that only you can answer. If I'm going to help you, I need to know everything."

"There's nothing else to tell." Travers considered the weapon in his hand again, turning it in both hands as if inspecting it.

"Sure there is. Tell me why you—" He didn't want to say it. "Tell me why you did what you did to those women."

Travers cocked his head and looked up sideways. "You mean removing their flesh?" Jack nodded. Travers laughed under his breath. "Up there on that mountain, do you know how I survived?"

"All of the articles I read said you hunted."

Travers shook his head. "There's nothing up there that time of year. There was only one way."

Swallowing hard, Jack asked, "I get it, but what did all those women have to do with that?"

"I told you. I had to be with them. They had to change me."

"I remember, but it didn't work so you killed them. But why deflesh them?"

"Do you know what I brought back with me from my time on the mountain?"

"Besides a warped sense of right and wrong?" With Maria now out of the room, Jack felt emboldened to speak his mind.

"Don't get cocky with me, Jack," Travers warned, waving his gun, as if reminding Jack he was armed.

Jack stood his ground. "I've got one too. Let's get past this posturing and get to the heart of the matter."

"And what's that?"

"Both of us walking out of here alive."

"That remains to be seen. Could be neither of us," Travers said.

Jack didn't rise to the taunt.

After what seemed like a Mexican standoff, Travers finally spoke. "What would you do in the same circumstance but it was your precious Leah who had been the one to die? Would you *eat* her so you could survive?"

In Travers' situation, Jack knew he'd give himself to save Leah, but had the tables turned . . . "Honestly, I don't know."

"Well, I do. I was forced to eat my lover or die up there with him," Travers said with a raised voice. "Do you know what that felt like? Every time I had to force pieces of Joe into my mouth, it destroyed another memory of us together. I didn't want our last memories together to be like that, but I had to keep reminding myself if I wanted to live, that's what I had to do."

"You did what you needed to do to survive, Paul. Joe would have understood."

"Maybe so, but what about his wife? I know they went back up and found him. They thought the wildlife got to him. That's what they told her . . . told everyone. They may have suspected what I'd done, but no one asked or talked about it. At least, not to my face. Can you imagine how Joe's wife would have felt knowing what I'd done . . . what we'd been doing behind her back?" Jack shook his head. "But Joe didn't just give me life. He gave me something else."

"What was that?"

"He gave me a hunger."

Jack was almost afraid to ask. "For what? Are you going to tell me you're some kind of vampire now?"

Travers laughed fully now. "Wouldn't that be something? No, what Joe gave me was something greater. He gave me the gift of life. By eating his flesh, I survived. And to continue surviving, those women had to give me life too." Travers laughed again. "Kinda fucked up, right?"

Just then, Jack understood why the Spreckels Lake victim's flesh was parceled out the way it had been . . . serving sizes. The thought turned his stomach. Jack swallowed hard to keep the bile down.

Through clenched teeth, Jack said, "Ya think?" Travers had just admitted to killing twenty women and defleshing them for the purpose of eating them? *Fuuuck!* He wasn't just a serial killer. He was a serial cannibal. "You know, Paul, I don't think you have to worry about going to prison. Where they'll put you, you'll wish you were behind bars. It's just too bad Alcatraz isn't still open."

"Oh, I'm not going anywhere." With his gaze on Jack and the SIG firmly in his hand, Travers lifted the weapon.

Two shots rang out, each finding their target.

CHAPTER THIRTY-THREE

Friday – a week later

"Bless me, Father, for I have sinned." Jack knelt on the cushion in the confessional at Father Nick's church, his hands clasped before him.

"Go on, Jack." Father Nick's deep voice filtered through the screen.

"I was forced to kill a man."

"You also saved a woman's life. And that of her unborn child."

Jack squeezed his eyes shut and shook his head. He'd wracked his brain over the paradox. "Does God absolve a man because he was forced to take one life to save another?"

"Would you feel better if I gave you penance?" Father Nick asked.

"I don't know what else to do. I can't get past the guilt. God has to know I did everything in my power to try to get the gun off Travers." Jack beat his forehead against his clenched hands. "He forced my hand."

"All right, Jack. For your penance, say three Hail Marys and three Our Fathers. And then thank God He gave you the strength you needed to take that son-of-a-bitch down." Father Nick said the last with passion.

Jack's gaze shot up and looked through the screen. The priest's steely gaze stared back at him. "Father?"

"God, the Father of mercies." The priest recited the Prayer for Absolution while maintaining a stern gaze with Jack. "I absolve you from your sins in the name of the Father, and of the Son, and of the Holy Spirit. Amen." The priest crossed himself, then said, "For the rest of it, I think my office is a more appropriate place."

Jack crossed himself then rose and met the old priest just outside the confessional. As tradition dictated, he followed Nick through the church to his office.

Everything in the Church had its ritual, and for Jack and Father Nick, it included the act of the priest pouring them both a short whiskey and sitting together to talk as friends.

Once his glass was in hand and Nick had seated himself in the chair beside him, Jack felt at a loss for words. Nick was patient and let him think.

Jack spun the glass in his fingers, focusing on the swirling amber liquid. "It's funny. I can't seem to remember most of this last week. But every moment of that night, every word, replays in my head, over and over again until that's all I can think about."

"Sounds like you're in shock. It's been a while since you had to face this on a daily basis."

"Thank God I rarely had to draw my weapon while on the job, and rarer still was I ever forced to kill someone. But this—I gave Paul every chance I could think of to get him to hand over his weapon. I thought I'd got through to him." He rubbed his eyes with his fingers. "I thought I had."

The priest's voice remained low and calm, but as always, he was firm and forthright. "If he wanted help, he would have asked for it long ago. If what I've been reading in the papers is correct, this had been going on for many years."

Jack nodded. "I haven't read many of the articles, but what I have, their facts are correct."

"You're confident he didn't have anything to do with Leah's disappearance, or Zoë's—"

"I am," Jack cut in. "He was on the mountain when it happened. It wasn't him."

Nick shook his head then gazed away. "I'm sorry for that."

"Why should you be sorry it wasn't him?"

He gazed back at Jack. "If it had been him, you could put your own troubles behind you. You might have discovered what happened to your wife, and why Zoë had to die. And Trax. But it wasn't him, so your journey must continue, as dreadful as it is. I'm sorry for you because of that."

Jack jerked his head, a sign that he appreciated the priest's sentiments. In a way, he wished it had been Travers too. That dark place in himself cried out to put it all behind him so he could make his way back to his family.

After a short silence, Nick said, "You seem to have recovered well."

Without thinking, Jack rubbed a spot over his heart. Prior to leaving his apartment, he'd had enough sense to put on his bulletproof vest before shrugging on his leather jacket. While the vest would have saved his life on its own, the impact at such close range would have knocked him on his ass, and no doubt broken a rib or two. But the thick leather along with the vest meant he'd only been winded from the impact, and left with a sizable bruise.

He'd been lucky that night. Travers, not so much. Knowing he was a cop, Jack assumed the man had been wearing his bulletproof vest too, so he made sure to aim directly at the bastard's head. A much smaller target, but Jack had always been the best marksman in the department. After three years and only a few times at the test range, his aim had remained true.

"Yeah," he sighed. "But there was still a lot I didn't find out." Like why he'd targeted these specific women, why he only killed every three months, and how had all of this gone on under the noses of his neighbors.

Nick put a shaky, arthritic hand over Jack's forearm, forcing him to look up into the man's dark hazel eyes. "Are they things you really need to know? You caught the bad guy, now let the department figure out the rest. Take satisfaction in knowing you had the additional insight they needed to make the city safe again." With a pat, he added, "And now the texts will cease."

"I suppose there *is* that." Inhaling deeply, Jack set the glass on the desk in front of him then put his elbows on his knees and scrubbed his face with his fists, trying to ease the pain behind his eyes and forehead. He groaned, then said, "I just can't get the image out of my head of his brains all over my curtains." Sitting up, he turned to Nick. "And all of those people in my house—"

Looking away, his vision became a moist blur. All this time, he'd been preserving the evidence of what had happened to his family, just in case something had been missed by investigators. What if a new technology had been discovered and something in the evidence could help him find who did *that* to his family? Back then, if he'd allowed crime scene cleaners to remove all of that evidence—

He couldn't think of it. But after he'd shot Travers, he'd been forced to let investigators into his house. Not only to collect evidence from what had happened—the collection also included what had remained in place since that long ago night. In the process, they'd ended up trampling through the entire house.

Now, he hated the thought of being forced to clean the house because there was no need in keeping any of it. Any evidence he'd hoped to preserve until Leah was found had surely been destroyed, or at the least, compromised to the point of making it impossible to accurately test, no matter the technology.

Nick must have known where Jack's mind was going, so he spoke again. "You're a good man, Jack." His gaze shot up to the priest at his remark. Was he a good man? He didn't think so. "Don't let what happened with Paul Travers sway your personal compass."

"My compass?"

Nick nodded. "We all live by a personal compass. We're all like ships on the ocean, Jack, and being guided by the compass of life. But sometimes the winds are strong and can put us off course. As with Paul Travers."

"Yeah, but his ship hit an iceberg," Jack said with a chuff.

Nick chuckled lightly. "There are many icebergs out there. But you've always been the captain of your life, and you've always steered your ship in the right direction. Don't let what happened be an iceberg. Navigate it. Push forward. In the right direction."

"How do I know what the right direction is, Nick?"

"You've always known. Listen to your instincts, as always. Now, what of the other case? The missing wife."

Jack knew he was still on the case, even though the department had officially taken it over. With the discovery of Bonnie's car and her clothes in the trunk, the case had landed in Ray and Travers' laps. But with Travers . . . out of the picture now, Jack knew Ray would be on his own with it, at least as far as the department knew. Or until Haniford saddled him with a new partner. Ray knew all the facts of the case, but as far as Boyd himself knew, Jack was still trying to find his wife.

Over the last week, Boyd had called Jack several times, but he wasn't taking calls from anyone. He even locked the door against Ray. He just wanted to be alone. Boyd's messages said he knew Jack had been involved in taking down Travers and he understood it took priority over finding his wife, but the man sounded truly frantic. Jack supposed he needed to call Boyd and give him an update. The man deserved as much.

But as much as Jack hated admitting it, at this point, Bonnie would probably never be found alive, if she was found at all. The very best he hoped for was that Boyd would be mollified with the thought that perhaps she had just up and left and started a new life somewhere. That's how Jack had been dealing with his loss. He just couldn't let his mind go to a dark hole in the ground, like those women buried in Travers' backyard. He had convinced himself Leah was still alive. Out there. Somewhere. Until she'd been found, one way or the other, this was the only way he could function. Would Boyd be happy with the same lie?

"I suppose I need to get back to that. I'll work with Ray. Hopefully, we can either put the husband out of his misery or put him in jail for killing her himself."

"That's a possibility, I suppose . . . that he did it," Nick added.

Jack nodded. "All the clues lead to him." He glanced at the glass on the desk that still held the shot Nick had poured for him. Ignoring it, he stood to leave. "I better go. I've taken up too much of your time already."

Without commenting on the drink, Nick stood and pulled Jack's hand into his own. For an old man, his grip was surprisingly firm, with Jack's hand in the palms of both of his, making him look into Nick's eyes. "You know where I am—"

Jack nodded, understanding that he knew Jack still lived in a dark place. "I do, Nick. You're a good friend. Thanks."

CHAPTER THIRTY-FOUR

Monday

Jack was done feeling sorry for himself. While he hadn't yet gone back to the Sunset house to start cleaning, he'd taken the weekend to refresh himself with the Boyd case—going over all of the video and audio he'd taken, from Boyd himself and his walk-through of the Boyd residence, the BWC footage, the interviews with Julian Sumner, Doctor Harvey, Boyd's neighbors, as well as officers Harris and Johnson.

Then there were his notes, and the case wall he had to finish putting back to rights after Travers had destroyed it.

Jack had been so buried in the work that the weekend passed in a flash.

He'd thought long and hard about it, but he'd taken down his family's case wall in the process. All of the places the texter—Travers—had sent him to were now moot. The only evidence he had was what had remained in the house. And now, even that was irrelevant.

Jack should have felt lost at having his family's case ripped out from under his feet, and he was, to a degree. Travers aside, Jack was grateful he'd never receive another of those texts. For so long, Jack had lived under that shadow, and now . . . now it was like a weight had been lifted from him.

That didn't mean he didn't still live in a very dark place. His heart, mind and very soul ached with the loss of his family. That pit of despair was still deep and only finding out who took his family from him would help him move on.

He refocused on the screen before him. The more he watched the video and listened to the audio, something still wasn't sitting right with him. Something about that house . . .

He needed another look inside.

Checking his watch, Boyd would, or should, still be at work. Assuming he'd returned to work with his wife still missing. Jack had been a mess after Leah went missing, but with his daughter's murder, it put the men in slightly different categories. Jack tried working and failed. Everyone had their own ways of dealing with tragedy, but could the man have pulled himself together enough to face the office?

Jack picked up the phone and dialed Boyd's cell. The phone rang twice before Boyd answered. "Mr. Slaughter." Boyd must have had his name and number programmed into his contact list.

"Mr. Boyd. I'm sorry for not getting back to you last week—"

"I understand. You were involved in a far greater case than mine."

"All cases are important," Jack assured him. "As it happens, it was while investigating your wife's disappearance that I was led to the other case. I can assure you that it was my top priority to make sure Bonnie wasn't one of those victims."

"Please, tell me she's not." It didn't pass Jack's notice that what he previously perceived as panic was still evident in Boyd's voice.

"No, she wasn't one of those victims."

"Thank God. Where does that leave us now?"

"I'm still investigating. I have a few more leads to chase, and I'm doing that this week."

With a shaky voice, Boyd asked, "Is there anything I can do? I want to help . . . if you think I can."

Yes, you can. Tell me if you killed your wife. "Are you home? I can swing by and go over a couple things with you." What those things were, Jack had no idea.

"Umm, no. I had to go to Monterey. I was going crazy just sitting at home."

Yeah right.

"I went back to work to give me something else to focus on. I've had to come to Monterey to see a client. Can we meet tomorrow?

I'll be home late tonight. Probably too late for a meeting."
Perfect. "Tomorrow would be fine. How's 10 a.m.?" he
suggested, pulling a random time out of the air.
"Excellent. I'll be waiting at home. Is that all right?"
"Yep. See you then." Jack disengaged the call, then opened a
desk drawer and pulled out his spare phone. He switched it on
and waited for the icon that said the phone was ready to use. He
dialed in Boyd's home number and waited.

He kept the spare phone for instances exactly like this. If he
rang Boyd's house with the phone he'd just used to call the man,
and if he had caller ID on the home phone, then he'd know Jack
was checking up on him. By using the spare phone, the number
would come up as unknown on Boyd's end. And if he answered,
it would be easy to just hang up and hope Boyd assumed it had
been a wrong number.

But if Boyd didn't pick up, he'd know the man wasn't home.
Given the age of the house and the man's proclivity for living in
the past, Jack doubted there was an answering machine. After eight
rings, he knew he'd been right on that account and disengaged the
call.

Rising, he threw on his spare jacket—his other sported a
sizable hole in the chest—and tossed both phones into a pocket.
He gathered his gear then headed out.

Fifteen minutes later, Jack reached the Lower Haight district
and Dubose Park but he didn't turn up Carmelita. Instead, he
circled the park onto Scott Street.

The houses along the west side of Carmelita were unusual to
most other residences in the city. Their backyards didn't butt up
against those on the next street. Instead, these yards butted up
against the part of Dubose Park that wrapped around the Harvey
Milk Center onto Scott Street. Jack found an empty space near
the Labyrinth, hung his helmet and gloves on the handlebar, and
dismounted.

The Labyrinth was a ground level activity area for kids, with a
single winding path leading into the center then back out again.
Years ago, he'd thought to bring Zoë here when she was old

enough. She would have been old enough now.

Renewing his resolve, Jack pulled out the spare phone and rang Boyd's home number again, just to be sure he was still out—he was. Jack slipped past the exhibit and faded into the trees and walked along the fence line, counting the houses until he knew he was behind the right one.

Typically, homeowners preferred their fences to have a smooth finish, but that usually meant their neighbor's side had the cross timbers. In this case, those cross timbers were on the park side. While he used those cross timbers to lever himself over the fence, he wondered how many criminals had done the same thing in order to gain access to these properties.

He landed as quietly as he could and gazed at the neighboring houses to be sure some of Boyd's nosy neighbors hadn't seen him. When he was sure it was safe, he quickly moved to the back porch.

As with everything else about the house, the doors still retained what appeared to be the original knobs. A quick look showed Jack there wasn't an alarm on the house, so he used the lock picks he carried with him and was inside the house in seconds, quietly pushing the kitchen door closed behind him.

The house had that certain atmosphere telling Jack it was empty but he still waited a solid minute before he was absolutely positive he was alone.

Making sure he wasn't tracking dirt into the house, Jack strode across the kitchen floor. He stopped suddenly. Something *had* changed. He felt his heart rate kick up a notch.

Turning, he noticed Boyd had done some upgrading—a new range and fridge, both retro in style, just as Jack had suggested. And the floor had been re-laid. It was still linoleum, but it was a lighter shade, giving the space a brighter glow. *Interesting*.

He moved to a door that led into the entry hall. The stale, musty odors from his previous visit had been replaced by something lemony overlaying some form of solvent. It wasn't just in the kitchen but continued into the entry hall. He let his gaze take in the polished timber floor and banister. The walls had been repainted. It didn't escape his notice how the lighting coming through the glass lights beside the door gave this previously shadowed space a cheerier, welcoming appeal.

Newly-carpeted stairs took him up to the landing. Through open bedroom doors, he saw the entire upstairs had also been re-laid and repainted. Light from the bedroom windows shone into the center of the house, lightening it. Even the bathroom smelled clean and fresh with new tiles and paint.

If Jack didn't know better, he would have thought he was in the wrong house.

In the master bedroom, Jack opened a few drawers but didn't see anything unusual. The closet was another story. What he assumed had been Bonnie's side of the space now had several new dresses and coats hanging from the rail.

Had Boyd already moved on? Had *he* been the one seeing another woman, and Bonnie found out so she left him . . . or he killed her? This case was becoming more complicated than he'd ever expected.

Closing the closet door, he returned downstairs and let himself into the living room. As with the rest of the house, this room, and the dining room visible through the open double doors, also had polished floors and new paint. While the furnishings remained the same, they had definitely been cleaned, as had the huge carpet in the center of the room.

Again, Jack wondered what was going on. Boyd had gotten rid of his wife's clunker, dumping her clothes at the same time. The house had had an intensive cleaning and refurbishing. And he'd moved in a new woman.

On his previous visit, and that of Harris and Johnson, the stuffed chair was still in place at the far end of the rug. While the rug had been cleaned, the chair was still in its usual place.

Something about that chair.

Jack strode across the carpet to examine it. As he approached, a creak broke the silence.

Until then, the silence had only told him he was alone in the house. Now, the creak seemed to boom across the room and made his already heavily-beating heart pound in his chest.

He kept his focus on the chair and continued across the room. He circled it, leaning down to look closely for anything that shouted it didn't belong there. But there was nothing. Like the rest of the house, the chair had been cleaned professionally. Anything that had remained on the chair before Bonnie's disappearance was now long gone.

"Shit," he said under his breath. He put his hands on his hips and gazed around the room, and the dining room behind him. Nothing.

Nothing but that odd creak under the carpet.

He grasped the chair on either side of the backrest and carefully pulled it off the carpet, trying not to leave drag marks.

Kneeling, he took the edge of the rug and started rolling it back. Almost instantly, something that hadn't been there before hit the back of his throat. It clung to the scent that dominated the house since its intensive cleaning and repainting. It was a vaguely familiar scent, but hovered just beneath the fresh smells.

With the carpet rolled toward the front windows, Jack looked at the whole floor now. Nothing looked wrong, but he knew it creaked when he walked over it. He slowly strode across it again, taking his time to test each board until he found the noisy one.

Gazing out the front windows from where he stood, he made sure no one was coming. Confident he had the time, he knelt to examine the boards. They didn't appear to have been sanded very well before restaining, as there were a few nicks on the ends of several boards in front of him. Using the edge of his apartment key, he was able to lift one of the loose boards. It came away easily. Using a hand, he tested the neighboring board to see if it was loose. It was.

There was the smell again. Stronger. Had a squirrel died under Boyd's house? It smelled like a family of them.

Flipping on the light on his phone, he shone it into the space, as he'd done with the attic space on his first visit here. The light reflected off a brand-new yellow suitcase.

Jack immediately knew where Bonnie Boyd had disappeared to.

CHAPTER THIRTY-FIVE

By the time Jack saw Carl Boyd rush through the front door, the house was swarming with officers, investigators, and forensic personnel. Jack checked the time. The sun had set a few hours ago and it was now going on midnight.

"Mr. Slaughter," he called from across the room where officers Johnson and Harris were preventing him from entering. "What's the meaning of this?"

Jack followed Ray down the hall to where Boyd stood.

"Are you Mr. Carl Boyd?" Ray asked.

Boyd struggled to get out of the officers' grasp. "Of course, I am. Mr. Slaughter, what's going on here?" Boyd quickly gazed between him and Ray several times, waiting for a reply.

Officially, this was now Ray's case. Haniford had only allowed Jack inside the house once it had been secured, and only because Jack had originally taken the case to find Bonnie Boyd. Jack had admitted to Haniford that he'd withheld some of his evidence when the case had been given to Travers. Haniford hadn't been happy about it, but he understood. And because Jack knew much more about the missing woman, Haniford agreed to work with him. Jack knew that if he'd been anyone else, Haniford would have put him in cuffs and sent him down to the station for obstruction, withholding evidence and anything else he could think of.

"Where have you been today?" Ray asked.

"In Monterey. Tell him, Mr. Slaughter. You know." Jack could tell Boyd was growing more agitated by the scared look on his face and the pleading tone of his voice.

Ray looked up at him. "Is this true, Jack?"

"I rang him earlier today to arrange a time to come by and talk about my findings on his missing wife. He told me he was in Monterey. I was nearby, intending on interviewing a few more of Mr. Boyd's neighbors, when I saw the front door was open. Suspecting Mr. Boyd really was home, I went to the door and called out for him. I thought I heard something suspicious, so I entered the residence as a concerned citizen. When I found the house empty, I rang the police." Well, some of it was true—the part about him entering the house.

Right on point, Ray said, "So you don't have any proof Mr. Boyd was out of town." Jack shook his head. Turning back to Boyd, Ray asked, "Can anyone verify your location today, Mr. Boyd?"

"No . . . I . . . oh, wait—" He grappled an arm out of Harris' hands then reached into his pocket and withdrew a wad of crumpled paper, and thrust them in Jack's direction. "Will these do?"

Ray took them and carefully unfurled the thin paper strips. Jack inclined his body to get a better look at what was written on the slips of paper. Two different parking garage receipts, one for 10:49 a.m. and the other for 5:06 p.m. A lunch receipt was time-stamped at 1:32 p.m. Each receipt with a Monterey address at the top. The final receipt was from a burger joint outside Morgan Hill for 7:49 p.m. And all receipts were dated for today.

Jack gazed down at Ray. They both seemed to be of the opinion that Boyd had been telling the truth about being down in Monterey all day. He certainly looked tired and bedraggled, as if he'd had a very long day, and a longer late-night drive home. His face had obviously not seen a razor since the morning.

"Mind if I keep these?" Ray asked as he filed the receipts into his notebook before Boyd could reply. Then, making notes, Ray said, "Tell me about your day."

"I was up at six and on the road before seven. It took me nearly three hours to get to Monterey. I hit rush hour traffic getting out of the city and slow traffic through San Jose. It wasn't until I hit the 156 out of Prunedale before the traffic thinned enough to

reach the speed limit. I nearly missed my 11 a.m. appointment."
Boyd fished around in another pocket and pulled out a business
card, handing it to Ray. "Here, this is my client. You can call him
to confirm the appointment."

Ray took the card and made some notes in his book before
stashing it with the receipts. "And someone at this number will
confirm seeing you there?"

Growing exasperated, Boyd's voice rose. "Like I said, I nearly
missed my appointment. Yes, I was there. The secretary will
confirm it, as will my client. And look at those receipts. One is
for the parking garage near his office. I barely had ten minutes
to spare. What is all this about? Why are you all in my house? Is
Bonnie back?" He stood on his toes to try looking over the tops of
people around him.

"And what about the return trip? The last receipt here says you
were in San Martin around 7:30 p.m."

"No, I was in Morgan Hill," Boyd said, irritation tingeing his
voice. "I stopped at a fast food place off East Dunne for something
to eat and to use the facilities. I think it was just past 7:30 p.m."

"Right, Morgan Hill." Jack knew Ray had been testing Boyd.
"Assuming you stopped for half an hour, let's say that was 8 p.m.,
you should have made it home in about ninety minutes. Where
were you during the other two . . . two and a half hours?"

Good question, Jack thought, gazing down at Boyd.

"Like I said, I was up and out the door before 7 a.m. By the
time I reached Morgan Hill, I'd been on the go for more than
twelve hours. I used the bathroom and got something to eat. I ate
in my car and intended to get back on the road when I was done.
All I remember is leaning back for a moment and when I woke up,
it was going on ten. I would have been here sooner but there was
an accident on the 101 just before the Seventh Street exit."

Ray gazed up at Jack with a look he knew well. Boyd's story
would probably pan out for today, but that didn't explain how his
wife's body got into the suitcase under the floorboards in his own
home.

"We'll check out your story," Ray said, cocking his head at

Harris. The officer nodded and stepped outside. "In the meantime, Officer Johnson will read you your rights and then he'll be taking you downtown for questioning."

Boyd's face went ashen. "Wait—what? Why? Mr. Slaughter, *please* tell me this isn't happening. What's going on?" he pleaded, gazing at all the people surrounding him.

Ray gazed up at him again. Jack knew his friend hated delivering bad news. He did too, but in this case, Jack already had a rapport with Boyd. "Mr. Boyd," he started, then repeated himself louder to get the man's attention. "Mr. Boyd! Your wife's body has been located. It appears she's been dead for some time."

It took a moment for Jack's words to sink in before Boyd swayed where he stood. He clutched at Johnson to steady himself. The officer grasped Boyd under the arm to keep him from collapsing onto the hallway floor. "What happened to her?" Boyd finally asked, his voice quivering. "Do you know who did it? How did she die?" Jack was used to the pathetic mewling of guilty suspects who pled their innocence, but Boyd was different. He wanted to know what happened to her. His emotions seemed genuine. Tears streamed down the man's now red face, and his body shook violently.

Just then, Harris arrived back into the hall. "It checks out. They're still up there cleaning up the debris. Traffic is backed up to the 280 in Portola." Both Jack and Ray nodded. Harris fell in beside Boyd once more.

"Please," Boyd begged. "What happened to her? Where is she? I want to see her." Tears began streaming down his face.

"I'm sorry, Mr. Boyd. That won't be possible. Her remains have been removed and taken to the medical examiner," Ray said.

"Removed? What—?"

Jack put a hand on the man's shoulder. He didn't know how to break it to the man. Boyd genuinely didn't seem to know what they'd found, yet all the evidence led to him. "Mr. Boyd . . . Carl," he said, using his first name to try reaching him on a personal level. "Listen to me. This is important. We found Bonnie. She's been here the whole time."

"No," Boyd shouted. His now red-eyed gaze flicked toward the living room then bore into Jack's. "Why is there a hole in my living room floor?"

"We found her under—"

"Oh my God, no!" Boyd's legs gave out from under him and he sank to the floor, scrubbing his fists over his eyes. "Bonnie . . . Bonnie . . . Bonnie . . ." he sobbed as Jack knelt down to tell him what they'd found.

The man's racking sobs were like a punch to Jack's gut. Boyd's reaction to the news that his wife was dead was much like Jack's walking into the bloody scene in his own home and finding the bodies of his daughter and Trax, and not knowing where Leah was.

"Are you all right, Mr. Boyd? I know this has come as a shock," Jack said, rising and apologized for what would happen next. Officers Harris and Johnson lifted the man from the floor and Johnson read him his rights.

When Harris went to cuff Boyd, Jack stilled him with a shake of his head, before the officers escorted Carl Boyd from the house and into the back of a patrol car.

Jack turned to Ray, who had a dark scowl on his face. Keeping his gaze on the patrol car as it pulled away, Ray said, "He didn't do it."

Jack turned his gaze in the same direction. "All the evidence points to him."

"Yeah, but he didn't do it."

"I know."

CHAPTER THIRTY-SIX

Two weeks later

Taping the last of the boxes closed, Jack sat back on his ass and looked around the now nearly empty bedroom.

When he arrived, he'd hesitated before entering the house, but he knew he had to do this. He supposed he'd known it all along, but it took Travers' brains getting sprayed across the front windows and curtains for him to realize it was time to step away from everything that had happened in the house—good and bad. And after that long ago night nearly three years ago, the evidence he'd hoped to preserve was degrading every day. Not to mention Travers' DNA contamination and that of the investigators and forensics teams.

It wasn't until after closing the Boyd case that Jack took some time to think long and hard about what came next. He'd even returned to Saint Frank's and sought Father Nick's advice. The priest had helped him come to many decisions over the last two weeks, but the most important ones were still in the front of his mind—find his wife then find that round with his name on it. The latter bit of information he kept to himself.

Knowing these things, he also knew there was no reason to hold onto the past, nor its possessions. Not many of them anyway. So it was time to clean up. That meant stripping out everything covered in blood and replacing with new. He'd take a leaf out of Boyd's book and repaint the whole house to bring some brightness and light into the place. And then he would put it on the market.

He'd already taken the first major step by contacting some

classic car enthusiasts who jumped at the chance of a nearly stock 1965 Mustang, even with its rust, flat tires and cracked windshield. He hadn't even tried starting the car to see if it still ran. Despite the dilapidated condition, he accepted what he thought was an obscene amount of cash, then deposited it into a trust account he'd set up for Ray and Maria's baby. He had no one else to leave it to, and he didn't need it to restore the house. The account he and Leah had set up for restoration had been lying dormant in the bank; he'd tap into that to do what needed doing.

A dumpster now sat in the Mustang's former place in the driveway, already filling with all the accumulated crap Jack hadn't seen in the last three years and would never use again. He donated tools to local community groups, and clothes, toys and furniture went to charity shops. Everything else was for the trash. Everything except what he'd put into boxes, like the one before him, and taped up.

Jack checked the time. Ray was bringing over his Silverado pick-up which they'd load the boxes into and take to his apartment. The boxes would probably go beside the other boxes in the backroom that he intended on going through more thoroughly. One day. The apartment only had two rooms and a bathroom though. He didn't know how he'd fit a three-bedroom house into that space, even after downsizing. Unless he moved, what remained of his life would remain packed in boxes.

He gazed to where their bed had once sat, divots still in the carpet. His eyes glazed over with moisture, his mind flooding with memories—wrapping himself around Leah to keep her warm on cold nights, watching her sleep, and making love with her . . . creating Zoë in that same bed.

Squeezing his eyes shut, he brought up his hands to his knees and rested his forehead on his balled fists. Memories flashed in his head like lightning and stabbed him in the chest. It was not a dissimilar feeling as the one that grabbed him when he bagged up Leah's and Zoë's clothes for charity. Even after three years, he swore their scents still clung to the fibers, just like those few hairs on Leah's favorite sweater. He'd boxed that up, along with Zoë's favorite stuffed rabbit, to take with him to Wong's. Everything else went to those who could use it.

A light, cool breeze drifted over him and he swore he felt Leah's fingers in his hair. A child's soft laugh enveloped him. He missed these things, and for a moment, he pretended it was his girls.

"Jack! You up there?"

His head shot up and he scrubbed the tears from his eyes. The breeze must have been from Ray opening the front door and letting fresh air into the house. Kids played out front. But for a moment . . .

"Yeah, be right down," he called. Rising, he took a deep breath before lifting the last box into his arms then headed for the stairs.

"How's Maria and the baby?"

"The doctor said the baby is still doing fine. Maria's okay. She's agreed to some counseling though," Ray said, watching Jack descend the stairs.

"She's a strong woman. And she has you. She'll be fine."

Ray nodded with agreement then jerked his head in Jack's direction. "You letting that raccoon grow? You'll be Satan Clause by Christmas."

Jack chuffed, scrubbing his fingers through his beard. Lately, shaving had been the last thing on his mind. "Satan Clause, eh? Maybe."

"Looks like you already got a head start." Ray nodded toward the living room. "I thought you were waiting for me to help you."

Jack sat the box down beside a few others on the now bare subfloor. "As soon as the dumpster got here a couple days ago, I started throwing stuff into it." Jack thrust his thumb toward the heap in the corner. Pulling down the curtains, rolling up the carpet and clearing out the unsoiled furniture had been the first thing he'd done when he came back to the house. He had yet to tackle the dining area and kitchen though. "Haniford is sending the department's HAZMAT team over to collect anything with blood on it for incineration."

Gazing at the boxes, Ray asked, "Is this all you're taking to your place?"

Nodding, he said, "I think so. Let me take this stuff down to the garage and then we can get started. All the painting stuff is upstairs already. I figure it'll be easier to start up there. When the downstairs is done, I can close the door and walk away."

"You wouldn't rather get your stuff over to your place now? That way we can blitz this place without worrying about throwing something out by mistake," Ray suggested.

"Nah. I'd rather just get them out of the way for now. We can take it all when we leave. I just want to get this done before I change my mind."

Ray threw a hand onto a hip and rubbed his eyebrows with his free hand. "You're really going to do this?"

Jack nodded, looking around. "Yeah. It's got to be done. After what happened here, there's no reason to keep any of it anymore. And I'll never live here again, so why keep the place? Let some other family live here and be happy."

With a clap on Jack's back, Ray said, "I hear ya, *amigo*. Tell me, what do you want me to do first? I brought the stuff the crime scene cleaners use to sanitize the place. It's down in the truck."

Jack nodded. "Grab a couple boxes and follow me out. We can bring all that stuff in on the return trip."

"Works for me."

Ray lifted a pair of stacked boxes and followed Jack out the front door. He wouldn't be ready to use the interior garage door until he got a chance to pull up the blood-soaked linoleum on the kitchen floor. He'd walked through Trax's blood twice—that night three years ago and when he'd come through the kitchen to confront Travers—and it was two times too many.

Ray had backed his red Silverado in beside the dumpster but there was still plenty of room to get into the garage. They set the boxes against the wall just inside the door then went out to the truck to gather the cleaning supplies.

"Oh, hey," Ray said. "I'm not sure if you'll think this is good news or not—maybe Haniford told you already, but Boyd is off the hook for killing his wife."

Jack stopped in his tracks and turned Ray by the shoulder to look at him. "What? I mean, I was sure he didn't, but . . . all the evidence pointed to him."

Ray shook his head. "We all got it wrong. He didn't do it."

"What happened? I can't see anyone going into the department willingly and confessing."

Ray chuckled. "No, nothing like that. When Cutter got the body, he pulled evidence off the suitcase before removing her from it."

Ray reached for a box but Jack stilled him. "And?" He didn't even try hiding his exasperation.

"And there was blood on it."

"Not Boyd's?" Jack asked.

"Not Boyd's. We got a hit on it pretty fast thanks to that new Rapid DNA over at Cutter's. This guy has a history of narcotics violations, a few drunk and disorderlies, and it seems he likes to beat on the ladies."

"Who was it?"

"That guy you thought was a woman—Julian Sumner."

CHAPTER THIRTY-SEVEN

"What the fuck!" Jack exclaimed. "He checked out. I interviewed him myself."

"You must have missed something." Jack gave him an *I don't think so* glare. "Seriously, the DNA was his. It was embedded in the teeth of the zipper and on the pull tab."

"How do you know it wasn't on the suitcase before she was killed and put into it?"

"Because Cutter is good at his job," Ray said with a smirk. "And because Sumner's blood was also found on Bonnie's clothing. Some of his hair was still in her fist along with some trace evidence under her nails. Cutter ran it. It's definitely Sumner's."

"Well, fuck me sideways." Jack let his gaze wander away from Ray, trying to make sense of this turn of events. Where had he fallen down on his end of the investigation? "Did he lawyer up?"

"Yeah, but he still wanted to tell us what had happened. Turns out, he has an active warrant out for his arrest in Florida where he raped and beat a woman to death. Sumner only confessed under agreement that we wouldn't extradite him. He'll fry there."

"California has the death penalty," Jack reminded him.

"Correct, but we haven't used it since 2006. There's a better chance that he'll die in prison of natural causes while going through all his appeal options—or catch a shank—than being euthanized."

Jack nodded. California was a very liberal state but there were a lot of pro-lifers when it came to capital punishment. If Manson could stay off the table, certainly Sumner would. "What did he say?"

Ray chuckled. "He broke down like a *pequito coño.*"

Looking back at Ray, Jack chuckled. "A little pussy, eh? Did he say why he did it? He was like a lovesick puppy when I interviewed him. He showed me pictures of them together. They looked in love. His story made absolute sense to me, especially knowing what I did . . . thought I knew about the husband. And the abortion. I just don't get it."

"He admitted that he was the one who was knocking her around. He took the pictures to blackmail Bonnie. If she told anyone he was anything other than her boss, or that he was hitting her, he'd take the pictures to the cops and say her husband had done it to her. She didn't want her husband knowing she was cheating on him, so she kept quiet." Ray pulled a box of cleaning supplies closer to him.

"Wait, what about the abortion?"

"Sumner thought he'd convinced her to leave her husband, so he bought the suitcase and took it over to the house that day. When he got there to help her pack, she told him she'd changed her mind. She loved her husband and wanted her marriage to work. She told Sumner the baby had been his and that she got rid of it because she didn't want to see him again and didn't want anything tying her to him for the rest of her life. According to him, they fought, he pushed her, and she fell into the corner of the hearth. When he realized she was dead, he stuffed her and the towels he used to clean up the blood into the suitcase. He didn't want to be seen leaving the house with the case, so he jimmied up the floorboards and stuffed her under the house."

Jack could've kicked himself. "When I interviewed him, he had a bandage on his hand. He said he cut his hand trying to handle a big pot in his garden shop. I didn't question it. But a couple weeks ago when I was going back over all the interviews, I looked online to see if he had a website for either of his shops. The souvenir shop's site had the usual tourist crap, but the garden shop's site looked like it catered to locals. It should have sold the big pots that he mentioned, but I didn't see anything remotely large enough to hurt himself with."

"Forensics went back to the house, but the hearth was clean. According to Cutter, Bonnie died from internal bleeding caused by a beating. It's possible he cut himself when he was fighting with Bonnie, that could account for his bandaged hand at the interview, and his blood on the body and in the suitcase. Or he could have hurt himself at work and the wound broke open during the struggle," Ray said.

"What about under her nails? I didn't see any scratches on Sumner. Just the bandaged hand." Jack jerked away from the truck, punching the air. "Goddamn it! How could I have missed it? When I met him, his sleeves were wrinkled, as if they had been up but had been rolled down before coming to meet me. They could have been hiding scratch marks. If they were deep enough to leave trace under her nails, they wouldn't have healed in the couple days it took me to find him. Damn it! The signs were there."

"Don't beat yourself up. It's not your fault. He was damn convincing. He has a history of this, which also means a lot of practice lying so that people believe him. I'm just sorry that little *puta* isn't going to fry."

Jack felt like an idiot. He used to be good at reading the signs, even the subtle ones. Was he slipping, the more time he was away from the force? Maybe he was just getting too old for this shit. "What about the car? The clothes and the remodel? Why did he tell the neighbors Bonnie was at her sister's? And," he stressed, "why do the neighbors still think there's something going on with Boyd's own mother?" He shook his head at so many unanswered questions.

"When he was interviewed that night, he told us that he was trying to win Bonnie back. When she came home, he was taking her to buy a new car. The clothes in the upstairs closet were the ones she'd bought herself. As for the neighbors, he was too embarrassed to tell them she'd left him."

"And his own mother? The neighbors were sure he'd been hiding her in the house, but I never saw her."

"Alzheimer's. She's been in a home for a couple years. Something else he was embarrassed about, I guess."

Jack finally took a long breath and forced himself to relax. "At least Boyd has been exonerated. The poor man can go back to his life, what's left of it. I'll stop by this week and see how he's getting on."

"Do you want me to go with you?" Ray offered.

Jack shook his head. "Nah. Thanks, man. I think what I need to say should be done *hombre-a-hombre*."

Ray chuffed under his breath at what he called Jack's *gringo Spanish*. "Okay. So, what do you want to do here first? You mentioned starting on the upstairs. Is there anything left to bring down before we can start prepping for painting?"

Jack turned toward the house, leaning back on the Silverado's tailgate and looking up at the now clean living room window, then over to Ray. "Let's get the cleaning stuff into the house, then move the rest of the boxes into the garage. Before we head upstairs, I want to start pulling everything out of the dining area and kitchen. I've been putting it off, but Haniford's guys are coming tomorrow and I want it all taken at the same time. You okay with that?"

Nodding, Ray lifted the box of cleaning stuff. "Whatever you say, *jefe*. You just tell me what to do."

Laughing, Jack reached for the rest of the cleaning stuff and motioned for Ray to follow him into the house.

Jack stood in the same spot he had a few weeks ago when he'd shot Travers—the threshold between the living room and the dining area. Only now he was facing into the dining area and kitchen beyond. He wasn't just at the threshold between rooms, he was at a threshold in his life. Once he crossed it, there was no going back. But he had to do this. He'd already started by clearing the upstairs and the living room. These rooms had to come next. And he was on a deadline.

Ray moved in beside him. "Are you ready to do this?"

Hesitating for a moment, Jack nodded and said, "Gotta be done," before he stepped into the dining area.

Following, Ray asked, "Do you want to do this room first or the kitchen?"

Good question. "I suppose this room first. By the time we start bringing stuff out of the kitchen, we're not walking through the mess in here."

"Makes sense."

In his peripheral vision, Jack saw Ray walking toward the kitchen, but he couldn't take his gaze off the highchair still sitting at the head of the dining table—it was all contaminated so would be going with the rest of the debris when HAZMAT came. He squeezed his eyes shut, forcing away the memory of the moment he'd found Zoë on that long ago night. He didn't want to remember her that way but there was no way to erase it. He'd spent nearly three years trying.

Ray talked to him from the kitchen, but Jack barely heard him. He let himself get lost in his memories.

He'd thought long and hard about what he did want to remember, especially the one final memory of his family he'd take with him as he left this world. What he'd decided on was the image he clung to every night before falling asleep—one he saw every night coming home after a long day at work. It was that instant and minutest moment just as he opened the door leading up from the garage into the kitchen, when his family turned to greet him with their loving smiles.

Trax would have heard the Harley coming up the road. Knowing Jack always entered through the interior door, the dog had always sat, waiting for the moment the door opened—his eyes wide with excitement, tongue lolling in his doggy smile, tail frantically sweeping the floor, and a quick hello bark.

Whatever else Leah did before he got home, the moment she heard the bike pull into the garage, she'd rush to the kitchen to finish dinner. As it had been that night, something wonderful smelling always greeted him as he crossed the garage from where he parked the bike. The moment the door opened, she'd turn with a big smile; the joy that he was home was so honest that it reached her eyes and made her face glow.

And as he crossed the small floor to embrace the woman he loved, Zoë would bounce in her booster chair, arms outstretched, and her laughing eyes, saying in her two-year-old vocabulary, "Zoë want kiss too, Daddy."

That was the moment he'd remember forever—coming home to his family. It made his chest hurt, but in a good way. He knew what absolute love was. Even now, his heart swelled with it. It was what drove him, every day, to find his daughter's and Trax's killer, and to find Leah. She was somewhere out there. He knew it. More, he *felt* it.

Then, images of Zoë flashed in his mind and his heart pumped a little faster and caught his breath. It wasn't the memory of her smiling face, the sound of her laughter, or the feel of her tiny hands on his cheeks when she pulled him in for butterfly kisses. He wished he could have one more moment like that with her.

Instead, his eyes flashed open and he stared at the highchair.

Not the booster seat.

The goddamn highchair.

In that moment, fury burned through him, realizing that whatever had happened in the house three years ago, it had all been staged.

ABOUT K.A. LUGO

K.A. Lugo is a native of Northern California who grew up on the Central Coast, with San Francisco just a stone's throw away.

Like most writers, Kem has been writing from a young age, sampling many genres before falling into thrillers, mystery, and suspense.

Kem loves hearing from readers and promises to reply to each message. Please visit Kem's socials to stay up-to-date on this exciting new series.

FIND K.A. ONLINE

Website
www.jackslaughterthrillers.com

Facebook
www.facebook.com/KALugoAuthor

Twitter
twitter.com/ka_lugo

Blog
jackslaughter.blogspot.com

Goodreads
www.goodreads.com/KALugo

BookBub
www.bookbub.com/profile/1147179734

Tirgearr Publishing
www.tirgearrpublishing.com

K.A. Lugo also writes romance as Kemberlee Shortland
www.kemberlee.com